IRON HEARTS

ST. AUGUSTINE CHAPTER

ROYAL BASTARDS MC
BOOK ONE

A.J. DOWNEY

BOOK ONE

ROYAL BASTARDS MC

A.J. DOWNEY

Published 2025 by Second Circle Press

Text Copyright © 2025 A.J. Downey

All Rights Reserved

ISBN: 978-1-95022-50-6

〜

Editing & book design by Maggie Kern @ Ms.K Edits
Cover art Dar Albert at Wicked Smart Designs

DEDICATION

To everyone who has been waiting for this day. I feel like Pinocchio — like I'm a real author now! Which I know is silly, having been at this whole thing for a decade. It feels good to be recognized and brought into the fold. I'm a Nomad no more. I guess that means this one is for the authors of the RBMC that came before, too. I hope I do y'all proud.

AUTHOR'S NOTE

Hello, my loyal readers! We're on a new adventure with this one, but I'm here to disappoint you. If you're yearning for my Kraken boys or for Reaver to slide on through these pages, it's not going to happen.

You see, the world of the Royal Bastards MC is so well built, and I'm so late to the party, I can't cross the universe of the Sacred Hearts et al. with the Royal Bastards' world. I just can't make my brain work in that direction – so I'm here, and I'm going to give you the best fuckin' story I can in my own style working within this universe, but I didn't want you turning pages with bated breath looking for my boys when they just aren't going to be here.

Cutter and his faithful crew of the Kraken MC are doing just fine on the inner coastal in their little town of Ft. Royal, Florida – but they are worlds away from my RBMC boys in St. Augustine, both literally and figuratively.

If you're a new-to-me reader and already familiar with the RBMC – welcome in! I hope I do you proud and meet and/or exceed the quality you've become accustomed to within these worlds and that by default, when you're waiting for the next one, I manage to introduce you to whole new worlds with my other series.

At any rate, if you're new to or familiar with my work, turn the page and settle in. I hope you enjoy the ride. I do my best to make them a wild one!

XoXo,
    A.J. Downey

CHAPTER ONE

Striker...

It was a sun-shining and beautiful fuckin' day in St. Augustine as I breathed in deep the salty sea air of the Atlantic, looking at the steel-gray waves coming in from the far distant horizon. I felt better than ever about being out here.

I'd had some trouble back in my rearview with how my last chapter had been going about doing things. I was lucky enough that the big dogs had taken pity on the situation enough to throw me the bone of laterally transferring here to help with the start-up of this new chapter under Renegade.

I'd found that we thought along the same lines, and there wasn't a better fit for me if it'd been custom made. The beach life suited me just fine, too.

I leaned way back in my creaking old desk chair and rocked a little, satisfied with the *creak-clack, creak-clack* sound that it made. I was sitting up top above the garage in the office space of the club-house for the St. Augustine chapter of the Royal Bastards MC.

It was a good building – strong bones, enough to withstand the worst kind of weather. With steel girders along the ceiling down below and a series of chains and pulleys – enough to lift the bikes out of harm's way should any of the more brutal weather that was prone to pop off during hurricane season decide to put a bullseye on the oldest city in the continental US.

By day, the floor below operated as a custom bike shop specializing in new builds and bitchin' skins to meet the dreams and demands of any motherfucker with enough coin to afford what we were offering – which was sicker than any other bike shop out there was capable of producing as far as we were concerned.

There were shelves up near the ceiling with dust-covered trophies from just about every bike week and fuckin' expo all over the US and some even international, too.

Renegade had an eye for making wicked sick and beautiful bikes and kept quite a few of us employed – at least on paper.

Above the garage was the office space – partially for the business downstairs and partially for the clubhouse upstairs. Upstairs is where it was at, though – a full bar, couches, a couple billiard tables and a row of dart boards. Even one of those arcade rock 'em sock 'em games where it measured how hard you could punch the speed trainer bag. It also measured speed depending on the setting.

We had weights and other equipment up there, too, and a room or two dedicated to the odd fuck, or some slap and tickle.

Best part about it, like down here, it was roofed, but the whole side of the building was open to the salt air and cooling breeze off the water. The ceiling fans spun lazily above to move some air on the more humid and stagnant days.

A lot of us spent the majority of our time here, working days and wild nights – like me. I handled a lot of the logistics for the shop below – inventory and the like, in charge of ordering supplies and keeping stock up to standard. I was also in charge of the books, taking payments, shipping and delivery of products. Shit like that.

For the club, I was the road captain – putting together runs and keeping the rides cohesive and safe.

Yeah, I was here more often than not, but I was good with it. I never got tired of it, that's for sure. Not with a view like that.

Some of us worked outside the shop, like the Butcher Brothers – our sergeant-at-arms and enforcer. They were born-and-bred bayou boys, transplant gator hunters from out in the Louisiana swamps, set on making a name for themselves hunting invasive species out here in the Glades.

They did pretty good for themselves, but they did even better working at the Gator Farm tourist attraction around here, which was kind of a trip for me. Those two, hanging around gator enclosures, wasn't what was weird to me. No, it was the thought of those two entertaining the kiddies and families from all over. That part was just fuckin' *bizarre.*

I dragged my eyes away from the preserved gator head chilling, sticking out from the wall above the archway that led out to the open deck with the view of the Atlantic beyond it, and sighed. My gaze fixing on one of the Bucher – pronounced *boo-shay* – brothers' trophies had drawn my thoughts to the brothers.

Skull, government name Jacques Montrose Boucher, never hesitated to correct you if you mispronounced his name. He said it was pronounced *Joc-keest* and not like Jaque Cousteau or whatever. The "Montrose" was where his great-granddaddy had been born.

His taller, lankier, and more unhinged younger brother, Bones, was Luis or *Loo-eese* Carentan Bouche – and had been named after where their great-granddaddy had *died* somewhere in Normandy.

It explained a few things. It seemed like their whole fuckin' family was a pack of morbid weirdos. Didn't help that the boys were only ten months apart and in the middle of the pack of something like seven kids.

Like their father and mother – their favorite pastime was fucking – either a pair of best friends or, most of the time, the same girl at the *same time.*

It reeked of some deep-South cousin-fucking type of shit to me and gave me the willies. Still, even with their weird-ass sexual proclivities and the fact they were both certifiably and deeply unhinged, they weren't bad guys.

I mean, they were, but *we all* were, at least by citizen standards. That just was what it was.

The world hadn't done many of us any favors, and a lot of us were pretty much *fuck the world* in response. We did things our way, and that's just the way we liked it.

I was an Army veteran, and my moment where the wool was stripped off from over my eyes came when I got back stateside after my last tour. My battle buddy, he wasn't doing as good as me with processing all the shit from over there. Tried like a motherfucker to go through all the proper channels through the VA, but they kept giving him the run-around. They kept putting him off, declaring parts of his body and mind failing him were *not service-related* when it had every-fucking-thing to do with what we did for this country over there.

He tried, man. Tried like a motherfucker to get them to fucking *help him*, which was what was fucking *owed* to him. He sacrificed everything and then some on the altar of Uncle Sam – his mind, his body, his fuckin' spirit – and they just wouldn't fucking *help*. Wouldn't give him the care that he was owed.

He died on his bathroom floor of an OD that was entirely preventable if they'd just fuckin' done what they were supposed to fuckin' do – but *no*. Three fuckin' tours, and he died of an overdose of some street drug he'd started on just to get some fuckin' *relief* from the monsters in his head and the pain racking his body.

He was still active duty when it'd happened. The Army quickly declared it a suicide and stripped his wife of survivor benefits, and had put him out bad with a less-than-honorable discharge or whatever.

It was an added insult to injury. One that she and I were fighting to this day because *fuck...*

I hated the fucking world for that one. *It should have fuckin' been me...*

My thoughts were pulled from their meandering path by the door to our VP's office opening. I was out in the open floor plan with a smattering of a few other desks – mostly empty up here. I hated being boxed in and preferred the open, now that I didn't have to worry about snipers or roadside IUDs and shit.

Renegade and Shadow each had their own offices, the doors remaining closed despite their open-door policy with the rest of the shop and the guys in the club.

We didn't tend to bother either one of them with any personal shit. We tended to keep it official club business with our leadership.

Anything personal, we took to each other or to the club's Chaplain – Pope. Me, I just kept it to myself for the most part. I didn't feel like baring my soul to just anyone. I was always down to help anyone else who needed it, though.

If I couldn't have Byron back, I'd settle for preventing anymore to go like he did, or worse, from actual suicide. I was pretty sure Byron hadn't wanted to die. He was reaching out for help at every turn. I think he just overdid it. He had everything to live for in his kid... even if he and his wife were on the outs and sleeping in different rooms when he'd died.

I slammed the door on the thoughts of a twelve-year-old girl finding her dad like that on his bathroom floor and looked up at Shadow's approach.

"What's up?" I asked, raising my eyebrows at the look of consternation on his face.

"Do me a favor and get the guys in here."

"Full table?" I asked curiously.

"Yeah, non-negotiable," he said unhappily.

"Shit," I muttered and picked up the handset on my desk phone. Shadow marched past me and headed down the front stairs in the direction of the shop below, no doubt to scare up Renegade.

I went down the phone tree and let everyone know what was up, to get their ass in gear, and get in here.

At least it was always two birds with one stone when it came to Skull & Bones.

I rang up the two brothers first, and Skull answered on the first ring. I could hear an announcer in the background as he grunted into the phone by way of greeting.

"Skull, Striker here. You and Bones need to get in here yesterday. Something's up."

I heard him swear low and soft in a string of Cajun-French. "A'ight, be d'ere soon," he said and hung up.

I pressed the button on the receiver and punched the next speed dial down the line. It would ring through to Enigma.

"Yo," he said.

"Clubhouse, now," I said.

"What's up?" he asked.

I laughed. "Motherfucker, you know better."

"Right," he said and grunted. I could hear a bunch of bombs and gunfire going off in the background.

"Sorry to interrupt your stream," I said. "Duty calls."

"Copy that. Be right there," he said and cursed before hanging up. Sounded like the curse of every frustrated gamer when they took a kill shot to their toon's dome in-game.

Next was Kain.

"Yellow?" he answered in his deep, melancholy voice.

"Club. Now."

"I got'cha," he said and hung up.

Next was Pope, then Pud, Toad, Mugshot, and Forks.

I hung up with Forks, who laughed at me for calling him up when he was just downstairs, but it wasn't like I knew if he was here. It was lunchtime, and there was no telling where any of these fools were at in any given moment.

I got my ass up and stretched, casting a longing look at the waves outside the apertures that we zipped clear vinyl "windows" closed when it called for it. It almost never did unless the rain came in sideways or in the heart of winter when it could get a little on the cooler side.

I needed to eat, and it would take a while for all the boys to arrive. With that in mind, I opened up the drawer I kept my bike's keys and my favorite firearm in and tucked it safely in the back of my waistband up under my colors. Straightening up, I moved to the front stairs.

"Where the fuck 're you going?" Renegade demanded when I appeared in the garage and headed for the open bay door.

"Grab a bite around the corner and bring it back. You hungry?" I asked.

"Yeah, get me a burger," he said, and I nodded.

"Combo?" I asked.

"Just the burger," he said.

"Cool." I looked to Shadow standing behind him and asked, "You?"

He shook his head curtly.

I saddled up and rode out of the gate. The burger place we frequented was a mom-and-pop place called Smokey's Char Broil, which wasn't but two blocks away. They didn't have a drive-thru. You had to go in and to the counter – and it was a cash-only joint. One that we looked out for, free of charge. We liked the food, and we liked the dude who owned it. It'd been in his family since the fifties.

Every once in a while, they'd comp our burgers, and every once in a while, they'd hit the button Enigma had installed under their counter that would send an SOS to all our phones. Whoever was closest would answer the call. Usually, it was some dumb fuck punk kid trying to rob the joint or a drunk homeless crazy fucker hollerin' for some bullshit reason.

"Striker!" Wally called from behind the counter. "What can I get you?"

"Couple half-pounders, if you don't mind."

"Combos?"

"Fries with one of them, but no drinks."

"I got you!" he called, and he went back to flipping, hollering out to the kid manning the deep fryer to get me some fresh.

The kid came around the counter with a grease-stained brown paper sack and slid it across the counter at me. I put a twenty on the counter and threw Wally some chin.

"Thanks for your business!" he called out.

"Any time, man!"

I left. Two burgers and a large fry only came to like twelve bucks and some change, but they looked like they were running a little lean today on patronage. I didn't mind leaving a bigger-than-usual tip on top of paying for my food, which Wally had fully intended to make on the house for me.

I got back to the garage and jerked my head toward the stairs at Renegade, who stood up from the bike he was working on the electrical on and said, "Grab me a beer, and I'll be right up."

"You got it, boss," I said and took the stairs two at a time, crossing the open office floor and taking the back stairs the rest of the way up to the third floor.

The third floor was worlds different from the garage and the office space. You would never guess, looking at either of the two floors downstairs, how fuckin' *nice* it was up here.

The walls were a deep, flat black with red breaking it up from the crown molding to the chair rails to the baseboards. The tile was an easy-to-clean linoleum in big, fat, classic checkerboard pattern in the equally classic black and white.

The pool tables were black with red felt, with the MC's logo in the center of each.

The back wall had a black-and-white mural of the Royal Bastards MC logo and track lighting, giving our club's colors a subtle but respectful glow.

Above the doors leading into the private rooms for playtime were a line of photo frames, simple black, eight-by-tens of each and every mugshot we'd ever taken.

A lot of us had been arrested plenty, some of us had served time, but most of us didn't have so much as a misdemeanor on our record thanks to Shadow's connections and some damn fine club lawyers that Renegade kept on retainer.

I was up there once or twice. Still no convictions, though.

I slipped past the archway leading to the front half of the third floor and what served as our chapel. It was in the front of the building, with windows on three sides that were deeply tinted and mirrored to the outside world.

Despite the deep tint, the room could get toasty, and we had an HVAC unit on the roof pumping cool air into it to keep it nice.

The table was long, burnished steel, with the club logo cut out in the center. The steel was heat treated and rainbowed out around the cuts with enough room at each place around the table for us to eat, drink, or do whatever.

I set Renegade's burger at his place at the head of the table and looked down the row of six chairs on either side.

I set my food down at my place and went back out to the bar to open up and bring in a couple of beers to go with our food.

I cracked the top on the bottle of what I called *sex in a rowboat* beer for Renegade. The shit was so fucking close to water it wasn't even funny.

I picked myself a nice IPA out of the row of taps, poured myself one, and took glass and bottle to the table, setting out a couple of the stone coasters, likewise with our club logo embossed in the top, at our places and set our beers down.

I dropped into my seat with a sigh and belatedly checked my pockets for my cell phone, which I already knew resided in my desk drawer where I left it downstairs. Still, I didn't want to be the dumb motherfucker to catch an ass whoopin' for breaking the rules.

I dug into my food, ripping open the bag to use as a placemat as Renegade walked in, Shadow on his heels, and dropped into his seat at the head of the table. Shadow, a beer of his own in his hand, dropped into the chair at Renegade's right hand.

I didn't bother asking what was up. It wouldn't be discussed until everyone was present and accounted for.

Forks came in a minute later, wiping grease off his hands with a sorry, faded red mechanic's rag.

Next came Enigma, then the Butcher Brothers — Skull & Bones, and a little after that, Pope, Toad, Pud, Kain, Switch — and then we waited.

...and waited, and waited, and *waited*... Renegade got pissed, Shadow stepped out, making repeated texts and calls, and then *finally,* Mugshot brought his happy ass in.

"What the fuck took you so long, pretty boy?" Switch demanded before anyone else could with a sniff.

"Never mind that now. He's here, and that's all that matters," Renegade declared. Still, Mugshot wasn't entirely off the hook as Renegade shot him a dark look and said, "I'll want an explanation later."

Mugshot looked a little green around the gills, and I couldn't say I blamed him — because *fuck that.* No one wanted to be on Renegade's bad side, especially not someone who wanted to keep their face as pretty as Mugshot did.

Modeling was his main gig — thus, he did *a lot* to keep his face and skin in good condition.

The meeting was swiftly called to order, and I had a regret that I didn't grab a second beer or at least a soda before we got started.

Oh, well.

CHAPTER TWO

R arity...

"What the fuck, Charlie?" I demanded, loud and clear over the din of bikes down below. I glared over my shoulder at Charlie, the Iron Horse's manager, and he just gave me a lackadaisical shrug and turned around and fucked off the other way, which just pissed me off even more.

The rules were fucking clear, signs everywhere – *no colors!*

No colors didn't mean that these biker dipshit, grown-ass men behaving like toddlers, couldn't come in at all. It just meant they couldn't come up in here wearing their colorfully patched clown vests. It wasn't a hard rule to follow, but it *was* a hard and fast rule.

"What the fuck is right," Gemma muttered, passing behind me with a rack of clean glasses.

I shook my head, finished pulling my beer, and passed the glass to the waiting customer, who was probably fifty-something and was way more a tourist than an actual biker. A weekend warrior type. Sometimes called a RUB or Rich Urban Biker.

He winked at me and turned to watch the men who had just

rolled in with their orange-and-black dirty vests with a scorpion on the back.

I swallowed hard and exchanged a look with Gemma.

I was a born and raised Ormond Beach local. It was sort of an unspoken Switzerland or neutral territory of bikerdom – but none of us were stupid or crazy enough to overlook the fact that Biker Shangri-La or not, we all sat firmly in the middle of Royal Bastards country and the Bloody Scorpions were persona non grata where the Royal Bastards were concerned.

Walking up into the Iron Horse with their colors on may or may not have been an act of rebellion for the odd biker or two who came fresh into town and not bothering to read the sign, but for these guys? Oh, they *had to know*. There was no mistake. They *had to fucking know* that word would get back to the Royal Bastards and that it would be a declaration of all-out war or some shit.

I honestly didn't give a flying fuck what these whack jobs did or didn't do in their off time with their dick-measuring contests. I just didn't want to be here when the shit went down, and another battle in their ongoing war went down in the bar.

"Jesus Christ," Gemma murmured, coming up near me to watch as these assholes bellied up to the bar.

"Smile and serve, bitch. Duck and cover if we have to. I have no idea what the hell Charlie is even doing, allowing this shit to go down. And what the fuck? Where's Big Dawg and Grappler?"

"This many Bloody Scorpions?" she said incredulously. "Probably hiding."

I snorted in disgust. "Big Dawg doesn't hide from anything or anyone," I said.

"I don't know," she said.

"What can I get you?" I asked the first one up.

"Jack and Coke, sweetheart." He grinned at me and was missing his bottom two front teeth. The rest of them were brown, likely from a combination of smoking cigarettes and a major lack of hygiene.

"Coming right up," I said without smiling. Tonight was definitely going to call for a firm hand and my resting bitch face to be out in full force.

While I loved working at the Iron Horse, and I didn't mind it when the regulars and riders came through, these dipshits in the one percent tended to grind my gears. They were usually lewd, rude, crude, and – well, the tattooed part I never minded, actually. What I did mind was when they tipped like shit, or the only tip they gave me was one of their red handprints on the cheek of my ass, unasked for and unwelcome.

These yahoos had a reputation for *uncivil behavior,* and the guys with the Royal Bastards, while they had the reputation, they had at least obeyed the rules. To tell you the truth. I wouldn't be able to tell you who they were or one from the other because, again, they *followed* the *rules*.

Respect.

Some men had it, others... didn't.

It was a frustrating and interesting dichotomy.

"Switch to plastic," I told Gemma, and she nodded.

With these guys here, glass just seemed like a bad idea. Honestly, if I could get away with it, I'd probably hand one or two of these troglodytes a damn sippy cup.

As the night wore on, and these fools got drunk and drunker still, shit straight up started devolving into madness. Locals and regular customers started filtering out, and our security team and Charlie seemed disinterested in taking issue with the biker gang's rowdy and distasteful behavior – let alone their flouting of the rules in that each and every one of them *still* wore their colors *inside* the bar and no one seemed to want to say a word about it.

I tried, pointing out the sign to just about every one of them coming up to my bar to order another round. All I got was laughed in my face for it, which ground my gears even more.

Gemma was doing her best to placate one of them, who had their arms around her. Rolling her eyes clearly at me, she mouthed for me to get help.

I threw down my towel and went and found Big Dawg.

"My dude, either you get up off your big ass and *do* something to help Gemma out, or I'm fixin' to cause a scene," I snapped at him. My southern drawl was in peak performance with the temperature of my anger rising.

"Aw, shit," he muttered, looking in Gemma's direction. She was pressing both hands to the dirty rider trying to force a kiss on her and desperately calling for Big Dawg to come help her. He finally lumbered off his stool and, with a big, unhappy sigh, marched across the deck in the direction of Gemma and her brute.

He went over and calmly tried to defuse the situation, but shit went sideways pretty quick.

Faster than was almost even possible, the drunk biker thrust Gemma aside, and one of those collapsible batons materialized in his hand. I shouted a warning, but he brought it up, crashing into the side of Big Dawg's face.

Big Dawg hit the deck, and Gemma screamed. No sooner did she let out her bleat of panic and terror at watching our big friend and colleague drop like a sack of potatoes, the same biker *spit on my friend.*

I lunged, screaming at him to get the fuck out of my bar, and his hand flashed out of nowhere. It was lights out for me, too.

I'm afraid I missed the rest of whatever action took place because the next thing I knew, I had a medic who'd come out of nowhere shining some kind of penlight into my eyes, first one, then the other.

I blinked and winced, groaning. He asked, "Do you know how long she was unconscious?"

It was a whole lot of fuss after that. The world swimming in streaks and streamers as I felt like I was going to throw up.

"I'm gonna hurl," I managed, and did just that. I heard one of the medics say into the radio on their shoulder, "We're going to need a second bus for a female, possible TBI, over."

"*Copy that, 3148, dispatching that second unit now...*" I heard.

I turned my head, groaning, and Gemma's face filled my vision.

"I called your mom, don't worry," she said, and I groaned.

The last thing I needed was my mother coming up here with my three super little brothers having a conniption fit over my getting hurt.

Or maybe that's just what I needed. Who didn't want their mommy when they were hurt?

CHAPTER THREE

Striker...

"You gotta be shitting me," Enigma said, wide-eyed.

Shadow shook his head. "Not one bit," he said.

"Look at these fuckers, just bold as brass," Skull said in his thick Cajun accent, leaning back in his chair.

Renegade looked like his legit first name – Stormy. I was always a little jealous of the fact that Renegade's legit government name was something so cool.

"So, what we gon' do about it?" Pope asked with a savage grin.

Shadow had gotten a call from one of the waitresses down at the Iron Horse in Ormond Beach, about forty-five minutes south of us. Said the Bloody Scorpions had ridden in like they owned the place, and the manager, Charlie, had been too pussy to stand up to them. That one of those pig fucking sons a bitches had gotten handsy with her, and when security had finally gotten off their ass to step in, that the fucker'd knocked his ass clean out.

Now that? That wasn't really no thing. What'd happened next when one of the other girly little bartenders had stepped up? Now *that* was fucked up. He'd backhanded that bitty thing into next week.

So bad, both Big Dawg and the little girl had been taken to the hospital by ambulance.

It was clearly these dumb motherfuckers pissing on Ormond Beach like a dog marking its territory. Problem was, Ormond Beach wasn't a foothold we'd be willing to let the Bloody Scorpions have.

Granted, we had only a few chapters scattered throughout the Sunshine State. Us here in St. Augustine, the boys up in Jacksonville, and another chapter over mid-north of the state in Ocala. We were creeping our way down, establishing strongholds, but apparently, the Bloody Scorpions had their own designs on parts of Florida.

I didn't like that. None of us did. Not one bit.

The Iron Horse had always served the biker community, no matter who rode in or how they rode. You showed up on two wheels, you had their respect, and they showed you hospitality with pride and something like grace. They'd always operated as a sort of neutral ground – no colors, no fighting, and no fuckin' turf war garbage. So, this shit? This shit was fucked up.

Not just a slap in our face thinking they could just waltz this close to or even inside our territorial lines to fuck around, but the fact they thought they could do it without finding out.

This was blatant. According to Shadow's contact, they'd come in enough numbers that the bar had been afraid to even *try* to enforce their own rules with good reason. Those boys were used to fightin' and breakin' up fights. They knew when they were outmatched and outnumbered. My best guess is that they knew that the Bloody Scorpions were spoiling for a fight. One they hoped they could avoid by just playing it cool. Problem was, the Scorpions had no fuckin' chill, the big fuckin' babies.

"I'm going to put in a call up to Jacksonville and over to Ocala," Renegade said judiciously.

"What kind of numbers are we talking?" Switch asked.

"Shit," Pope said with a laugh. "Flip your switch an' you're good to take out at least seven of 'em dawg."

"Yeah, I'd say that's a conservative estimate," Switch said with a savage grin. "Problem ain't gettin' started. It's who's gonna stop me from merc'ing one or more of their asses. I like living on the *outside* if you know what I'm sayin'."

"Fair," Pope said. "More than fair."

"Jacksonville and Ocala," I said, getting right back on task. "Then what?"

"Then we ride on down there and put a stop to this fuckin' nonsense, yeah?" Skull asked.

"That's about the right of it, I reckon," Pud said, staring off into space.

"Sounds like a solid plan," I said. "Only going to work if we show up in more numbers than they got, which takes time."

"True story," Shadow said.

"So, what, we just going to lull them into some false sense of security? Let 'em run amok?" Toad asked.

"No," Renegade said. "We're going to move fucking *fast*."

"Element of surprise," Pope said, grinning. "I like it."

"Yeah, who doesn't?" I murmured, already running the logistics of this run through my brain. "Rally here?" I asked.

"Best bet," Shadow agreed.

"Cool," Renegade said. "Sounds like we don't even have to put it to a vote, but let's do it anyway – by the book. All in favor of riding down to Ormond Beach and fucking some shit up?"

Every hand shot up.

"By unanimous decision, let's make those calls, Shadow."

"You got it," Shadow intoned, pushing to his feet.

"You take Jacksonville, I'll take Ocala?" I asked.

"Time is of the essence," Shadow agreed.

"Bet," I told him.

CHAPTER FOUR

R**arity...**
"Rarity, oh thank God!"
Shit. Mom was here.

I sighed as she rushed to me in my hospital bed and wrapped me in a hug so tight I thought my head would squeeze off.

I was supposed to be an only child. My mom and dad had struggled with fertility issues, and when I'd been born, I'd been named *Rarity* as an ode to the fact I was supposed to be their only one.

I was twenty-four, and I had three younger brothers. A set of identical triplets that my mom had come up *surprise! I'm pregnant!* When I was *nineteen...* They were all four years old now, and right before they'd been born? Dad had died on us. A stupid accident. So here was Mom with three newborn sons, and I, her only daughter, was *still* a rarity.

Unfortunately, that sometimes meant that Mom went overboard on the overprotective helicopter parenting where I was concerned. At the same time, she was just as bad about the boys. She'd had them so late in her forties it'd been a dangerous-as-fuck pregnancy, and I'd been terrified I was going to lose her, too, in childbirth. And so soon after I'd lost Dad? *Woof.* Let's just say that when the boys had been born, I'd bawled more over the fact that Mom was *okay* than over the fact that I had three new, amazing baby brothers – but she didn't need to know that.

Some things were just best kept to yourself, you know?

Anyway, the whole thing had been a fucking rollercoaster. More so when it'd fallen to *me* to be the other adult and parent figure.

Dad had made damn good money when he was alive, and my salary at the Iron Horse and my other job at a craft store wasn't anything close. But we were making it. Barely. Some of it in part due to my mother's overbearing parents moving into the house with us, some by virtue of my mom's full-time job at the DMV.

Holy hell, was it rough making ends meet, though, even with the house being very nearly paid off thanks to Dad's life insurance. The homeowner's insurance was *wild* thanks to hurricanes picking up in frequency, speed, and destructive power, and they were *killing* us. Feeding three growing boys was no joke, either. Add cars aging out and blowing up, gas and groceries being sky high, keeping three boys in clothes and shoes when it felt like something new was having to be bought week to week, and the fact that the three of them were still young enough to want to dress alike and would throw a fit if they didn't always get to? Yeah, I know, I know, they should have to suck it up, but you try telling my mother that. Especially on top of her guilt of Dad being gone, which was in no way her fault.

It was just a stupid accident!

"Mom, Mom, Mom! *Stop!* I'm fine! I'm fine!" I got her to stop fussing. She leaned back, overwhelmed and mascara and eyeliner tracking muddy down her face.

"I don't want you working there!" she tried. I shook my head, grinding my teeth against the sudden wave of nausea that tried like hell to swamp me.

"No, no, no, and no!" I said. "Absolutely not. We're not doing this," I declared, and she scowled at me.

"It's too dangerous," she tried to argue. "Just look at you!"

"We can't make it without the tips. Besides, I'm an adult, and it's not your choice."

The curtain was whisked aside in the emergency room bay I was in, and the doctor came in, interrupting any further discussion of my employment status.

"Well, your scans did come back with signs of a mild-to-moderate concussion," he said.

"Oh!" My mother covered her mouth with both hands.

"Mom, stop!" I snapped. "I could have just as easily gotten it playing soccer."

The doctor chuckled. "That's true, actually, but that's not what happened here, now is it?"

I sighed. "No offense, but not you, too, Doc. I *need* my job."

"Well, you *need* to take some time off," he said, and I stubbornly shook my head, gritting my teeth. I needed to look fine. I needed to *be* fine. I couldn't miss any hours.

"I'm fine," I argued.

"You are most assuredly going to *be* fine, but you're definitely not fine right now," he said.

"My poor baby." My mom's voice cracked.

"I'm going to work tomorrow," I griped. "And there's nothing either of you can do to stop me."

The doctor sighed, lowering my chart and grasping the clipboard at his waist, arms crossed and gripping the edge.

"That may be true, but you'll need to follow the head injury and concussion protocol tonight..."

I impatiently waited for the doctor to fill my mother in on what needed to be done, since he clearly didn't trust me to handle myself, much to my frustration. I wasn't a child! But I got it. I wasn't exactly an adult, either – not at just twenty-four. I mean, wasn't it something like twenty-five before your frontal cortex or whatever fully developed?

Honestly, I was too tired to fucking care. I just wanted to go home.

The entire car ride from the hospital to home, my mother lectured me on being careful and told me how much I needed to look after myself. Which, okay, fine, alright, I would take that – but when she started in on my job, I shut her down cold.

"Nope," I cut her off. "We aren't going there!" I declared.

"Rarity Jane Mitchell!" she cried, and I glared at her. She faltered, her face awash in the red light of the traffic light in front of us.

"Boundaries, Mother," I said firmly.

She crumbled a bit and looked so lost my heart gave a twist.

"I'm fine," I reiterated. "It was stupid and a one-off thing. It's the *Iron Horse*. It's not always going to be one hundred percent safe. That's the world we live in these days."

Her eyes welled up, and I made a slightly exasperated sound.

"It's green," I told her as the light changed. Just anything to get her to stop looking at me like that.

Thankfully, we made the rest of the ride home in silence, albeit an uncomfortable one.

Once home and inside the front door, my mother sighed disappointedly and said to me, "Go to bed. I'll get you up like the doctor told me."

I nodded tiredly and sighed. "I love you, Mom."

"I love you, too, baby," she declared. We hugged in the kitchen, and I went into my room across from the kitchen island while she went into her room past the dining room table.

I took a long, hot shower before drying my long blonde hair and braiding it to sleep. I had the promise of a spectacular swelling bruise across one cheekbone, climbing up my temple and around my right eye. Right now, it was hard to see under the harsh bathroom light, the barest shadowing of blue under my skin with the chance to darken like a motherfucker given time.

I made a face at my reflection and looked at the rest of me. Long blonde hair, wide blue eyes, and a smattering of freckles across my nose and cheeks made me feel like I looked thirteen with my face scrubbed clean of makeup. It also made me look like some kind of preacher's daughter – all sweet and innocent.

Nothing could be further from the truth. My dad had lived fast, my mom had too, and I had been the apple of both of their eyes. I mean, I still was, I guess, but things were so different now without him.

Life kind of sucked, and I felt bad for my kid brothers. They would never get to know him, or me and Mom, and what we were like with him around. All they got to see was the both of us working ourselves to the bone, trying to keep things together. Man, we weren't the same. Life just wasn't the same... and four years on, it felt like the grief would never end.

I turned away from the mirror and clicked out the bathroom light as I moved into my bedroom, which had pictures of happier times of me, Mom, and Dad stuck to the walls everywhere. There were also pictures of Aden, Braden, and Caden – *yes, my mom went there. No, she wouldn't listen to reason. And yes, even though I was vociferously against it, I still thought the names were adorable, and they'd only gotten cuter the more the boys had grown.*

I crawled into bed, cuddled under my fluffy comforter, and closed my eyes. Before I knew it, I was asleep. I swear my mother was shaking me back awake in the blink of an eye. I groaned and flailed an arm in her direction and grumbled about being up. She made me get up and walk around the kitchen island before she would let me lay back down.

So stupid, which I know – she was worried – so it wasn't stupid... but still.

A full night of that shit, and I felt wrecked. Nevertheless, I got my ass up, got dressed in my uniform for the craft store, and slipped out before my mom could stop me. I marched resolutely an hour-plus walk back to the Iron Horse to get my keys, my phone, and most importantly, *my car* to drive myself to what I considered my first job.

Thank God for caffeine and sunglasses.

When I arrived, it was to a pretty serious cleanup effort and oh, yay, *Charlie* was still here and he was standing with the owner.

"Rarity! You're alright!" the owner called, and I nodded tiredly.

"Concussion, but I've got to work, and I'll be here tonight."

"That's my girl!" Charlie tried to sound enthusiastic but my withering look and pulling off my sunglasses shut that shit right down.

"I'm just here for my keys, phone, and car," I told him.

Rob looked a little green around the gills because of my face.

"Nasty shiner, girl. You sure you're alright?" he asked me.

I looked at him. "I'll be better if Charlie Boy and security would actually enforce the rules around here. I mean, for real, *what the fuck was that* last night?" I demanded.

"It'll be taken care of," Rob grunted, and I believed him. Charlie at least had the grace to look embarrassed, which was something, I guess.

"Oh, yeah? What's the plan?" I asked.

"Extra security tonight," Rob said. "And I'll be on-site later."

I nodded slowly and said, "It's a start. How's Gemma?" I asked.

"Fine! Fine! She's fine. All good," Charlie stammered nervously.

"Big Dawg?" I asked, raising my eyebrows.

"Fractured orbital. He'll be out a while," Rob said, and he didn't sound happy about it.

A little instant karma, I thought to myself. I knew it was bitchy, but damn – he's the head of security when he's on shift, and he let that shit go for far too long. So as bitchy as the thought was, it was also *true*. Of course, Charlie was the manager, as he always liked to remind us. He was the one in charge and held the power. We were just to do what we were *told*. That had definitely tied Dawg's hands to an extent, and for *that*, I low-key felt bad for him. But still, Big Dawg could have crumpled Charlie between his hands and thrown him into the garbage bin. He should have told Charlie to fuck off and pulled rank as *head of security* when it came to the bar's, *you know,* actual security?

Wild concept, I know – but *ugh.*

"It'll all be good tonight," Rob declared. "I doubt they'll be back after the cops were called last night."

Well, shit. I wished I had as much faith as good ol' Rob, but lord.

"I'm going to grab my phone and keys. I'll be back tonight," I said. I ran upstairs to my bar and punched the keypad of the cubby under it. The door beeped and clicked, popping open. I retrieved my personal belongings and scrolled through the burst of messages and texts that'd come through the night before.

I walked back to my car, answering everyone, but it was Gemma's text that caught my eye.

You know, fuck Charlie, fuck Big Dawg, and especially fuck Rob for not firing them after that shit show. Don't worry, girl. Tonight's going to be different, I promise. I took matters into my own hands and made some calls.

Interesting...

I texted her back that I was okay and let her know about Rob's big master plan to supposedly keep tonight different.

I got back an eye-rolling emoji from Gemma and a **yeah, right, for real, just you wait.**

I couldn't think about it anymore. if I wasted any more time, I was going to be late getting to work. I twisted the key in the ignition to my dad's old Jeep, and it fired up, old reliable. I loved that it was an old standard shift. He'd taught me to drive it before he'd died, promising me if I could drive a standard, I could drive just about anything.

With a sigh, I worked the clutch and gear shift, putting it into reverse and backing it out of the grassy, sandy parking space on the side of the road across from the gas station next to the bar.

There was no real parking for cages at the bar, just bikes. After last night, I expected the place to be *packed* tonight. I mean, it was going to be a typical Saturday night at the Iron Horse, but with the added excitement from last night? It was probably going to be packed even *more*.

Yay. I hoped the tips were at least good. I had a shiny new ambulance bill to pay, and that shit ain't cheap.

At least I was still on my mom's insurance for the hospital visit.

Being a broke-ass adult in Florida sucked ass.

CHAPTER FIVE

S triker...

"Hey, hey! What's up, my dude?"

The greeting, more than the voice, tipped me off that I wasn't speaking to anyone but Kash Kendrick of the Ocala chapter of the RBMC.

"Wish it was a social call, Kash—" I halted a moment and said, "Well, actually, for us, it kind of is. But all the same, this is club business and serious business at that."

"Oh yeah?" he asked. "Gimme the 4-1-1."

I filled him in on the situation in Ormond Beach and what the Bloody Scorpions were up to. He was quiet on the other end of the line.

"So basically, what do you say? Feel like coming up our way to party and maybe do a tap dance on some Scorpion's face?"

"Dude, fuck yeah! You know I like a little violence with my beer. You guys have a master plan?"

"Renegade's on the phone with Jameson, and Shadow's calling up to Jacksonville. Man, you know we got a plan."

Kash laughed.

"Dude, I'm sure Jameson is just going to *love* Renegade being in charge of this one," Kash declared.

"Fuck your West Coast. Ain't no party like an *East Coast* party on this one," I told him.

He laughed again and said, "Lemme get with The Bishop and see if we can't get the rest of the boys on board."

"Might want to leave the ol' ladies out of this ride," I told him.

"Aw, bet, bet. They can be as fuckin' pissed off as they wanna get, but this is for sure not a ride for them."

"No. No, it is not," I affirmed.

"Hit me back in about fifteen minutes."

"Copy that. Talk soon," I said.

"Cool, cool," he said.

I checked the clock and sat back in my chair, staring at the burner on my desk and waiting the allotted fifteen minutes. It rang after barely ten. I picked up.

"Dude!" Kash called on the other end of the line.

"Yeah?" I asked.

"Fuckin' count us in," he said. "What were you guys thinkin'? Tonight?"

"Tonight," I affirmed. "We wanna be fashionably late, add a little insult to injury by whooping their asses when they think they got the high ground. Y'all have been to the Iron Horse, right? You know how it's set up?"

"Yeah, yeah!" Kash affirmed. "We got you. Let's fuck some shit up! Text you when we roll out, dude."

"Keep the shiny side up, brother."

"And the dirty side down," Kash quipped, and the line went dead.

Shadow came out of his office, and I gave him a thumbs-up. He threw me some chin and called out, "Jacksonville is mobilizing."

Renegade came out of his office, and I asked, "How'd it go?"

"The usual," Renegade said. "Jameson told me to do it his way. I asked him if I'd ever let his ass down before, and he told me to fuck off and get it done and don't fuck it up." Renegade gave a shrug.

Shadow and I laughed.

Renegade and Jameson had a... *contentious* relationship sometimes.

Jameson wasn't exactly known to be the trusting sort, but if there was any president of any chapter of this fuckin' club that was trustworthy – it was fucking Renegade.

Ren had taken up for Jameson under Rancid's rule as far as he could without getting out bad under that fuckstick's megalomaniac charge.

Of course, Renegade always did shit his own way and in his own time, and damn if he didn't have a knack for coming up roses. It tended to gripe Jameson's ass, who was particular and liked shit done his way or the highway. It caused Ren and Jameson to lock horns on more than one occasion, but Jameson had to grudgingly admit Renegade had it going on. Slowly but surely, Jameson'd learned to loosen the reins.

Funny thing was, the more he unclenched his fist around Renegade, the better Renegade brought the kind of results and then some to lay at our king's feet. Now, Jameson begrudgingly let Renegade have free rein, and yeah – that's how Renegade had gotten his name. It was more than fitting and a badass honorific.

When Jameson had looked at the map of North Florida for a strategic place to fortify our club's holdings, Renegade, who was already a local for St. Augustine, had been Jameson's choice to anoint as president of the St. Augustine chapter.

The rest, as they say, was history.

Now it was just a bunch of hurry-up-and-fucking-wait for Jacksonville and Ocala to show up. Since our chapter was hosting this run, I had my work cut out for me to put it together and lay out the ride's master plan. I got on Google Maps and busted out the graph paper to put down the formations.

Truth be told, I was jazzed. It sure beat the fuck out of the boredom and staring out the alcoves wishing something would happen.

Of course, the phrase *be careful what you wish for* certainly entered the back of my mind while I worked.

CHAPTER SIX

R arity...

All I wanted was some goddamn sleep when I got off work at the craft store, so I went home to get a nap before getting ready to work my shift at the Iron Horse.

The house was blessedly quiet when I went in. Mom was out with the boys, probably at the beach, and Grandma and Grandpa were up in Tennessee for a weekend getaway in the Smoky Mountains.

Worked for me.

I set my alarm and lay down.

My eye had purpled up, but the swelling had gone down. Still, I'd been chastised by my manager at the craft store for being "clumsy." I didn't have the heart to tell her, *Wanda, I got clocked in a bar fight – I couldn't avoid that. Clumsy had nothing to do with it.*

Of course, Wanda came from a time and place when a woman was "clumsy," it was because her husband had swung on her. Typically, divorce wasn't an option, but oopsie, her hubby would go on to die doing something stupid, like falling off a ladder, or would simply go to sleep one night and not wake up. A tragic turn of events... and yeah, I'm rolling my eyes so hard, I just checked out my own ass.

It is what it is, or rather, *it was what it was* back then. Nowadays, if a man laid a hand on me, I'd do exactly what my daddy taught me to do. I'd mace his ass, get him right in the balls, or break a damn bottle over his head.

My father had taught his only daughter to breathe fucking *fire* and it was a lesson I wouldn't soon forget.

Of course, my mother, on the other hand, worried enough for the both of us.

I got up from my nap and honestly felt *more* tired, but that wasn't anything an energy drink from behind the bar wouldn't fix.

I was in my bathroom, pulling my long hair into a high pony, when I heard the front door open. My bathroom had two doors. One that opened just inside the front door, and another that opened directly into my bedroom. I typically kept the one inside the front door locked.

I unlocked it now and pulled it open to my mom and a gaggle of triplet toddler boys piling in the front door of the house.

"Rarity!" Aden, or Caden cried. Braden came right to me and hugged me tight, his hair still dampened with seawater, Mom juggling their life vests and floaty wings and whatever other beach floaty toys she'd taken with her.

"Hey, baby girl, how are you feeling?" she asked.

"Tired as hell, but determined to get to work on time and finish tonight's shift."

I let Braden go. He was the quiet one. Mom ordered the boys into their bathroom to rinse off in their shower.

They went but under protest, at least one of them throwing a tantrum when I told them I couldn't help, that I had to go to work.

"Good luck," I told my mom, and she rolled her eyes.

"I'm going to need it," she said and, worriedly, made a last-ditch effort to change my mind. "I wish you would just stay home..."

"Nope!" I declared.

She sighed. "Stubborn, just like your father."

"Thank you!" I yelled at the compliment. She laughed and hugged me back, and out the door I went.

The drive out of the neighborhood took the longest when it came to the commute to the Iron Horse. I got a premium spot, which was lucky, considering how fast they filled up on the weekend.

I trudged across the gas station parking lot in my comfortable Converse, my long legs slathered in sunscreen, wearing the short jean shorts that I tended to prefer behind the bar. I was in a ladies-cut Iron Horse Saloon bartender's tee, and I could already hear the band, loud and blaring out from the open-air venue.

The roar of bikes made me wince. As I climbed up to my bar, I noticed it wasn't as crowded as you'd expect it to be.

Why did that unnerve me so much?

Gemma hugged me and wrinkled her nose at my shiner that I hadn't even bothered to try and cover with makeup. Could it hurt my tips? Maybe. Was it likely to garner me more? Maybe.

I didn't care much about that, though. I cared more about the fact that every time I looked in Charlie's direction, he would get really uncomfortable and immediately look away.

Feeling a little guilty? I thought to myself in his direction.

I could be the Queen of Petty when I wanted to be, and on this? Oh, I wanted to be petty. Yes, I did!

Fucking asshole.

The energy of the Iron Horse picked up as the sun started to dip in the sky. Business started to become brisk, but there weren't many bikes down below – at least not yet. The distant roar rumbled out there at the road and signaled their approach. All too soon, that growl that could have been mistaken for thunder resolved into bikes, a real *big* damn pack of them. When they rolled up, the whole deck that bar number two, the bar that I worked, vibrated with ferocity as they spilled underneath. They rolled across the packed dirt of the yard down below, sending up plumes of dust in their wake as they all piled in and parked close to fit everyone.

I heard shouts, our security flowing down steps and out into the crowd coming in, and I felt my heart sink.

"What club?" I shouted over the combined music and roar of bike motors.

"Same one as last night!" Gemma hollered back at me from across the bar as she set the tub of bar glass on the bar's top and slid it across to me.

We took turns bartending and bar-backing. It was going to be my round of bar-backing next, which meant taking a tub with me out into the crowds on the deck, picking up any errant mess, and bringing the empty glasses back in.

By the sounds of it, this would be the *last* round of bar-backing for our glassware. It was time to switch to plastic. We tended to go full plastic when the crowds thickened up like this.

I felt my heart sink even more when the first biker from down below crested the top of the steps, and *yep* – he was wearing his *fucking* colors.

"Stay behind the bar with me. Let Grayson barback if he's not going to work any kind of *actual* security," Gemma said dispassionately.

"We'll give it a round or two, and then I'll go out," I called back. "I'm not letting anyone scare me from doing my job!"

"Oh, my *God*! Rarity! Just *who* are you trying to prove yourself to?" Gemma exclaimed, exasperated.

Myself, I thought grimly. I was trying to prove to myself that I could, and would, do my damn job and that these motherfuckers didn't scare me.

I didn't answer Gemma out loud. I just started slinging drinks with as much grim determination as I had about getting my skinny ass out there to gather up any remaining stray empty glasses.

After the pile of bikers had been served their tequila, beer, and Jack and Cokes – or whatever the hell else they were swilling down – I grabbed a bus tub and ducked under the end of the bar to head out into the crowd.

The music blaring from the stage down below was distorted and completely drowned out too quickly by a fresh pack of bikers pulling in. Only instead of a sea of black and orange, these guys wore black and red.

Shit.

I swallowed hard and moved fast. I did *not* want to be out in the crowd when the Royal Bastards MC hit the top of those steps.

This was going to be a shit show.

CHAPTER SEVEN

S triker...

Riding into the Iron Horse, up under the decks and bars on their stilts, and watching the faces on the security guys arguing with the Bloody Scorpions, and the faces of the Bloody Scorpions themselves fall flat – that shit was *priceless*.

The plan had been discussed, the game was set, and it was time to *match*.

The thing about the Bloody Scorpions was these motherfuckers were out here playing checkers while the Royal Bastards were out here playing a fucking master class in *chess*.

The idea was simple as far as plans went. We were here to have a fucking drink. That was all. We pulled up, in our cuts, and sure – we were breaking the rules, *but* – they broke them first, so fuck it. Right? The rules applied to all of us, or they applied to none of us. The precedent had been set last night when no one got kicked out for sporting colors inside the bar. The slippery slope was slicker than owl shit, and we would have divested if we hadn't rolled up and seen the Scorpions still sporting their colors proudly without any clapback.

They had theirs, and we'd keep ours, but we'd also keep it PC and play it cool.

We were remaining respectful, throwing little verbal barbs, sure, but we weren't going to be the ones to throw down first. Couldn't claim self-defense if you threw the first punch.

That wasn't in the cards. That wasn't how things worked.

We rolled up, heeled down our stands, and parked, effectively blocking these losers in. We smiled and nodded politely and took our asses upstairs to have a drink.

We stuck together for the most part, and as we hit the top steps, I spotted her.

She was short, but *stacked*, her tee fitted and showing off the girls with the deep V of the neckline. Her blonde hair rode in a high pony-tail, the beachy waves swinging back and forth as she passed by. She had an ass to match those tits of hers.

What didn't match was the deep shadow of blue, rotting into purple, surrounding her right eye.

She must've been the waitress or bartender who'd been knocked out the night before. I appreciated the pair of brass ovaries she was sporting to be back at it so soon and vowed to get her name.

"Rarity!" the brunette behind the bar called out, and the blonde quickly turned her head.

Well, that was easy, I thought to myself.

Rarity, the barmaid with the black eye, jogged back over to the central bar up here and passed the tub of glassware across it to the brunette before ducking up under the end of the bar and taking up post behind it.

I bellied up to it on her end and smiled at her, turning on what little charm I had.

"Hi!" I called across to her.

"What'll you have?" she asked, almost *demanded*, all while looking bored.

That was fair. She'd been clocked into next week just last night. I'd be sick of shit, too.

"IPA," I called back, and she set about getting me my pour, her face a mix of uninterested, weary, and *wary*.

"Thanks kindly, baby girl!" I called to her, and she made a face.

"Sweetheart?" I tried.

"Worse!" she called back.

"Beautiful?" I hazarded.

She snorted, clearly, but whatever indelicate sound accompanied her facial expression was drowned all the way out between the band and the din of customers.

"That'll be eight dollars!" she called.

"Oh! Highway robbery!" I joked.

"Yeah, well, it's a three-dollar charge just for putting up with you!" she called back. I put both hands over my heart and half stumbled back as Kash came up beside me and laughed at my getting shot down.

I handed her a ten and called back, "Keep the change, baby!"

She didn't look at me, just rang me up and stuffed the extra bills into her back pocket, moving down the line to help the next paying customer.

"Watch this," Pud said, tugging on his cut, and he moved in to shoot his shot with her.

"Ten dollars!" she called out.

"You just charged him eight!" he cried.

"Yeah, well, you're worse!" she yelled back at him, and a bunch of us fell out laughing. He paid her with a twenty, and she gave him back the correct change – which was actually more than ten dollars. Kash stopped Pud before I could.

"C'mon, dude! Tip the lady!" Kash called.

"Here's a tip," Pud called over his shoulder, and the girl raised her eyebrows. "Don't be such a bitch!"

A chorus of *ooohs* went up around us and she just waved the lot of us off, unimpressed.

I handed her a five and, raising my voice over the din, said, "Sorry about that. He can be a dick."

"You mean I'm all dick!" Pud said, grabbing his crotch in my direction. I rolled my eyes and was looking forward to him throwing hands with someone who maybe went for his balls. I would let Karma sort my brother out.

I turned back to the pretty little bartender and looked her over.

"I have to guess you know what's coming," I said. I tried to keep my voice low and for her only. She leaned in to listen, and I said, "When shit gets started, I want you and the other girl to duck and cover. I don't want you to come out until after the sirens get here and it's gone quiet. You understand me?"

She looked up at me sharply, her blue eyes flashing keenly, but she gave a single curt nod.

"Good girl," I said without thinking, and the prettiest blush worked its way across her nose and cheeks, and she got flustered. Her ears turned bright red as she pushed away from me and the bar and made her way to the other end.

I couldn't help but grin as I watched her go, and I took a sip of my pale beer. It was crisp, hoppy, and dank as fuck, which is what I liked in an IPA. I would have to try and remember to ask what she'd poured me. It was some good shit.

I drifted on over to stand with some of my Royal Bastards brethren. We were scattered in knots among the varying bundles and micro-groups of Bloody Scorpions. The tension was so thick in the air that you could cut it with a knife.

Dudes in plain clothes were scattered throughout all of us patched bikers in even smaller knots of twos and threes. They were all hugging the railing or edging toward the stairs, casting a watchful eye on the rest of us up here, rightfully waiting for the thing that'd make one of us snap and the free-for-all to begin.

They were victims of arriving here before the rest of the lot of us, their bikes blocked in, unable to flee like I know they wanted to.

Instead, they started making their way down to the food, lower bars, gift shop, and down where the heavy-duty sewing machines with all the patches were set up.

They would likely barricade themselves into employee-only areas and duck and cover when the fists started to fly, which was smart. With how much the Bastards and the Scorpions hated each other – shit wasn't exactly liable to stay at just fists.

Now, we were taking a gamble – and had mostly left our firearms locked away in our bikes or left them off our person altogether.

Was that a major risk?

Fuck yeah, but it was a calculated one. Law enforcement from all over the fuckin' place was liable to show up, and shit was liable to get searched. It behooved those of us with felony records to *not* have an unauthorized weapon on our bikes or persons.

Of course, that was what the prospects were for. While St. Augustine didn't have any, we were relying on Jacksonville's and Ocala's to plant some street weapons on the bikes below for the Bloody Scorpions to make their day a real rotten one when law enforcement showed up. When the brawl started – which it *would* start – our boys in plain clothes who had gotten here early enough were to do their thing with the distraction going on up top.

While just about all of us would wind up in cuffs, and some of us would head to county while the others headed to city lockup for the rest of the weekend, we were prepared for it.

Renegade, The Bishop, and Creed, the Jacksonville chapter's president, would make their calls to the Royal Bastard's respective lawyers, and shit would get sorted out.

It all just predicated on us being cool and the Bloody Scorpions losing their shit to where they threw down first.

We knew where the cameras were, and we hung inside their view. That footage would be the first thing collected by the pigs and would likely be the first thing subpoenaed by our defense guys.

While the Royal Bastards were getting a stronghold formed up in North Florida, we'd been doing it carefully and quietly, working mostly above board and legal – nothing that law enforcement could get us on for RICO or other organized crime charges.

That was on purpose.

Strategic.

We were moving the pieces across the board. Building empires took fucking *time*.

Something these idiots in their Halloween costumes couldn't understand. I shot a dirty look in the direction of the nearest set of black-and-orange colors and turned back to Switch. He was a sarcastic motherfucker, and his verbal barbs were just loud enough and scathing enough that you could see that tempers were starting to flare nearby.

Wouldn't you know it? They started edging away from our knot like the pussies they were, and we had a good laugh about that.

I felt eyes on me and glanced in that direction to catch little miss Rarity pulling a beer, but her true-blue eyes fixed on me, staring unabashedly.

I swilled down the rest of my beer and sauntered in her direction to grab another.

A Bloody Scorpion tried "stumbling" into me and knocking me pretty good. I stopped, put a hand out friendly like on his shoulder, gave him an easy smile, and called out, "You good there, buddy?"

"I ain't your fuckin' buddy!" he slurred and jerked his shoulder out from under my hand. I put my hands up in surrender, the boys in my knot of brothers and a few other Bastards watching like a hawk.

"No harm, no foul, bro!" I did say that *bro,* with all due disrespect, even though I kept my tone light and polite.

"I ain't your fuckin' bro, either! You son of a bitch!"

"Hey now, let's keep my momma outta this. She was a good woman – God rest her soul."

Actually, my mother was alive and well, and I was her main disappointment in life, but that was neither here nor there.

"Fuck you!" he snarled, and I bobbed my head.

"You have a good day now!" I called as one of his brothers who could actually read the fuckin' room dragged him away.

So close, I thought to myself as I made it to the bar, tossing my cup into one of the nearby trash chutes and asking for another one.

"Sure thing," she said coolly, eyeing me.

"Mind telling me what that is? It's dank as fuck, and I *like* it!"

"Salt Waves & Spanish Moss Brewing. It's their Haunted Crypt IPA," she said.

"I'll be damned. Ain't they out of Savannah?" I asked.

She nodded. "Split off from the Moon River Brewing Company after a falling out."

"You know your beer culture," I said, taking the glass from her and handing her a ten. "Keep the change."

She threw some chin and operated the till, stuffing her tip in her back pocket, ignoring the shared tip jar in the back which was pretty empty.

I found that interesting – *smart,* considering the tension riding the air. For real, the sky was blue and clear for miles in every fuckin' direction, but still, there was a crackle-like electricity in the bar's atmosphere.

Like the barometric pressure was rising or dropping – whatever the hell it did with an impending thunderstorm about to let loose.

"Your shift ending soon?" I asked her.

She shook her head. "Just started."

"Well, damn," I said.

"I heard you loud and clear," she called back and moved on to help a Scorpion.

I guess concern had entered my voice because legit – I was worried about a pretty little thing like her getting hit again, or worse. If one of these dipshits opened up, it was anybody's game. Here was to hoping they'd keep it at fists.

We could be so lucky.

CHAPTER EIGHT

Rarity...

Tension rode my shoulders and tightened everything along my spine the more these yahoos danced around fighting each other. It wasn't a matter of "if" but *"when"* – the one with the name flash *Striker* had pretty much said as much. I didn't know how I felt about that.

On the one hand, a heads-up *was* always nice... on the other, all I could think was *could we just... not?*

I swear to God, it was a confusing scene in front of my bar. The men in red and black, their crowned skull of a logo on the back of their cuts, were fairly respectful. I didn't pay any mind to the one who tipped me by way of telling me not to be a bitch. That was banter at its finest around here, and besides that, Striker had made up for it. Honestly, I think his brother had been trying to be Striker's wingman.

I glanced up the bar to where Striker had left his place, wandering back to his little knot of fellow Royal Bastards.

He was older than me – but in that way that made it hard to tell if it was a lot, a little, or somewhere in between.

He had a good smile, all of his teeth in his head, but imperfect – a guy who had definitely never done the whole braces thing like I had, for which I was a little jealous. He had good teeth, too, just a couple crooked in the bottom set, and nothing crowded or gapped up top.

Checking a guy's teeth around here was almost a necessity. There was a lot of hardcore drug use in the area, and *no fucking thank you.*

I didn't ever want to hook up with some meth, ice, or worse – a budding flakka user.

I didn't want to end up like that poor homeless man with his face eaten off. Florida man was a real thing down here and I wanted no part in that crazy.

Judgmental of me? Probably more than a little bit, but that's how things had to go if you wanted to stay *safe* in this day and age.

About the only thing I liked about watching Striker sidle up to my bar was watching him *go.* He had a fine ass, and he knew how to wear his jeans. Wranglers by the look of them, and they fit him like a fucking *dream.*

He was ruggedly handsome with chin-length brown hair and a set of keen hazel eyes that leaned more to green than any other color. His white tee underneath his dirty, patched vest hugged all the right places, and he had a nice set to his shoulders and swell of his chest.

Made me want to lift the tee and see what was under the hood – which was kind of obnoxious. I didn't have time to date or for a fling or any of that. Not with Mom and the boys depending on me. My family was my whole world, and with Dad gone, I felt wholeheartedly like it fell to me. You know?

I know, my mom was supposed to be the adultier adult, but it'd taken two adults to keep things going and together when Dad had been alive. Even though his going had hit me hard – and I do mean *really* hard, my mom? It'd all but *destroyed* her. So, with him gone, a lot was my responsibility now. There were three boys who would someday need to go to college and live their best lives. While we'd set some chunks aside for them in some high-yield savings from

Dad's life insurance, it was only a drop in the bucket with things going up, and up, and up.

I automatically contributed a hundred dollars a month to each account, and that was a chunk of change times three.

Their future was *everything*... just like mine had been everything to my parents as I'd been growing up. I had no problem putting college on hold for a while to make sure the boys were taken care of. The plan was that things would get easier, and I would be able to do the whole school thing when *they* got into elementary school, which was only next year or, at worst, the year after.

Until then, I would work, work, work, work, *work*.

There was no way I could even pull in *half* of what my dad had when he was alive. Hell, I didn't even think I pulled in a third of his salary between both my jobs *and* tips, but something was definitely better than *nothing*.

It was scary and frustrating, for sure, but what else was there to do? It was like wading through quicksand anymore.

I focused hard on keeping both Gemma and me behind the bar as much as possible. If these idiots didn't throw down, it would make for a big fuckin' mess to clean up later and would keep us here well past closing to do it. But this was definitely the *safer* option.

The cops didn't really respond to bar fights here anymore – as long as things stayed to just fisticuffs. The *bikers* sure as hell wouldn't be the ones to call them in, and the staff didn't if we didn't *have to* because our employment depended on the bar remaining operational. Too much violence or too many calls into PD would get our liquor license suspended.

The only time we called the cops was if we had to call an ambulance, and even then, it was iffy on if we called the cops, too – generally preferring to white lie and say whatever altercation took place *outside* the bar behind the gas station up front and out at the road.

No, the cops didn't come unless shots were fired, which was a very real possibility tonight with how the vibe felt. If one of these assholes from *either* side started popping off, I wanted to be *behind* the bar ducking and covering behind the thick planks and steel refrigeration units back here.

I hadn't had to deal with more than just fists being thrown. There was one night, a knife came out, and a dude got his arm slashed bad enough that the wee-woo wagon had to be called in. But that was because he couldn't ride and our bouncer was holding his arm basically together and keeping the pressure on through three blood-soaked bar towels, and that was with an emergency tourniquet applied to his upper arm.

Had to hand it to the dude that got slashed, though.

None of us were really the wiser that anything was serious down on the ground where it'd happened. He didn't scream, cry, or holler at all. He just sat patiently and waited while Big Dawg held his shit together, and he puffed on a cigarette, waiting to get taken away.

That was the wildest thing to go down, and that was in the thick of Bike Week and Spring Break. Not this past year, but the year before.

This was my third summer working the outdoor decks. I usually found seasonal retail and stock work in the winter months when they stripped back the employment around here to the main indoor bar space up front.

"We're out of Jack!" Gemma called. "I have to go down!"

"Don't!" I called back. "Radio down to the boys. They need to bring some up! Neither one of us is wading through that." I jerked my head in the direction across the bar and to the thickening crowd up here.

She nodded and got on the radio.

The boys were generally runners and gophers anyway. Their main objective was to keep the trash chutes and garbage bins emptied, run liquor up here, or tap new kegs or new boxes of syrup for the soda machines when we ran dry. All of that was on the ground level and let us do what we were supposed to up here which was smile, flirt, and serve customers.

Neither of us was in a flirting mood up here today, though. Not with this crowd.

It was a tightwire act on a *good* day, and today was definitely *not* a good fucking day.

The feeling was palpable and indescribably dark. The energy shifted from wary to a careful circling of two hissing and spitting wildcats. The verbal barbs were sharper, the hatred so thick, it oozed up between the cracks in the boards and rolled out underfoot, climbing up each and every one of the bikers in a miasma of negativity.

It was such a thing, it was almost *physically visible* to the naked eye.

The biker, who was older than me but still hot, caught my eye from where he stood in a knot of his brothers and gave me a serious look and a wink, dipping his chin *just so* to let me know that this symphony of discord was about to hit its crescendo.

I nodded, imperceptibly enough, I hoped, and then it happened – a ruckus at the far end of the deck, between our bar and bar number three. It started with shouting, then devolved into shoving. I looked from the turbulence in the bodies to Striker. He made a hand gesture in my direction to get down, and I grabbed Gemma's wrist and pulled her down with me.

"Oh, shit," she said, and I nodded. We huddled small behind the bar and did the only thing we could - radioed downstairs to call in the cavalry... if they weren't too chickenshit to get their asses up here and throw down.

I didn't have high hopes for that. Clearly.

CHAPTER NINE

S triker...

It was on.

I looked over my shoulder to the bar and locked eyes with the barmaid. She looked a mix of angry and determined, but it all held a dash of caution and an edge of anxiety. I winked at her to hopefully give her a sense of *some* security and pushed my hand down to signal her to take cover.

She disappeared down behind the bar and dragged her bar mate down with her.

Good fucking girl, I thought to myself, and then the wall of bodies scrapping in front of us undulated and crashed into our little knot of brothers, sweeping us into the fray.

It was a whirlwind of hands and fists flying in every direction. I looked for orange and grabbed hold of a fucker swinging on Feral, the treasurer for the Jacksonville chapter. He grinned at me, gave a nod, and started laying into the Scorpion I had a hold of who'd been trying to punch Feral's lights out. Feral grinned with ferocity, his teeth coated in his own blood as he hooked his fist up and into the solar plexus of the fuckwit that I had a hold of. The guy sagged in my arms, winded and so much dead weight. I let him go as another one of *his* brothers swung at my head.

I managed to lean back, his punch going wide, and Feral, true to his name, tackled the dude and took him to the ground, his fist pistoning into the guy's ribs over and over again.

A hand grabbed me by the shoulder and spun me. I saw stars as a fist, heavy laden with big, chunky rings, connected with my cheekbone, and *ow* that fuckin' hurt. I didn't even bother with my hands. I just head-butted the fucker and felt a satisfying crunch out of his nose at my hairline.

The hand he had wrapped in the shoulder of my cut let go, and he staggered back, both his hands to his face. I brought my boot up, cunt punting him right where his cock was supposed to be, but I figured he housed a pussy in his jeans.

Fuckin' coward. Thought he could dish it, but he sure couldn't take it.

While some brawls undulated and grew closer, moving like a mosh pit, others knotted together in a Gordian knot of fists, kicks, blood, and whatever other trappings of a bar fight. They seemingly *exploded*, moving out from the nucleus where the fight began and spreading throughout the space virulently. The violence metastasized like a swift-moving cancer.

That's what this fight did.

Some guys went over the railing to drop to the dirt or on top of bikes a story below. Others moved out of the open air, under the shelter, and closer to the bar – which is the direction I most definitely chose to go in - closer to Rarity, who was ducked down out of sight for now.

I pulled a Scorpion off of Renegade, who was duking it out with two of them, and spun him, throwing a right cross into his face and squaring up as he came back around, fueled by as much adrenaline as I was and heavily numbed by the booze he'd swilled – or maybe more than both booze and adrenaline. He Hulked out, screaming at me and posturing – teeth brown, face as red as a fuckin' tomato, eyes wild and bloodshot. I had to wonder if he was on something harder than just booze and the venom of his ire.

He lunged at me and caught me around the middle. We went crashing back into the bar. The bar's lip caught me across the back painfully, but thankfully higher than my kidneys with how I'd been falling. So it was painful, yeah, but not in a way that was incapacitating. He threw a punch into my side, and I grunted and deflected as much as I could by skirting to the side as I brought my elbow down in between his shoulder blades. He grunted but kept at it, and we struggled. I kept taking hits to where I felt my fuckin' bones creak in protest but managed to get a knee up between him and me as I kept wailing with my elbow into the back of his neck, his head, between his shoulders – which didn't seem to be working much.

Finally, *pow!* I switched things up and boxed him in his fuckin' ear with my fist, and *that* broke him loose.

He backed off, and hands grabbed him. I managed to look up into Kash's face, savage with anger, as he ripped the dude off me and threw him back into the fray.

Kash reached down, we clasped hands, and he helped me up.

I went my way, and he went his. He caught a Scorpion and bodily lifted him and threw him. The guy went sideways over the bar and disappeared behind it to two feminine screams.

Shit.

I went for the bar, a guy getting in my way, and we boxed it out for half a round before I knocked him into a pair of fighters by the railing. They went at him just long enough for me to break free to the dude climbing back over the bar and jumping off it onto Kash's back, who flipped him forward off himself and into the Scorpion he'd been squaring off with.

Relieved the problem took care of itself, I went back at it with a Scorpion who got shoved into me. He clipped me a good one in the chin, making me see some stars before *another* motherfucker in black and orange went over the bar. Except, he didn't pop up right away, and the girls screaming didn't stop over the din of the brawl going on all around us.

I stood up and kicked the guy in front of me down like I was kicking in a fucking door – and I mean, it was accurate. Dude was in my fuckin' way.

I took two steps, another Scorpion entering stage right to get in my way, and I swung on him, cold cocking him and sending him to the floor like a ton of bricks. The bigger they are, the harder they fall.

I leaped the bar and got the motherfucker over the one girl in a choke hold, squeezing down on the sides of his neck. He took his hands off the girl, who *wasn't* Rarity. She was kicking and struggling underneath him as he fought to shake me off while I worked on putting him to sleep. I was riding that bitch like Yoda on Luke's back when a bottle crashed over his head, and he dropped out from under me.

I let him go and looked up to Rarity, her chest heaving, a broken bottleneck in her hand as the stench of Wild Turkey left me nearly retching. It was that alcohol that reminded me of that time I almost died from drinking it – I couldn't help it, okay?

"Time to get you girls outta here," I decided as another motherfucker came across the bar and landed at the other end. I looked behind me and relaxed when I realized it was Skull. He looked at me, devoid of emotion, and got up like the fuckin' terminator he was.

"Help me get them out!" I hollered at him. "Clear a fuckin' path!"

He nodded once and skirted past me and both of the girls, lifting the end of the bar and forging ahead. I ushered the girls out behind him and ended up thrusting Rarity behind me as something crashed into the bottles behind the bar, breaking bottles in a shower of liquor and shattered glass.

I pulled her along behind me, and we went out into the fray.

Bones had met back up with his brother, and the two of them were making for the stairs, bodily throwing Scorpions out of the way and guiding Royal Bastards out of our path with a lighter shove or a shout.

The brunette barmaid followed them, stepping lightly, jumping at everything, her arms drawn in and trying to defend herself as she danced across the deck like it was something more than plastic cups and jostling bodies coming at her.

Rarity followed me, and I pulled her around to my front and shoved her ahead as we started down the steps.

Bones threw a Scorpion over the railing and laughed, even as Skull pushed the brunette past and ahead to the bottom of the steps. She made it to the ground, Rarity right behind her, and we started making our way through the bikes and bodies throwing down, down here.

We lost Skull and Bones to a charging Scorpion coming at me and the girls. He was as big as a fuckin' mountain. They met his challenge with a determined battle cry, taking him down to the ground and pounding him.

Rarity pulled her friend along and shoved her out in front of her. Before I could shout at her to fuckin' *go* rather than turn around to check on me, she dove, taking my legs out from under me as three shots rang out, whizzing over both our heads.

I landed over her and held her down to the ground, shielding her with my body – but *fuck*. She'd seen it, and she'd just been the one to save *my* ass.

Sirens were approaching, and more shots rang out, but up higher. I got up and screamed at her, "Stay low! Go, go, go, go, *go!*" She did what she was told, staying low, using bikes as cover, shrieking and jumping as a round pinged off the bike next to us.

She made for the exit, and I stayed right on her six, dodging bodies and leaping back as a blade flashed and caught me in the stomach. Pain seared along the knife's edge, and I punched the little Scorpion in the face who'd come at me. The knife flew out of his hand, and Rarity picked it up, tossing it into the garbage collection bin hitched to the back of one of the bar's Gator ATVs.

She ducked as cups and shit flew down from the upper deck but never stopped surging forward, dodging past Scorpions and other

Royal Bastards alike, until we surged down a narrow passage between the original bar's squat building and the fence next to it.

"Aw, shit!" she called and stuttered to a stop. I crashed into her back and held her steady as we faced in front of us the cops coming our way.

More shots popped off behind us, more screaming, and the cop shoved Rarity and me aside screaming, *"Move!"*

Didn't need to tell me twice. I shoved the girl forward as her friend barreled ahead of us and into the arms of a medic, sobbing and hyperventilating. The medic, another girl, turned her away from the furor and shoved her in the direction of her waiting ambulance.

Rarity grabbed my hand, pulled me behind her, and called, "This way!" I went with her, running across the parking in front of the gas station, through the pumps, and across the road.

She had her keys out and was dragging me toward a black Jeep Wrangler with a lift kit. I let her, curious, and she hit a button on her key fob. The lights flashed, the locks popped, and she looked at me and said, "Get in or get a ride from the cops. Your choice."

"My brothers," I said.

"Your choice!" she called, and she got in.

"Hey!" a cop shouted in my direction. I pretended not to hear him and dove for the passenger door.

She was reversing before I'd even fully pulled myself into the passenger seat, throwing it into gear and taking off as cops ran in our direction, only to duck as more popping went off.

They abandoned us and went for the real danger. I worried about my brothers and crew but knew that Skull and Bones would have my back.

"Shit, that was fucking close," I said.

"Too close," Rarity agreed.

I felt the burn of the deep cut in my front, all sorts of other points of pain starting to blossom, popping up like mushrooms after a rain all over me. I sucked in a breath and pressed a hand over my stomach, coming up with blood in the darkening gloom of the cab of her Jeep.

"Shit!" she cried. "Are you stabbed?"

"Cut," I said. "It's not bad. It'll be fine. I've had worse."

Maybe two miles up the main drag into Ormond Beach, she turned into a housing subdivision, and I didn't say anything. She looked like she knew where she was going.

CHAPTER TEN

Rarity...

Jesus Christ, this was a bad idea, but I didn't know where else to go and he was fucking *bleeding*.

I pulled into the driveway, relieved my grandparents were still out of town, but Mom and the boys were home. *Shit.*

"Listen, we're going in the front door," I said. "But *you* are immediately going in the door on the left just as soon as we get in there as quickly and as *quietly* as you can. Shut it and *stay there.* Okay?"

He eyed me and warily said, "Alright."

"My mom is going to freak out bad enough as it is that I was even there during that mess. I need to mitigate the damage with quickness. If she knew I brought a Bastard home? Let's just say *fuck my life,* I would never hear the end of it, and if I have to give her a heart attack, I try to limit it to one per day."

He was grinning at me now and started to laugh softly.

"I mean it," I said. "Inside, and immediately through the door on the left and *not a fucking word!*"

"You got it," he said, and we bailed out of the Jeep. We shut the doors in perfect unison, and that was just a happy accident – unless he'd done it on purpose.

We went through the front gate, and I punched in the code for the front door and pointed as we went through it. He slid inside the door to my bathroom, which was blessedly unlocked for once and cracked from where I'd come out earlier before heading to work.

"Rarity?" my mother called questioningly from the living room, where something Disney was playing.

I went around and said, "Yeah, Mom – it's all good. I'm okay."

"What do you mean?" she asked, going on high alert as no doubt the smell of alcohol wafted across the living room to her, a hundred times stronger than I usually smelled of it, considering I'd taken quite a few full-fledged fucking showers and baths in it since the brawl started.

"There was a biker brawl at work. Worst one I've ever seen. A bunch of bottles got broken, and booze everywhere. They started shooting, but I was already out, thanks to security, and on my way home before things got that bad. I just took a bath in some of the booze. I'm fine! I promise! Look!" I turned this way and that as she stared on in horror and slowly got up from the couch, untangling herself from my brothers and the nest of blankets they were in. She set her bowl of popcorn aside.

"A *shooting*?" she asked, voice shaking, her tan floating on top of her skin as she paled, like an oil slick on the water.

"I'm fine!" I reiterated and went to hug her.

She was already keening with her panic and crying.

"Scared the shit out of me, too, but I'm fine. I promise!" I told her, hugging her back with bruising force.

"You stink," she warbled, and I nodded.

"I know. Just... just let me get a shower really quick, and I'll come back out. I promise."

"I'll put the boys to bed," she said, and I nodded.

"Okay." I agreed.

I went into my bathroom and discovered it empty... *shit.*

Panic rising in my breast that he'd ditched, I slipped through the door to my bedroom and found him sitting on my rumpled bed, talking low and quiet into his phone.

"Yeah, no, I'm on it," he said. "Get you all out as soon as I can."

He hung up and looked up at me.

"My mom is putting the boys to bed," I said. "I've got to take a shower and be out there with her for a while. There's... stuff." I shrugged kind of lamely, and he arched a brow.

"Stuff?" he asked.

"A long story," I murmured.

"Do what you gotta do," he said. "I've got to call in the lawyers."

I nodded and said, "Okay. Thanks for being... cool, I guess."

"You saved my ass from getting *shot* back there," he said. "I can be cool with a lot of shit after something like that."

"Fair," I said, slipping back into my bathroom, starting the shower.

I stripped and got in, trusting that he would be busy with whatever phone calls and that I would have enough time to get in, clean up, and get back out again in a jiff. Maybe I could let him clean up if he did it quickly, then turn off the shower, letting my mom think I just stayed in it for a while.

The shower door slid aside, and I froze.

"Chill," he said. "I need to clean this up and figure out how bad it is. Figured you didn't want this running too long or to stop and start it to tip off Mommy dearest."

I scowled at him. The fact we were both naked and standing within a foot of each other was completely irrelevant with what he'd said about my mom.

"It's not like that," I said darkly. "She worries like a mother..." I stopped and said, "Should. Probably more since my dad died."

"I'm sorry," he said. He just stood there, hands at his sides, and kept his eyes on mine.

"You good?" he asked.

"I've never showered with anybody," I said. "It's weird."

He grinned. "Well hurry the fuck up and get out so it'll be less weird," he said, and he fought not to laugh.

"Can you even see it?" I asked.

"My dick?" he asked, and I snorted, shaking my head and closing my eyes.

"The *cut*," I said.

"Eh, I'll manage," he said.

"Well, *I'm* not looking at your dick, I promise," I said and dropped my eyes down a well-formed chest across a nice flat stomach with just a hint of abs and to the narrow bleeding slash mark across his stomach.

"Shit, I can't be sure, but this *might* need stitches."

Okay, I looked at his dick, but mercifully, he was sorta being a gentleman, and he wasn't hard. Still, even flaccid, he had a nice-looking peen as far as peens went... at least, I thought so anyway.

God, Rarity! I thought to myself and continued chastising my stupid brain even as my pussy gave a throb.

Thank fuck you couldn't really tell when a woman was hot – not like a guy. His cock jumped, and so did I. He fought not to laugh.

"Made you look," he said, and I looked up at him as he flexed his stomach or did whatever he did to make it jump the first time, except blood spilled when he did it this time.

"Ha, ha, very funny, but whatever you're doing, *stop it*. You're making yourself bleed more."

"Noted," he said, and I slid out of his way so he could get under the shower spray. He hissed between gritted teeth, and the water swirled with pink at his feet.

"I don't know what to do," I said. He turned his head, cracking an eye, and looked at me.

"Got a clean washcloth?" he asked.

I slid open the shower door on its runners, just a crack, and pulled one off the bar outside the door, holding it out to him.

"I'm going to clean this with soap and water, rinse it real good.

I'm going to need you to hold on to that. When I'm done, hand it to me so I can hold pressure. Got a first-aid kit in here?"

"Yeah, under the bathroom sink," I said.

"You done?" he asked.

"Yeah," I said, and he nodded once.

"Get it out for me after you dry off."

I slipped out of the shower, careful to keep quiet, and pulled a fresh towel off the bar, drying off briskly and thinking, *whelp, he's already seen it all,* before wrapping my hair up.

"I'm going to get dressed," I said, and before he could say anything, I ducked into my bedroom.

I pulled a clean pair of undies from my top drawer and pulled them up my legs, then picked up my leggings off the floor from the night before. I dropped onto the edge of my bed, pulled those on, and was just sliding my sweatshirt with the neckline cut out over my head when there was knocking at the front door.

I went into the bathroom, and he shut off the tap at my signal after one final swipe of his shoulder through the spray to rinse the soap he had on him off.

"Just a minute!" my mom called on the other side of my bathroom door before I heard the front door open.

"Rarity!" she immediately called.

I called back, "Two seconds! Let me get dressed!" I thrust a towel at the biker and pushed him into my room, quietly closing the door behind him, then counted slowly from one to twenty before opening my bathroom door and stepping out.

Two cops were standing in the doorway.

"Rarity Jane Mitchell?" the one asked.

"Yeah, that's me," I said.

"You work at the Iron Horse?" the other one asked.

"Just got home not twenty minutes ago," I said. I gave them a look, rolled my eyes in the direction of my mom, and said, "Left right before the shooting started. I don't get paid enough for that shit."

"Ma'am," one of the officers said. "Do you mind stepping out here and talking to us about what happened?"

"Not at all," I said. I turned to my mom, my heart thundering in my chest so hard I could feel my pulse in my temples. "Mom, it's all good. Go finish up with the boys. I'll come help as soon as I'm done."

"Okay," she agreed, but I could tell she didn't want to.

I stepped out onto the front porch and closed the door behind me.

"Some of our officers said that you were running and that you had one of the Royal Bastards with you."

"Never saw him before tonight," I said. "But yeah, he helped me get out."

"He said that you both took off after you were ordered to stop."

"Okay, yeah, that part was stupid, but I was scared out of my mind, and there were shots going off. I wasn't stopping for *no one*. Just please, *please,* don't tell my mom I was there when there was shooting going on. She worries enough as it is, and I don't want her anymore freaked out than she is right now."

"What about the man with you?" the first officer, a light-skinned, shaved-head Black man with a dimple in his chin, asked me.

"I got around the corner, and he bailed out," I lied. "I don't know what happened to him after that."

The cops exchanged a look, and the second one nodded, writing something down in his notebook.

"Like I said, I'd never seen him before tonight. I didn't even get his name."

I swallowed, and the second cop asked, "Do you know how the fight started?"

"No," I said. "I was behind bar number two. I heard shouting over on the other end of bar number three, and then there was something happening on the deck. Someone yelled at me and Gemma to 'hit the deck,' and so that's what we did."

I was telling the truth, except for the part where it'd been Striker telling us to get down and that he hadn't shouted it but had gestured for us to do so.

The rest, from there on out, was all true. How dudes kept flying over the bar. How the second one had tried to hurt Gemma and how Striker had come to the rescue and enlisted two of the other Bastards to get us out.

"They got us down to the first floor, and we were—" the front door opened. I turned to look back at my mom and said, "All good, Mom. Just a few more minutes."

She looked from me to the cops and back to me and said, "I don't know if I like this..."

"She's right. It's all good, ma'am. Your daughter's not in trouble. She's just a witness. We're just getting her statement."

"Five more minutes," I said. "It's okay."

She went back into the house and closed the door.

"Where were we?" I asked.

"You got down to the first floor and..."

"Right, and one of the guys in black and orange with the Scorpion on his back slashed at the Royal Bastard trying to help me and Gemma with a knife. I don't know if he cut him or not. Then, one of the other ones in black and orange had a gun, and I hit the deck and took the guy trying to save us with me."

"So, you saw one of the shooters?" the police officer asked.

"Yeah," I said, hugging myself. "Anyway, we can keep that just between us?" I asked hopefully.

"Afraid not," baldy-locks said. "You're a witness."

"Shit." I sighed. "Okay, well... *fuck,* my mom is going to kill me."

"I can't say about your mom, but back to this... do you think you might be able to pick the guy with the gun out of a lineup?"

"Um, I don't know. I could try?"

"Okay, here's my card. Detectives will probably be by tomorrow, and we'd like to have you come down to the station and go over all this again. Have you look at some photographs and see if you can identify anyone. Would that be alright with you?" he asked.

I didn't know what else to say except, "Sure, yeah... okay."

I took the card and gave them my information – phone number, mailing address, email address, and sometimes that would work for me.

"We're very sorry you had to experience what you did tonight," the other cop said, running a hand back through his light brown hair, his light brown eyes looking me over as I huddled on my front step uncomfortably.

"Hazards of working a biker bar, I guess. You know, I've been there going on three years, and this is the worst thing I've ever seen."

"Might want to look into another line of work," he said, and I nodded.

"Might," I said. "But the pay is some of the best around here, and I can't beat the tips. Still, we'll see how much they're going to be willing to fork over by way of a raise to keep me... because *that*? I deserve a raise."

"You're a tough girl, Rarity," the first cop said, and I smiled.

"Thanks," I said.

CHAPTER ELEVEN

Striker...

I heard most, if not *all,* of what she told the cops out of the cracked bedroom window. I'd cracked it carefully and as quietly as possible to hear what I could of their conversation. I had to say – Rarity did me another solid, you know, aside from keeping my ass from getting shot. She kept me hidden, made up some bullshit on the fly about me bailing out of her Jeep around the corner at the first stoplight.

I could deal with that. It was smart.

You did a Royal Bastard a solid, let alone the few that she'd already done me, and you had a friend for life.

My phone buzzed as she came back in the front door, and I answered.

"Yeah?"

"It's me," Renegade said.

"You at the jail?" I asked.

"Lawyers on their way?" he asked by way of confirmation.

"Yeah, should be there any minute," I told him.

"Good. They ain't got shit on us, but you know this is liable to be an all-night thing."

"Yeah, I'm good," I told him. "I'll be there first thing with transport."

"They're impounding the bikes," he said.

"Figured that," I told him.

"Where you at?" he demanded.

I told him, knowing full well the line was being recorded, "Someplace safe. I'm good, P. Let the lawyers do their thing and give 'em hell."

"Right," he said. "I'm getting looks. They took the Scorpions left standing to the county lockup. We're in city lockup for Ormond Beach."

"Smart," I said.

"Certainly wasn't dumb," he said with a chuckle.

"Any of our boys hurt bad?" I asked.

"Cuts and bruises mostly," he said. "Nothing super serious for either Jacksonville or Ocala. They took Enigma and Switch to the hospital. Switch has something broken in his hand or arm. I didn't get a clear answer on that. Enigma was out cold, so they took his unconscious ass for scans to make sure he didn't lose too many brain cells. I saw it happen. I'm pretty sure he's gonna be fine."

"Good, good," I said.

"We'll see if they turn up here or if they turn them loose directly from the hospital."

"Okay," I said.

There was an indistinct voice on the other end of the line, and Renegade grunted. "That's my cue. Gotta go."

"Talk at you later," I said, and the line went dead.

I brought my head up at the sound of inconsolable weeping from out the way that I had to presume was the living room, and I worried for a minute that it was Rarity.

"You're my firstborn and my only girl!" came a raised voice. "Of course, I worry!"

"I know, I know!" I heard from the door across from Rarity's bed and guessed that she had to be in the kitchen or something. A guess that was confirmed by the kitchen tap turning on and then off.

Shit.

I wanted to talk to her and find out what the plan was on her end, but I couldn't do shit about fuck without diming her and myself out. She'd earned not only my respect but my patience and silence as well.

I pulled the washcloth away from my stomach and looked. I was still bleeding, but it had slowed considerably. While I didn't have access to anyone who could suture the wound, I could get by with some butterfly stitches or super glue to hold shit together.

I went back into the bathroom and slowly, carefully, and quietly opened up the first-aid kit to see what I had access to – no glue, but gauze, disinfectant, and a shit ton of band-aids. There was antibiotic ointment, burn cream, a chemical ice pack, a chemical hot pack, and *BINGO*... butterfly bandages.

It was hard as fuck staying quiet and standing far enough back from the mirror and yet close enough to see what the fuck I was doing.

There was no real *sweet spot* to do both, and it made for a difficult time using one hand to pinch the edges of the wound that gaped the most together while I used the other to affix a bandage and get it tight enough to actually be fuckin' useful.

I have no idea how long I was at it or how many I wasted trying to get it right.

The women's voices outside the bathroom door shifted from the living room to the kitchen while I worked, trying to concentrate, and eventually, she came in her bedroom door while I edged further into the bathroom, waiting on her.

"Yeah, Mom?" she called over her shoulder, looking past the open door across to what I had to presume was another.

"I love you, too," she said in response to whatever her mother said, but I couldn't make it out.

She came fully into her room and closed the door, her shoulders dropping and her breath coming harshly as she threw the tiny tab of a lock on the inside of the doorknob.

"Help me with this, would you?" I asked.

She turned to me and said, "Yeah, sorry."

"All good," I said.

She frowned and said, "Come lay down so I can do this. There's no way am I getting on my knees."

I snorted softly. "Afraid I'd bust out the sexual innuendo?" I asked.

"No, the tile is cold and hard." She rolled her eyes.

I fought not to laugh and told her, "Don't make me laugh. It's pulling."

"Sorry," she said.

I came into the room and sat down, the towel riding low on my hips, gaping dangerously as I swung my legs up. She pulled the bottom sheet up over me and said, "I've never used these before."

"They're easy. Just do your best to get one side affixed, pull the wound together, and strap down the other side so it holds things close," I told her.

"God, that sounds like it's going to hurt," she said and looked a little green around her gills. She'd taken down her hair, and the towel was gone, but her hair was still damp, falling in snaking locks around her face. *My little mermaid...* the thought came to me unbidden, and I shoved it away. Still, right on the heels of that, I thought, *I guess that makes her green around her mermaid gills.*

"I am so sorry!" she hissed when I coughed to try and cover my laugh at my own joke.

Ah, shit, she thinks she hurt you, dumbass!

"All good," I said. "Just keep going and get 'er done."

She smirked and asked, "Just how old are you?"

I grinned and said, "Probably old enough to be your daddy."

She rolled her eyes and said, "I'm twenty-four, so I'm betting not."

"I'm forty-two, so I say it's possible."

She blinked at me, bewildered, and said, "There is no way you're forty-*anything*."

I chuckled and asked, "Aw yeah? What makes you say that?"

We both froze as we heard a sound in the kitchen, and I pointed to the television mounted to her wall. She leaned closer, picked up the remote off the nightstand, and turned it on for noise. She quickly scrolled through streaming services, landed on some educational one, and turned on some true crime.

"Never understood women's obsession with true crime," I muttered and she looked at me bewildered again and blinked.

"It's so we don't become victims ourselves," she said, and I raised an eyebrow.

"You won't catch a true crime girly falling for a dude with his arm in a cast asking for help – the wounded bird shtick was so Bundy and nope, nope, nope – not falling for *that*."

"But you'll pick up a Royal Bastard, help him hide from the cops, and doctor him up in your bedroom?" I raised my eyebrows, a slow grin overtaking my lips.

"That's different," she said, rolling her eyes. I tried to keep my laughter silent.

"Hold still!" she chastised me in a harsh whisper.

"Make it make sense," I shot back.

"Are you a rapist piece of shit?" she asked, giving me a baleful look.

"No!" I answered quickly without thinking.

"Well, okay, then. I guess we're good." She had a faint smile on her lips, and I was officially mollified.

"You're something else," I said and let it shine in my tone that I was duly impressed. Her smile flexed in response before she could hide it at the praise, and that made mine flex in return.

"There," she said with finality and leaned back. "I think that's as good as it's going to get."

"Thanks," I said softly.

"My name's Zach. Zachary Carlin. Everybody calls me Striker, though."

"Rarity Mitchell," she said, holding out her hand to shake. I took it, and her grasp was light but firm. "Everybody calls me Rarity, or just Rare."

"Pleasure to meet you, Rarity. I gotta ask. How did you get a name like that?"

"How did you get Striker?" she asked in return.

"Okay, Touché, but working at the Iron Horse, you should know the rules on that."

She smiled a bit coyly and said, "I'm a dumb blonde twenty-something. Depends on the day and the crowd."

I chuckled at that and said, "You got me there."

"So?"

"A couple reasons," I said. "One, I'm a trick shot." Her eyebrows went up.

"What like an Annie Oakley type of trick shot?" she asked.

"You know your history, and yeah. I can shoot the face off a quarter spinning in the air, or take out the spade in the middle of the ace of spades at a hundred paces. Shit like that."

"You said two reasons," she said. "What's the other?"

"I used to serve in a Stryker Brigade when I was in-country," I said.

She frowned, perplexed. "You mean *out* of the country, right? Like, you served over *there*."

I nodded and told her, "Except in the military, we call it 'in-country' when we're over there – as in 'in the other country' away from ours."

"Okaaaay," she said, drawing out the word.

"So... Rarity?" I asked, and she shifted on her shapely ass on the edge of her bed. She had something like forty-nine hundred pillows like some girls liked to do, and I was comfortably propped up looking at her.

"My mom and dad were having hardcore fertility issues when

they were trying to get pregnant with me. They were doing IVF and the whole nine yards. The doctors told them I was, for sure, going to be the only one if they managed to get me to term. My mom decided, since I was going to be such a rarity, that the name fit."

"So, are those your boys that you referenced your mom putting to bed?" I asked curiously.

"What? No!" She laughed a little. "They're my brothers. Triplets. Identical – it was wild. When I was nineteen, Mom got pregnant with them and wasn't even trying." A shadow crossed her face. "My dad never even got to meet them. He died before they were born."

"I'm sorry to hear that," I said, reaching out and taking her hand off her knee, smoothing my thumb over the back of it.

"Thanks," she said. "That was a little over four years ago." She sniffed. "We miss him every day."

"I bet," I murmured.

"Anyway, I drive his Jeep now. It's paid for so..." she shrugged.

I said, "That's cool."

We lapsed into an awkward silence, and I squeezed her hand when her deep blue eyes lapsed into a sightless stare. I didn't want her to retreat into bad memories. I knew a thing or three about that... and so I squeezed twice to bring her back. She looked at me solemnly.

"He'd be proud of you, you know?" I asked.

"What?"

She frowned, and I told her, "For keeping your cool back there. You were braver than some soldiers I know."

"No." She looked like she didn't believe me.

"*Yes,*" I insisted.

"He'd probably be pissed I was even there," she said, trying to play things off, and I shook my head.

"Well, yeah, that too, but being proud and pissed aren't mutually exclusive to one another."

She giggled lightly.

"How about this?" I asked. "*I'm* proud of you and grateful. You really saved my ass back there. Kept me from getting *shot*. You got some brass ovaries, girl. I've seen grown-ass men fall the fuck apart under less pressure than being unarmed during a live fire incident."

She blushed prettily and sounded a bit awed when she asked me softly, "Really?"

"Really," I whispered, raising her hand to my lips and kissing the backs of her fingers. She turned a deep, deep red from the pretty pink she'd been initially, and simply stared at me wide-eyed.

"I can sleep on the floor," I said after a moment, and her face contorted into one that said she'd heard something utterly absurd.

"Move your big ass over," she said. "Stay under the sheet. I'll sleep on top of it."

"Nice compromise," I said, but it was still a pretty tight fit. She only had a full-sized bed, not even a queen.

CHAPTER TWELVE

R arity...
I tried to give him some space and stay on my side of the bed, but it wasn't exactly comfortable, two people on a full. It was hard not to touch.

"Come here," he said. "Turn over." I did as he asked and turned over. He turned, too, to lay flat. He pulled me up against him and said, "Lay your head on my shoulder." I did, carefully, my body coiled tight with the awkwardness of being cuddled up to a stranger I barely knew.

I mean, he *was* older – a lot older than I thought. *Forty-two,* I thought to my *twenty-four.* It took me an embarrassingly long time to do the math right in my head and I felt myself shift and even quite possibly pale when I realized *eighteen.*

He had been *eighteen* when I'd been *born...*

He was closer to my *mom's* age than mine, my mom being forty-nine.

But he didn't look forty-two. I wouldn't have put him a day over thirty-five.

What does it matter, Rarity? I asked myself silently. *It's not like you're going to hook up or whatever. You're just feeling a little bonding from going through the same trauma. No big deal.*

"You're thinking awfully hard," he murmured. "What's up?"

"You're really forty-two?" I asked, and he chuckled.

"Yep."

"That means you were *eighteen* when I was born," I whispered.

"See, I told you I was old enough I could be your daddy."

I snorted. "Still could be if that's your kink," I joked.

He was entirely *too* silent, and I sat up sharply. He snorted and shook with silent laughter. I laid back down and muttered, *"Asshole,"* which just made him shake with laughter more.

I couldn't keep a smile off of my face if I tried.

"What were you even doing when you were eighteen?" I asked, curious, after we'd both stopped our giggle fits.

"Enlisting in the Army before I'd even fully graduated high school," he said, heaving a big sigh. "I wanted to get out of my small town and travel the world."

"Bet your parents were proud of you," I said demurely.

He snorted.

"Mom was *pissed*. Dad was proud, though."

"Why was she mad? Afraid of losing you?" I asked.

"No," he said. "She wanted me to take up the family business, get my dad closer to retirement."

"Did your dad want to retire?"

He chuckled. "Not even close," he said. "Mom was always super overbearing and wore that man down. What she wanted, she got, and I was done. I was eighteen and so close to freedom I could *taste* it. So, I grabbed on with both hands and held on like a motherfucker. Blew that town and everyone in it and blazed my own trail."

"I could *never*," she said softly.

"Why not?" he asked.

"My mom may be a helicopter parent sometimes, but she *loves us so much*. It would *kill her* if I bounced. And I couldn't leave her with Caden, Aden, and Braden. They're a handful on a good day."

"Are you serious?" he asked.

"What?" I rolled my head on his shoulder to meet his downward look.

"*Caden, Aden* and *Braden*?"

I snorted and fought not to giggle.

"How many fuckin' *'Live. Laugh. Love,'* signs would I find if I went through this house?" he asked. I snorted and clapped both hands over my nose and mouth to keep from laughing too loudly.

I looked up at him in the blue glow from the television that still played, and he grinned down at me.

He was achingly handsome, but *no way*. Not only was he *forty-two* to my twenty-four, but he was also a *Royal Bastard*. I could *never!*

"At least three," he said judiciously.

"Nailed it," I said, counting in my head and coming up with... yeah, three.

"Unbelievable," he said and chuckled.

"My mom believes in holding on to positive vibes," I said.

He nodded and asked, "Is she a hippy chick?"

I thought about that for a minute and said, "No, I don't want to say *hippy* chick, more like a little sage and hood and wish a mutha-fucka would."

He wheezed, and I put my hand over his mouth. His lips were soft, the faint stubble growing rough against my palm.

"*Mm, mm-mm mmm, mm-mm-mm, mm!*" he said against my hand, and I didn't get *any* of that.

I moved my hand and asked, "What?"

"You gotta stop making me laugh," he said with a grin, and I scoffed.

"I can't help it if I'm a funny bitch."

That touched off another set of snorting and giggling.

"You're something else," he said, and it sounded like praise the way he said it. I felt a glow suffuse me, and I cuddled a little closer. His arm tightened around me vaguely, and it was nice. Warm and cozy.

It was a weird sensation. Felt good. Safe. Like I hadn't felt safe since my dad had been around. That part weirded me out a little bit, but not, like, enough to move away or anything.

I closed my eyes and listened to the droning announcer's voice narrating the show, but didn't pay much attention to anything he was saying.

Instead, I was fixated on the warmth of Striker's hand smoothing up and down my arm as he closed his eyes, too.

~

"RARITY!" my mother called and I jumped out of bed, my feet hitting the floor as she tried my doorknob. "Why is this door locked?" she called out, bewildered.

I went and cracked it open, standing in the way. "Jeez, Mom, I don't know. I'm twenty-four and trying to spend some quality time with my vibe and didn't want you walking in?" I rolled my eyes. I knew I was flushed with embarrassment at having to lie, yet again, to my mother, whom I loved and adored, but for real – I didn't want her stressing any more than she already did.

"TMI!" she cried. "TMI! I don't need to know these things!"

I snickered and asked, "What's up?"

"I'm heading into work. Grandma and Grandpa will be home sometime today. Are you good to watch the boys?"

"Of course!" I said, then asked, "They up?"

"Not yet." She sighed. "I'm trying to get out of here before they do, and I have one attached to each leg and the third hanging like an albatross from my neck, begging me to stay home."

I snickered again and said, "*Go!* Be free!"

I heard my bathroom door click faintly, and I rattled my doorknob on purpose to cover it, opening my door to give my mom a hug before she went out the door.

"I love you, my sweet girl," she said with a gusty sigh.

"I love you, too, Mom." I hugged her tight.

"Okay, I've got to go," she said.

"I'll have dinner on the table," I told her.

"You're a lifesaver," she said as she went to the door between our rooms and out to the garage through our laundry room.

A second later, I heard the garage door trundle open and her truck fire up.

My shoulders sagged in relief.

"Coast is clear," I said when the garage door was making its descent.

He came out of my bathroom in his jeans and boots, his cut on over his bare chest.

"You got the kiddos to look after," he said. "I *definitely* got shit to do."

"Yeah," I said, feeling almost sad that he had to go.

"Can I see you again?" he asked, and I raised my chin.

"I don't see why not," I said. "You know where I work. Maybe next time, just follow the rules and don't wear your colors, yeah?"

He chuckled and nodded.

"Surprised you're going back," he said.

I shrugged. "After something like that, it's probably the safest place I can be."

"Aw yeah, how do you figure?"

"Cops are going to be keeping an eye on things, and you know security is going to be doubled if not quadrupled for the time being. They don't want to get shut down any longer than they have to be."

"Fair points, but are you sure?" he asked.

I smiled, and I knew it held no humor. "Best place to work around here when it comes to the tips if not the actual wage. I need the money. Dad was the big earner and Mom and I are barely keeping up."

"I see," he murmured.

"You need to call an Uber or something?" I asked. "I can give you the address."

He shook his head.

"No, I already got one of the guys on the way. Bikes have been impounded, so..."

"Gotcha," I murmured.

"I'll see you again," he vowed, and I shrugged.

"Maybe I'll see you around."

I didn't expect him to want to come around. My life was a hot mess.

He nodded, and I let him out through my bedroom door and led him around to the front door. He left with a little salute and I shut the door behind him, sighed, and locked up.

I had no idea what the rest of my day was going to look like, but I knew it started with getting the boys up and getting them breakfast.

CHAPTER THIRTEEN

S triker...

Kash and Enigma had me up in the Uber they'd ordered. Kash'd been taken to the hospital for a chunk of glass he'd had stuck in his forearm from a bottle coming down on him. He'd blocked, so it could have been a lot worse. He reeked of tequila when I got into the back of the car with him and Niggy, and we were off to St. Augustine.

We needed to pick up the shop van we used to transport our shop guys who didn't ride to bike shows to get the boys at the Ormond Beach jail and then head on over to the impound lot to get our bikes out.

That was going to cost a pretty penny in towing and storage fees, but that was just the cost of doing business for something like this. Renegade and the Bishop were more than good for it.

Kash and Nig had been far more in the loop at the hospital than I'd been at Rarity's place and filled me in.

Enigma had a concussion, but ain't no worse than anything he'd had before. He wouldn't be riding or driving, so we would have to figure *that* out but that was easy enough. Switch was *still* in the hospital. He'd broken his hand so badly on a Scorpion's face, they were talking surgery and waiting on an orthopedic surgeon to come look at it and make a final determination.

The Scorpions had five in the hospital, the rest in lockup, and one of their numbers was a goner – from friendly fire. One of the dipshits who'd started popping off had hit one of his buddies and taken him out.

Our lawyers were eating investigators for fuckin' breakfast, and our boys were free to go now. Kash and Enigma were both saying how they'd had cops at their bedside all night and how they'd been cuffed to the bedrail until the word had trickled down that they were free to go.

"I tell you, the hospital was a lot more comfortable than lockup, brother, but I could have stitched this shit myself. I didn't wanna go."

"Yeah, but they would have been all sorts of up your ass in lockup. At least in the ER you had pretty nurses to look at," Enigma said, his head laid back and eyes shut against the bright sun.

"I hear that," I said, leaning back to show the butterfly bandages holding my own slash mark closed.

"Eh, what did that?" Kash asked.

"Knife."

He nodded, but he was already thinking and hard.

The Jacksonville chapter had come up smelling like roses out of the lot of us. No injuries enough to go to the hospital, but all of them had been picked up.

The rest of the day was spent in a logistical nightmare of getting everyone where they needed to be and matched back up with their bikes.

Renegade and The Bishop were power teaming the impound lot, arguing with them about the jacked-up rates and the fuckin' damage to several of the bikes from their careless handling.

The lot backed down pretty quick and gave the two presidents what they wanted by way of cut rates to pretend some of the damage didn't happen. Our shop would take care of it, no problem, for the cost of parts. It was the least we could do.

By the end of the day, we'd all wound up at this burger place, stuffing our faces, having a laugh over some of the more stupid shit and swapping war stories about the night before.

"Then *this* motherfucker right here..." FOCUS stabbed a finger in Pud's direction. "Pretty much drops trow and starts pissing all over the poor fucker he knocked right the fuck out. And all I can think is *get a load of that dick!*" He held up his hands and leaned back in his seat like praise be to the good lord above for bringing him this bounty. "Swear to God, if he ain't got a boner and he's that fucking big. *Fuck*, we gotta get him in front of some lights, get the cameras rolling – you know what I'm sayin'? We could make some damn good money."

All the guys from every chapter were falling out laughing except Kash, who was squirming in his seat and looking downright tempestuous.

"What's the problem, Kash?" Renegade asked, and Kash's expression soured further.

"Man, I just wanna get back down to Ocala and inside my ol' lady. No offense, but after a scrap like that, it's all I can fuckin' think about."

"Don't you worry. We're heading right on out from here," The Bishop told his man.

"Speaking of pussy," Sundown said with a grin. "I heard you made off with the blonde bar chick. How'd *that* go?"

All eyes were on me, and I shifted in my seat.

"Man, it ain't like that. She's barely twenty-four," I said with a shrug.

"So?" Highway, the road captain for Jacksonville, said.

"Last time I checked, anything over the age of eighteen was both legal and acceptable," Creed, the Jacksonville president, said.

"I know," I said with a laugh. "But it wasn't like that."

I explained the whole thing, how she was just trying to make it, about her mom and three siblings. How she'd helped me out. Not just keeping me from getting shot, but also how she'd lied to the cops and fudged some of the details. How she was going to bat for us on our side as a witness, for all the good it might do, seeing as she'd been smacked around by a Scorpion the night before. I mean, biased much?

Some impressed looks went around the tables that'd been pushed together to accommodate three chapters of the Royal Bastards in the joint we were at, and some silent and thoughtful nodding threaded through, too.

"Still, I'd like to shoot my shot I think – if y'all don't mind," I said. Mostly because Rarity *was* a rare beauty, and I didn't want too much competition nor any of these guys bugging the fuck out of her when I was already half sweet on her.

"So you going to see her again?" someone asked, but I couldn't tell who.

"Yeah, I think I might," I said.

"Not at the Iron Horse," someone else said, and Renegade snorted.

"What's that?" I asked.

"We've been 'trespassed' off the property," he said, putting *trespassed* into air quotes with his fingers.

I laughed. "Like they're gonna remember any one of our faces if we go in there slick-backed."

"That's what I was thinkin' too," Shadow said, grinning.

The Bishop stood. "Well, gentlemen, it's been a good time. Let us know if you need anything. Gotta get in the wind so this big beast can get his dick wet."

"Yep, it's been swell," Creed said. "But the swelling's gone down some and it's time for us to make for home, too."

There were nods around the table and we settled up our bill with the establishment, tipping well above board for all their hard work in feeding our hangry horde on the fly.

We rode home, Ocala splitting off to go their way, Jacksonville riding with us as far as our exit before waving and heading on up further to their home base.

Renegade gave the signal as we hit the St. Augustine city limits that we could all fuck off back to our respective homes if we wanted to. I was relieved about that. I just wanted another shower and to put something on the developing sunburn across my shoulders and down my arms from riding with no shirt all damn day.

I lived in a small but neatly kept apartment in a big house two streets away from the lighthouse.

The house was owned by a rich fuck who owned a bunch of fast-food franchises. He and his wife only wintered down here in Florida, a pair of regular snowbirds. All spring and summer the place was a vacation rental through one of those online deals. They liked having me around to make sure that shit was kept low key and respectful in their home. Other than the odd rager I called in to let 'em know about, I was pretty well left to my own devices in the carriage house apartment set back and to the left of the house.

I went in and dropped my keys in the bowl on the table just inside the front door. I hung up my cut on the hook I'd set in the wall above that and set about emptying my pockets. Change? In the bowl. Receipts? In the little trash can I kept by the door. Wallet? On the table. Random cash? In the bowl.

I kicked off my boots on the tile and padded across the living room carpet, sweeping up the remote off the coffee table, and switching on the seventy-five-inch television.

"– Horse Saloon is closed tonight and until further notice after two rival motorcycle gangs decided to fight it out which resulted in a shooting last night," the male television anchor said. "We're going live on scene with Cocoa Abrams."

"Yes, hi, David. We're here live in Ormond Beach, where the investigation is still ongoing into the incident that took place here last night that sent multiple people to the hospital and left at least one dead."

I dropped onto the couch and watched, looking past the reporter into the background, although for what, I had no idea. Maybe a glimpse of Rarity? Which was stupid. I had to bet she was nowhere near the place.

"It all started when two rival groups of bikers showed up to party and drink at the well-known biker bar that's popular here during bike week. Things were civil to begin with, according to management, but then things took a sudden turn for the worse..."

The scene cut to a guy named Charlie, who looked upset as he stood hands on his hips to talk to the reporter and give his side of the story.

He threw both the Scorpions and the Bastards under the proverbial bus, which I expected. Talkin' how we showed up in numbers flouting the '*no colors*' rule of the bar. He wasn't necessarily *wrong* in how he framed things up. About how his security staff was outnumbered, and how everything had seemed to start out well enough.

Still, he didn't paint a flattering picture – which big fuckin' surprise there.

His loyalty was to keeping his ass employed, after all.

I watched the news in a bit of a daze, fucking tired as hell, and waiting for any indication we might be somehow fucked. But all they said was that the fight and subsequent shooting led to multiple felony arrests and that charges may still be pending for some individuals involved.

I wasn't worried about us.

Renegade had it handled. Shadow was probably already doing his thing. It was all above my paygrade from here.

CHAPTER FOURTEEN

R arity...

The boys were in rare form today. Just *wildin'*. It made for a long one, for sure. My grandparents got home and managed to take them off my hands long enough to talk to the detectives who had come calling, and I stuck to my story like *glue*.

I couldn't help but feel like they smelled bullshit, but I guess things were close enough to Gemma's account that they were willing to overlook a few inconsistencies between us.

Honestly, I'd stuck to the truth as much as possible except for a few slightly fudged details – but bleh, they were going to believe what they were going to believe. There was nothing I could do about it.

When they left, I was vaguely worried, but I had dinner to make and more shit to do where the boys and housework was concerned.

By the time Mom had gotten home and dinner was hitting the table, the boys were in such a foul temper that it was all-hands-on-deck to get them to finish their dinner. It was bedtime early since they didn't want to behave.

Thankfully, Mom, Grandma, and Grandpa took the boys and left me to clean up the kitchen in some peace.

I was listening to the boys scream, holler, and generally throw tantrums throughout the entire process and really should have seen it for the red flags that it was – but *nope*.

Boy, would I live to regret that later on, but for now, I just tuned them out as best I could and let my thoughts drift while I rinsed dishes and put them up in the dishwasher.

I let my thoughts drift, and of course, they drifted right on over to Striker. He hadn't been far from my thoughts all day, and I wondered, vaguely, if I would ever see him again. I also wondered if I should stay at the Iron Horse. There was supposed to be a staff meeting the next day, and I was going. My mom was *not* thrilled, in the slightest, but we weren't talking about it. If anything, we'd carefully danced around the subject. Especially considering – *"Boys! That is enough!"*

My mother's stern voice reverberated up the hallway from the hall around the corner where she was in the boys' room trying to get them to stop whatever it was they were or weren't doing. I rolled my eyes and sighed.

"Do I need to come in there and bust somebody's butt!?" I called, which Mom and I almost *never* did. The mere threat of a spanking usually did the trick.

"No!" I heard a chorus of small boy voices call back.

"I will!" I called back, and waited, but there was no more shouting or fussing.

I finished loading the dishwasher, added a soap tab, and closed it up.

I sighed and hit the buttons on the front to get it going and went around the corner just as Grandma, Grandpa, and Mom filed out of the boys' room and shut the door behind them.

"We're going to bed," my grandmother said and she looked like her patience had been *tried* – woo boy.

"We go away for a long weekend and just look at things," Grandpa agreed, and cast a worried look in my direction.

"Hey, I'm the golden child. I ain't been misbehaving," I said, my thoughts adding silently, *that you know of...*

My mother snorted at that and rolled her eyes.

"Goodnight, Mom. Goodnight, Dad. It's good to have you home," Mom said and gave hugs and kisses to her parents.

"You keep yourself outta trouble, kiddo," my granddad told me, and then he and Grandma went through the door at the end of the hall that separated their suite of rooms from the rest of the house.

They had a bedroom with an attached bath and their own little living room space back there.

It had its own door leading from their little living room to the sunroom along the back of the house. It also had an entrance off the back of the dining room next to the kitchen, and then there was a single entrance that went out onto the back patio.

Mom and I spent more than a few evenings on the patio with its strung-up line of Edison bulbs, firepit, and lazily spinning ceiling fan.

All it took was one look from my mom and I said, "I'll make the drinks."

"I'll get the supplies." We both made for the kitchen area. I went to the cabinet devoted to liquor and started concocting a couple of mixed drinks. One for me and one for Mom while she went around the dining room table and disappeared into her bedroom to grab her rolling tray and joint supplies.

We convened outside, both of us dropping onto the big section patio furniture couch and lounging around the stone firepit table. Mom set down her stuff, and I set down our drinks on their coasters. She opened up the base of the table and twisted the knob to get the gas fire going.

It clicked and whooshed, and she turned the flame in the center of the table among the lava rocks to a steady golden glow.

While she did that, I turned the Edison bulbs to a warm white from the multi colors the boys had them set to.

"So," she said. "This staff meeting... you're turning in your resignation, right?" she asked.

I picked up my drink and took a fortifying sip.

"We'll see," I said. "Depends on what they have to say."

"Rarity," she chastised and I scoffed.

"I'm not trying to be a rebellious pain in the ass about this, I promise," I said. "Trust me, I know how bad it was. *I was there* and spent a big chunk of my day with detectives going over it all again. It *scared the shit out of me*, but even they said that when something like this happens, generally the place it happens is the safest it'll ever be in the months right after."

My mom snorted like she didn't know about that, as she worked on rolling us a joint to split between us.

My mom wasn't a hippy, but she partook of the herb on the regular. Had all my life. Wouldn't let me touch it until I was twenty-one, though.

I was one of those weirdos that had spent her twenty-first at home, getting drunk and high with her mom, falling out in fits of giggles over stupid shit and crying over Dad, wishing he could be there with us.

Honestly, there had been no place I would have rather been. It was a hell of a lot safer than going out.

For as much of an attitude as I had, I was your trademarked "good girl" and I didn't give a fuck what anyone had to say or think about it, because to me it was all made-up bullshit anyway. Nothing was really ever that black or white. My dad and mom taught me better than that.

My mom sparked up and took a hit, holding the slim joint out to me. I took it, and a hit of my own and held the green smoke in my lungs as long as possible. I coughed. I was never very good at smoking. Generally, I preferred edibles, but edibles were *wild*.

I handed her back the joint as she cackled at my coughing and I shook my head grinning, taking another slurp of my cocktail. She tried hers.

"Ooo! Good job, baby girl," she declared.

"I know, right? It's like it's my job or something." I rolled my eyes and we both dissolved in a fit of giggling.

"Not for long, I hope," she said with a gusty sigh.

"Mom, *if* I do decide to stay, I don't want you to nag me to death, okay?"

"I'm your mother," she said flatly. "You're my first born and my only daughter. I reserve the right to nag you to death when I'm worried you're going to get hurt or worse, *die*," she said.

"Alright, alright," I grumbled. "You have valid points, but at the same time, I'm not going to find a waitressing or bartending job anywhere around here that pays better, *especially* by way of tips. And in case you hadn't noticed, even with Grams and Gramps' help, we're *barely* making it without Dad and we still have what? Five or six years to go on the mortgage for you?"

"Six," she confessed with a sigh.

"There you go," I said. "Let alone saving for the boys' future. That shit can't wait. The fucking insurance going up, up, and up with the hurricanes, medical insurance, groceries to *feed* all of us and three growing little monsters – we don't have the luxury to be snooty about where I'm earning my keep from."

She stuck out her bottom lip and pouted.

"When did you get so grown up?" she demanded.

"When the fuckwit on the back of that crotch rocket slammed into Dad out on the boulevard," I said unhappily.

She sighed and nodded, took a drink and then another hit, and passed the joint back to me.

"I don't want to be sad tonight," she said around her held breath. "I feel like all we are is sad anymore, you and me."

I nodded, holding my toke in, and let it out without coughing this time. "We have a lot to be sad about," I said. "The struggle is fucking real and shit just keeps getting tighter. But at the same time, we have a lot to be happy about too."

"Yeah..." she sounded like she was struggling to come up with shit to be happy about so I helped her along.

"The boys are all healthy and happy," I said. "I'm doing just fine. Dad taught me well, and you did too," I reminded her. "I got out before shit had the chance to get too real and came right home. Fool me once, shame on you – fool me twice, shame on *me*," I reminded her. "There was no way I was sticking around for round two. Just my luck that I saw how it started and I'm stuck being a stupid witness."

"I'm proud of you for that," she said.

"For what?"

"Talking to the cops and telling them what really happened."

I shrugged. "All I can tell them is what I saw," I said. "I'm sure they'd be a lot happier if I told them what they wanted to hear. seems like they really have a hard-on for anyone wearing a cut, but for real – the Royal Bastards didn't do anything. It was all those other guys, the Scorpions."

My mom stared at me and shook her head. "I can't believe the bar didn't do anything to keep you safe," she said.

"I mean, yeah, that's part of it – but the other part is *what were they supposed to do?*" I asked. "When the 'customer is always right' and the customers outnumber managerial and security staff two to one, I don't think they thought they *could* do anything." I, of course, put "the customer is always right" in air bunnies with my fingers, because honestly, as someone who worked both retail *and* hospitality industries, whoever had come up with that little quip deserved a swift kick in the balls with steel-toed boots, as much as the sort of customer who liked to abuse the phrase.

"The manager should have called the cops and had them fucking trespassed the *first* night after one of them clocked you," she said.

I thought about that for a second and said, "You know what? Cheers to that." I held up my glass, she clicked hers against mine, and we both took a drink.

"This is what you get when the world is run by men," she said, her tone snarky, and I busted up laughing.

My mom only seemed to turn into raging feminist when she was drunk or high. It was funny as hell every time, especially coming from her, who had absolutely adored being a trad wife until I got into school and she started getting *bored*.

Boredom and my mom hadn't mixed. It'd led to an unhealthy amount of retail therapy that'd put my parents into a *scary* amount of credit card debt for a while. She'd gone to work, and that had both seemed to balance her out and helped by way of paying down said debt. She'd been careful ever since.

Now, we didn't have a choice. It was *stay frugal or die.*

My mom and I talked, sitting on the porch under the fan, the warm, sultry night full of insect and frog song as we *mellowed out* from the day. Still, my thoughts kept drifting to Striker.

The more I sat with and understood my mom's point of view, the more I realized I *didn't* want to return to the Iron Horse after what happened. I mean, I loved it there when the times were good, and the times *were* mostly good – but the last two nights had *definitely* dinged my confidence in feeling safe going to work. I mean, shit – I had the bruises to look at every time I caught my reflection, reminding me every time that I had just barely begun to gaslight myself into thinking things were or would be fine.

No, the only reason I even considered for a moment keeping my job, was the hope that I might see Striker again. Something about spending time with him had been... nice. It'd been comfortable, and it felt *safe.*

He hadn't let anything happen to me, and yeah, he made me feel proud of myself for helping him, too.

I sighed and leaned back in my seat, staring out into the dark as something zipped low to the ground on the other side of the chain link fence that we had around our backyard.

"Oh, did you see that?" my mom asked.

"Yeah, what was it?" I frowned.

"Coyote. Do you know if the cats are inside?"

I shook my head. "No, I haven't seen Sir Didymus or Jareth in a minute," I said.

Didymus was our fat orange cat and a coward. Jareth was a tuxedo who was long and lanky and not just in body. His legs were almost too long, and his ears too. He was one of the weirdest-looking cats that you'd ever lay eyes on, but I hadn't seen either all day. Didn't mean anything, though. They roved in and out at their leisure and sometimes would abscond for a day or two at a time.

I think Didymus had one or two other part-time families he hung out with in the neighborhood. He certainly was round enough to be eating in more than one place.

"Well, may the odds be in their favor if they aren't in the house," my mom said with a gusty sigh. "Nothing we can really do about it."

Yeah, it sounded callous, but it wasn't. It was just the reality of things. Knowing Mom, she would be awake worrying all night.

We went inside and found Didymus on the couch. He sauntered into the kitchen, waddling into Mom's room to go to bed. She let out a relieved sigh and let me know Jareth was in her room before she closed the door.

I put our glasses in the sink and went to bed, closing my bedroom door behind me.

I found the ruin of Striker's shirt in the corner on the floor. I picked it up and thought it was a shame. It was a good *Black Rebels Motorcycle Club* tee. It was a band, and I liked them enough that I had a few of their songs on my playlist. The shirt was in a size large. So, my size but only because of my chest. If my boobs had been just a little less, a medium would have suited me just fine for the rest of me, but my bazongas were just like my mother's and would *not* be contained.

I swallowed and self-indulgently brought the tee shirt to my nose, closing my eyes and breathing it in.

It smelled like booze, sure, but underneath, it smelled like him. Like whatever cologne or aftershave or whatever he used, but even below that, it smelled like *him*. I found the scent... *nice*. Comforting in a strange way.

I looked at the shirt in my hands, at the blood stain across the front where it'd been slashed, and thought about it.

I bet I could save it.

I mean, not for him – but I bet I could make it work for me. A few clever cuts, a knot or two, and it'd fit right in at the Iron Horse.

If nothing else, I had it to remember him by, even if I never saw him again.

I took a shower and went to bed, only to be startled awake at some ungodly hour by one of my little brothers hiccup sobbing by my bed.

"Baby, what's wrong?" I asked, sitting up, unsure which one of the triplets it was.

"Rarity," he said. "I frew up."

Ohhhh nooo... I should have known.

"Okay, bud, let's get you cleaned up."

I put my feet down and made a face. He'd failed to mention he'd thrown up in his room, and up the hallway, and through the kitchen, and in *my* room. I guess I was closer than Mom.

Fuck a duck.

CHAPTER FIFTEEN

S triker...

It was pretty much business as usual as soon as we got back to St. Augustine. We all went home, showered, slept, and met up the next morning at the club to a catered brunch. Renegade's way of showing us all appreciation for showing up and showing the Scorpions *out* of North Florida.

We ate around the table in the chapel, talking shit and cuttin' up, and it was a good time.

My thoughts were never far from Rarity, though. I'd woken up with one hell of a boner and missing the feel of her in my arms. She was a sweet thing, and I had one hell of a sweet tooth where she was concerned.

I was contemplating my next visit to the Iron Horse when Renegade caught my sightless staring while I was lost in thought.

"You ain't planning on going back down that way anytime soon, are you?" he asked, leaning back in his seat.

"I'd be lying if I said I ain't thought about it," I said, relaxing back into mine with a careless grin. "Think it's a bad idea?"

"Eh, you fly solo and slick-backed and see if their staff or security recognizes you. They do, you leave with some grace. They don't..." he shrugged. "I don't see a problem."

"I know what her car looks like. Could always leave a note," I said.

Renegade's mouth turned down like he was impressed, and he said, "That's using your head for something other than a hat rack."

I laughed.

"Man, fuck you," I said, and he grinned and winked at me.

I felt better about the whole thing having his blessing, you know? I didn't need it, but it was nice to have it.

"Thanks, man," I said, and he gave a little lackadaisical shrug.

"You aren't one to get sidetracked by pussy," he said evenly, and he didn't mean it in any sort of insulting way toward Rarity. It was just a fact.

"She's got a set of brass ovaries," I told him. "I don't think I've seen anything quite like it. She's got my attention. It's been a long time since that's happened."

"Yeah, yeah, it has," he agreed.

I'd carefully avoided getting too involved with anyone over the last, shit, almost twenty years. I'd had flings, sure – but never anything past a few weeks or months of fun while the girl looked for something better... more permanent.

I wasn't looking to *settle down* or anything with Rarity. Hell, I didn't even know what I *was* after where she was concerned other than I'd really like to get to know her. Or at least learn more about her.

She was this alluring combination of straight *fire* and yet held this sort of sweet innocence about her. It had me hooked, and I didn't know how or in just what way – not yet. I just knew I had this driving need to see her and to see if it *could* go anywhere. Part of that was feeling like I owed her.

I mean, for fuck's sake. She'd stood between my ass and getting *shot*. That was huge. She had the heart of a lioness, and yet she was just a cub. I wondered if that was part of the appeal for me.

I had a serious need to be a protector, and she'd pushed all the right buttons. By the same token, she was stand-up, could and was taking care of herself and her family. She wasn't just fling material, and I recognized that. But with the age difference, I didn't know if it was right to go further than just friends...

I just didn't know, but I had this serious urge to find out.

I had the impulse to go for a solo ride and decided to take the A1A all the way to the Ponce De Leon Inlet Lighthouse and Museum. If I needed a quick fix to clear my head, I would just climb the St. Augustine Lighthouse. That was a fuckin' workout. The Ponce Inlet Lighthouse wasn't nearly as grueling, but I wasn't in it for the climb when I went out that way. I was in it for the hour-and-forty-five-minute plus ride along some of the most scenic beachfront coastal roadway in North Florida.

I let the bike eat through asphalt, my mind a pleasant hum of replaying every memory I had so far of Rarity. I admit, I *almost* slid into the turn lane when I approached Ormond Beach to head more inland to where the Iron Horse and her place lie – but I resisted the urge.

For real, I couldn't bank on her feeling anything for me like I had her. I didn't even know if I *should* be this low-key obsessed, but I couldn't shake her beautiful blue eyes or the feel of her silken, soft blonde hair between my fingers. I *definitely* couldn't shake the memory of her soft curves pressed into my body as we'd lay in the dark, the only illumination the blue flickering glow from her softly playing television.

I thought for sure that I'd picked up on the vibe that she'd wanted to see me again at the end there when I'd slipped out and we'd parted ways... but now I was second-guessing everything.

She was *twenty-four*, I was *forty-two*. When I was enlisted and going through fucking boot camp, she was taking her first few breaths.

I knew the world wouldn't approve, and as much as I wanted to know her, I didn't know if I wanted the judgmental bullshit falling on her shoulders. Or mine.

Did I fucking care *that* much about being accused of being some kind of predator? No. I was a predator. A wolf among sheep. I didn't give a fuck what anybody thought about me to that end because I knew the truth.

As interested as Rarity had made me, which was a rare thing, I wasn't interested in her just because she had a bangin' body. She was beautiful – sure, but this was *Florida*. There were a shit ton of beautiful women here. No, her iron heart, her brass pair, her caring nature, and her total bravery were what had my attention.

...and yeah, maybe even the fact she was, by all appearances, some kind of a daddy's girl. I had the kink. I wasn't ashamed to admit that. I know a lot of people thought it was fuckin' weird, but again, I didn't much give a fuck what citizens thought. My brothers' sure – I cared what *they* thought of me, but for sure, when it came to things, we were a more... enlightened lot than most. If not downright unbothered about being hedonistic fucks.

Shit, look at Skull & Bones. They were *biological brothers* who liked to fuck the same woman *at the same time*.

The Ocala chapter had their little porn empire, so they were as open-minded as you got when it came to sexual proclivities. Pud was all for diving into the industry as one of their new stars, so I didn't see any stones coming from their direction.

No one said shit about any of *that*, so I didn't think anyone would blink at a Daddy/little girl dynamic.

Renegade...

That was my only concern. He had a daughter about Rarity's age. Dusty was pretty much the club's princess. All the guys would kill for that girl in a fuckin' heartbeat.

I think that was what wasn't sitting right with me.

I was worried about what Renegade would think – which was fuckin' stupid, wasn't it? Hadn't he been the one to give his blessing to return to the Iron Horse so early on just so I could try and slide in across Rarity at her bar and shoot some kind of shot?

Of course, did he *know* how old she was? Had he really gotten a look at her?

Fuck, man, what the hell was wrong with me? I'd never worried about shit like this before.

I let my thoughts meander all over hell and gone over the subject of Rarity, and I couldn't remember the last time I'd ever been in such a damn tizzy over a woman. It was confusing and yet... *delightful.*

She gave me butterflies in my stomach, and I couldn't remember a time that'd *ever* happened... except back in high school.

I made it to the lighthouse and sat astride my bike in the parking lot, my mind just *churning.* I had no idea if the object of my new obsession even spared a single thought toward me.

Probably not... I thought. I wouldn't be able to know until the Iron Horse reopened and that still depended on if I was recognized as one of the "bad actors" and tossed before I could even shoot my shot.

I could do things, get around it. I knew what her car looked like. I could leave a note like I'd said.

I thought about that, got off my bike, and stretched. I went into the Ponce Inlet giftshop and wandered around sightlessly for a while until I ran into a rack with notes and postcards on it.

I turned the rack and looked at the art, then stopped at one of the postcards.

It had a mermaid on it, and it made me smile. It was in the old-school art style of old travel posters and magazines from the '40s or '50s. Illustrated, watercolor painted, framed in white, the undersea background in the blues and turquoises of the waters around here.

The mermaid was beautiful, but a brunette, but still... she reminded me of Rarity and how I'd thought of her as a little mermaid, with her hair still wet from the shower, her face fresh and free of makeup, making her look younger, *more* innocent if it was possible.

I bought a handful of the cards and my ticket to go out into the yard that housed the lighthouse and its accompanying lightkeepers cabins down below. I wandered out and looked up at the light. It wasn't nearly as tall as St. Augustine's light, but it was still impressive. While Augustine's light was painted in a black-and-white barber pole swirl with a fire engine red cap, Ponce Inlet's was much more sedate. The tower was painted a uniform color. It was closest to a brick red, a few shades darker than terra cotta, with a tinge more earthy tone to it. The window cross bars and the lighthouse cap were black, but the window sashes and the framing of the door at the bottom were a gray stone hinting at tan.

The doors were flung wide and there was a beautiful golden wood with just a hint of red to them. The window above the door had classic gold block lettering and read *Ponce De Leon Lighthouse, 1887.*

There was one thing I loved about the Ponce light more than the St. Augustine light, and one thing only... the design and beauty of its spiral staircase.

It was imminently more photographable than the Augustine light, even if capturing it was tricky as the bottom of the staircase was cordoned off. You had to lean way over the railing to get the camera centered to get the snap, and it sometimes took several tries. But if you could get it, it was chef's kiss fuckin' perfect, the ridges and swirl up to the top as perfect as a nature-made nautilus shell.

It was wild to me that the Ponce lighthouse was *taller* than Augustine's light by a mere ten feet, but to reach her top? She had two-hundred-and-three steps to get to the top, which was sixteen steps *less* than it took to get to the top of St. Augustine's light.

I imagine it was some engineering thing but nothing that I thought too much about.

I started the steady climb to the top, and it didn't take long for the burn to set into my legs, my already stiff body from the explosive fighting of the night before protesting every riser as I worked my way to the top.

To say I had some serious fuckin' regrets about undertaking the climb by the time I reached the top was a *major* understatement of the facts – but by the same token, the view over the Atlantic couldn't be beaten from up here.

I leaned on the railing, catching my breath, the wind ruffling my hair and plastering my shirt to my body, cooling and drying the sweat on my back.

While the ride had let me work through a lot of thoughts, worries, and concerns and let me wonder and daydream freely – standing up here at such an unearthly height with the wind washing over me, the vastness of the water out in front of me, feeling like I was standing at the edge of the world itself?

My mind went blessedly quiet. Silent in its awe of the view and the churning waves ahead of me. I slipped into what could only be described as a meditative state as tourists snapped pictures beside me and made fools of themselves by playing up their fear of heights... which I thought was stupid as fuck. If you're *that* afraid of heights, why make the fuckin' climb in the first place?

I had respect for the one girl, though – she was afraid but was genuinely there to conquer her fear. I listened to her tell the atten-dant at the top how she had been to all the lighthouses you could climb in Florida, taking them from smallest to tallest, and she'd made it. She was here at the tallest, and that meant something – even if she clung to her boyfriend and shook like a leaf.

It brought me back to my fearless little mermaid and the peace I'd felt with her in my arms. Safe, cuddling into me like I was her prince... I liked it. Maybe I'd let my imagination run wild... maybe she'd meant nothing by it... but it sure felt like she'd *craved* that feeling as much as I craved to give it.

I didn't know.

I stood up there and let the wind and salty breeze carry my thoughts and troubles off over the water and trees out there. I took my time making my descent.

When I reached the bottom, I lingered, wandering over to the wrap-around porch of the lightkeeper's cottage and dropping into one of the rocking chairs on it for guest's enjoyment to look up at the lighthouse from down here.

I pulled the postcards out of my pocket and a pen out of my cut and sat with my thoughts, which were much calmer but fleeting now.

I had no idea what to write, but I was sure I would come up with *something*.

CHAPTER SIXTEEN

R arity...

"That's bullshit."

I didn't need to say it. Big Dawg had it handled. He wasn't about to take any gaslighting off Charlie, and I wasn't either. I didn't say anything. I just let my resting bitch face do all the talking.

Several of the Iron Horse's employees had already quit and walked out. I was still on the fence but would quickly make up my mind based on how the argument about to go down between Big Dawg and upper management shook out. Right now, Charlie was sweating bullets, and the old adage *people didn't quit bad jobs, they quit bad managers* was floating around in my thoughts.

I didn't think Charlie was going to survive this argument or the incident as a whole. The owner was doing the math, the calculations clearly going on in his deep brown eyes, even if the rest of his face was inscrutable.

I'd known Rob since I was knee high to a fuckin' June bug, as my gram and gramps would say.

He and my dad had gotten along. My dad even helped Rob with some metrics and financials at one point.

I could never remember being so *disappointed* in my "Uncle Rob" as I was right now.

He should probably fear my mom calling his ass up. I'm sure she'd thought about it. I didn't know if she had already or not.

Rob's eyes flicked in my direction and I knew he noted how unhappy I looked, but I just kept my mouth shut.

Did I *want* to keep my mouth shut? No. Did I know that if I did, it would bother the shit out of Rob, and he might take me more seriously and *ask* my opinion?

Yes.

I was playing the game to get the best results, and the best results would be to get rid of fucking Charlie and get somebody in here to manage the place who had the iron pair of testicles necessary to call the unpleasant shots.

Shit, *I* could do a better job than Charlie. I just didn't have the experience or even the *time* to until the boys were in school, and even then, I didn't know if that was what I ultimately wanted. Running a bar like the Iron Horse was... *a lot.* Way above my pay grade right now, that was for sure – but that was the point I was trying to make. Charlie sucked at it that bad. Sure, he made sure we never ran out of things or whatever, but the actual security side of things, and things besides just the payroll and ordering and stuff?

Yeah, he sucked.

"Rarity, what 'cha thinking?" Rob asked,

"Depends," I said. "Am I talking to Rob, my boss and the owner of the Iron Horse, or am I talking to 'Uncle Rob,' who I grew up with?"

He grinned at me and asked, "What's the difference?"

"Whether I'm being real or not," I said with a shrug, and there was a smattering of laughter.

"Let's start with Rob the boss," he said.

"Okay. The last couple of nights of operation were a train wreck on the security side of things. Charlie doesn't listen, and he doesn't always enforce the rules or he tells Big Dawg to let it slide. Dawg should have pushed back more on night one – but when night two went down?" I shook my head.

"And Rob the uncle?" he asked, looking uncomfortable.

"You should have been here last night from the time that we opened. The cops should have been called, and the Scorpions should have been 86'ed before the Bastards even showed up. You know how these cock goblins work. It's been the same shit since the fifties and the sixties. They might as well whip their dicks out and piss on their territory, and *this*—" I flailed my arms, gesticulating wildly. "*All* of North Florida is *Bastards* territory, so you *knew* they were coming. Big Dawg was already down for the count. Charlie," I looked at him with disgust, "clearly isn't up to the task, and if my dad were alive, he'd have some serious shit to say right now."

The staff around us all sat or stood with their mouths open, and Rob burned with embarrassment as he stared into my eyes, one of them looking even worse for the tinge of purple and deep bruising around it.

"Last night was *bullshit,* and everyone here knows it. You've already lost half your staff. You need to lose him." I pointed at Charlie. "And you need to be present for a while until you replace him. And if my mom doesn't stop bugging the shit out of me to quit, *you* can deal with her. I'm tired of hearing it, and honestly, you're on strike two – three strikes, you're out. The money is the only thing keeping me here. Your wages are some of the best ones around the area, and the tips can't be beat. That's the *only* reason I'm even considering staying because point blank? I want my brothers to be there when I get married. I *want* to be able to get married. I want to live a long life and die of a ripe old age and not die in some stupid bar fight turned firefight between a bunch of guys making up for their small dicks."

Rob's eyes shone with laughter, even though I knew he wasn't laughing *at* me – just at how I wasn't afraid to mince words and how I'd phrased things. He sniffed, nodded, and said, "Tell us how you really feel."

"I believe I just did," I said, grinning. Charlie looked like a landed fish and I shot him a dirty look.

"You're fired," Rob said, and for a split second, I thought he was talking to me, so I hopped off the bar stool.

"Not *you*, Peanut. This asshole." He pointed at Charlie, who sputtered. "You can come get your last check tomorrow," Rob said.

"As for the rest of you – if you stay, you're getting a dollar-an-hour raises, we're sticking to the *goddamned rules*, and if you know anyone looking for security work – we're hiring temps until we get back to normal."

It was a start, but like with most things anymore, I'd listen to my dad, who'd always told me *don't listen to what a man says, watch what he does.*

Seemed like solid advice, especially in a case like this.

"We're closed for the foreseeable future. Our liquor license is suspended for the next thirty days, so we need to get the booze off the shelves, and the place cleaned up and maintained. We'll reopen sans liquor- which we can do – so we need to book some entertainment." He ticked off on his finger. "Get the smokers going and the barbecue up and running." He ticked off another. "And get everyone back to serving and whatnot before those thirty days are up. I'd honestly like to be down for only a few days at the worst. Do you think we can handle that?" he asked.

I thought so. Heads nodded around the bar.

"Alright, if you wanna bounce, do it. If you plan on staying, let's make a plan, and if your ass just got fired, *get the fuck outta my bar!*" He barked the last at Charlie, who jumped and left forthwith.

I stood there, and Rob looked over at me and said, "I appreciate you calling me out on my bullshit."

I nodded. "It's what my dad would have done," I said.

"You're right, it is, kiddo." He looked over my face, disappointment on his own, as he shook his head and said, "I'm real sorry this all went down like it did, and you got hurt."

"Don't be sorry," I said. "Let's just not let it happen again."

He nodded, and I went around the bar and hugged him.

"I'm going up to bar two to pull the liquor and beer," I said.

"Appreciate it, kiddo," he said, and off we all went, scurrying like ants to pull the booze and finish cleaning up.

It was getting on toward evening when I walked out the side gate to head for my Jeep. I got in and, sighed tiredly, racking my neck back and forth.

I didn't know how effective a bar would run without alcohol sales, but I had to hand it to Rob. He was trying. I mean, I knew he'd been through this kind of thing before, but it'd honestly been *years* since a dust-up of *this* magnitude. We're talking more than a decade since trouble this bad. The last time the Iron Horse had its liquor license pulled was in the early 2000s around the time I'd been *born*.

Eugh... I thought to myself. *I really was just a baby.* I probably sounded obnoxious as fuck back there and should be grateful that Rob had *listened* and hadn't just fired me on the spot.

Fuck me.

I leaned my head back onto the headrest of my seat and sighed out, closing my eyes and just trying to take a minute for myself before heading home to three poorly little boys who had been an epic fucking yak-fest the night before all the way into the wee hours of this morning.

Whump! Whump!

"Ahgh!" I screamed and whipped my head around to my driver's side window, where the two knocks had come from.

"Jesus," I muttered and rolled down my window.

"Sorry, I didn't mean to scare you," Gemma said. I sighed, waiting for my heart to drop back down into my chest from my throat and nodded.

"All good," I said. "What's up?"

"I just wanted to say thanks. What you did in there was ballsy. You just made life a whole lot better for the rest of us, and because of it, I've decided to stay."

"Yeah?" I asked, and she nodded.

"That scared the shit out of me, but I actually feel like it won't happen again. Like, I'm hopeful. If Charlie had stayed on, I would have been *gone*."

"Not gonna lie, I have mixed feelings about what you're saying right now," I said with a tenuous laugh.

"Why?" she asked.

"Because if the shit goes down again, and you're caught in the middle, I'm going to feel like it's my fault," I said.

She laughed and shook her head.

"I'm a big girl, too, Rarity. I think as long as you're around, I'll be all good. You go, I know it's time to go, though. For sure."

I laughed at that and said, "If I go, that's your sign it was time to leave ten minutes ago."

She looked at me, her eyes going a bit wide, and we both started laughing.

"I guess I'll see you when we all get back together," she said, and I nodded.

"Yeah. Right now, I gotta get home. Aden Braden and Caden all have some kind of nasty stomach bug and were up pulling an exorcist all night last night."

"Oh, ew!" she cried. "Have fun with *that*."

"Oh, the fun just never stops," I cracked sarcastically, rolling my eyes.

She giggled and stepped back, going around the back of my Jeep to her little car on the other side. I let her pull out first, and when she'd gone, I carefully backed my Jeep off the grassy shoulder and onto the pavement of the side street.

No sooner did I put it into first and start to let up on the clutch, a motorcycle turned in off the boulevard. I rolled down my window to tell the rider that we were closed until further notice and to check our social media when he stopped next to my driver's side and lifted his mirrored aviators to hold back his dark hair.

"Well, well, well, fancy meeting you here," Striker said with a grin that looked a whole lot like the cat that ate the canary.

"Hey, you," I said with a soft smile.

"Wanted to come by and leave this for you," he said and produced a postcard from his back pocket. "I think I'd like to stay in touch," he said.

I plucked the card from between his fingers and looked at the mermaid on its face, *Ponce Inlet* written in block text below her. It was a pretty postcard.

"Anyway," he said, revving his bike motor, distracting me from the postcard. "Call me!" he shouted, and then he disengaged the clutch, gave the throttle a twist, and rode down the way past me. Mystified, I set the card aside on my passenger seat and pulled forward, stopping at the stop sign and turning on my right signal.

I watched in my rearview as he swooped in an elegant turn and rode up behind me before ditching off to my left to put on his signal to head back for the interstate. Likely to go north to St. Augustine.

I realized he wasn't wearing his cut as he pulled up even with me. It came as a shock when it hit me that he'd come incognito, especially to see *me*. *Why did that warm me to my damn toes?*

"I'll call!" I shouted at him over the combined noise of our engines, and his smile split into a wide grin.

I made my turn and headed for home. I'd be lying if I said I didn't hurry up to get there just to see what the postcard said.

I pulled into my driveway and parked, turning off the ignition and setting the parking brake. With shaking fingers, I picked up the card and let my eyes rove the mermaid on the front, the coral she was nestled among, the way her hair floated freely, her curving teal-blue tail, and how the fins swept out and around her. It was a beautiful piece of art, and I loved that he'd picked it.

I turned the card over and blinked in surprise at the elegant script it was written in.

Rarity...

Can't seem to get you off of my mind. Would like to just talk some and see where it goes. Gimme a text or call any time. If I don't hear from you, I'll take the hint, I promise.

Yours,

Striker

He left his phone number and then...

*PS. There's no time limit on this. Hours, days, weeks, months, or heck —
even a year or two. I can wait.*

I didn't know what to make of it. I certainly wouldn't keep him
waiting *years*. Days, maybe, depending on how the boys were doing.

Shit.

I better move my ass. The boys. I'd promised them snuggle time
on the couch and a watch of their favorite movie, *How to Train Your
Dragon.*

I got out of the Jeep and gathered up my stuff, taking it in with
me. I found Mom on the couch with three little blanket-covered
lumps around her.

"Still feeling bad?" I asked.

"Yeah," Aden called mournfully.

"We jumped the gun and already watched *How to Train Your
Dragon,*" Mom told me.

"Well, that's alright," I said. "I was late. I'm sorry. Let me go put
this stuff down, rinse off really quick, and I'll come out and join you
guys, okay?"

"Okay," the boys chorused and my mom nodded, but I could tell
by the look in her blue eyes, which were so like my own – she was
worried.

I tried to give her a reassuring smile and went around to duck
into my room. I sighed, set things down, put my phone on the
charger, and stuck the postcard in the edge of my mirror to keep it
displayed.

I showered, redressed in comfortable pajamas, and joined my
mother and brothers in the living room, cozy on the couch and
watching Disney until it was late enough and all three boys were
sleeping to the point we had to carry them to bed.

When their light was out, and Mom and I were in the kitchen
about to go for our own beds, the tension reached its peak. She

broke first, asking, "So, what'd Rob say he was going to do about it?"

"Well, I got Charlie fired," I said with a sigh. "The bar's liquor license has been suspended for a month, and we're scrambling to get the liquor and beer off the shelves and put away. We're switching gears to food and soft drinks, focusing on putting live talent on the stage and hoping we can weather the storm. Rob is hiring more security and buckling down on the rules like never before. I decided to wait it out, and if I even get a whiff of things going sideways, I'm out. For good this time."

My mom looked at me, and her expression was torn.

"On one hand, I want to be so *mad* at you for being so pigheaded. I swear to God, you're just like your father that way, and it was one of his *least* endearing qualities sometimes," she said, her eyes welling up with tears. "On the other hand, I'm *so* proud of you... and I honestly don't know what to say."

Of all the things she could have said, *that* wasn't on the list of shit I'd expected.

"You blaze your own trail, that's for sure, baby girl."

The waterworks really started then, not just from her but from me, too. I went around the kitchen island and hugged my mom tight, and we stood there and cried together. Definitely wasn't the first time and probably wouldn't be the last time, either – but it'd been a while since I'd cried for something that, to me, was a *good* reason.

I mean, *oh, my God!*

"I worry about you," she said.

"I know, Ma," I said, sniffing when we finally broke apart.

"Just keep being careful. I'd die if anything happened to you, too."

"I promise," I told her. "I'm not going anywhere."

She nodded, and we both sort of drifted to our respective rooms. I dropped onto the edge of my bed and looked across to my mirror with its mermaid postcard tucked in its frame.

I got up, went to it, and flipped it over, bringing up my phone from where it was charging to punch in the number and make a new contact.

I took my phone back to bed with me, snuggled under the covers, and texted out with shaking fingers... *I could use a friend...*

It was late, and I didn't expect a response, but I got one anyway, and in just a few seconds.

Talk to me. I'm right here.

CHAPTER SEVENTEEN

*S*triker...

I was at home, on the couch, with a cold beer perched on my knee, my boots off, and the television on. I hadn't bothered with turning on a light, so it was just me and some mindless action flick on the boob tube casting the room in a blue flickering glow.

Made me think of her. Made me think of holding her while the television in her room played.

I sighed and was about to switch it off and head on into my bedroom when my phone buzzed twice, walking itself in two short steps across the coffee table in front of me.

I picked it up, an unknown number, but Florida area code for the region, and I knew it was her just by the contents of the text... ***I could use a friend.***

I hesitated, a bunch of shit tumbling through my head on what would be a good response when I felt my shoulders drop as I told myself to stop fucking overthinking it.

Talk to me. I'm right here, I shot back.

She texted a novel, pouring out her heart and soul about her worries. For her mother, for her brother's future, about how she felt like she was letting them all down, and if her dad were here, how she wasn't so sure he wouldn't be disappointed in her. She said her mom had told her she was proud of her – but she just didn't understand or believe because of how her mom ragged on just about every choice she made and how confusing it all was.

I didn't think she'd had anyone she felt like she could talk to in a while, and for some reason, she'd decided that she could be frank with me. I glowed from the unspoken praise.

I wasn't used to being trusted. Not outside the club and even inside the club... sometimes trust was a rare commodity.

I did my best to shore her up and assure her that she was doing great. That yeah, it sucked, for sure – she was overworked, and she'd been through some shit that would leave a lesser woman crumbling, but not only was she holding it together and still showing up, but she was also doing it in a way that to the rest of us made her look like she was Supergirl.

Thanks... she texted finally after what felt like minutes of radio silence. ***Bars closed this week, and I only have two days at my other job. Looks like I'm free for a few days after the middle of the week.***

I hesitated, then started to thumb out a response. Deleted that and tried again. Deleted *that* and thought to myself, *you're fuckin' crazy...*

I held my breath and thumbed it out anyway. ***You should take some time for yourself. Come up to St. Augustine for a day. I'll show you around.***

I swallowed hard, staring at the text, then went to delete the fucker but fat-fingered it, and it sent.

Fuck. Me.

I felt my face flame with embarrassment and thought to myself, *you old fucker – she'll never go for it.*

Bet.

Do what now?

Bet? I asked, just to make sure I wasn't completely delusional.

I'd like that, she came back with and I was floored.

Okay. You just name the day... I wrote.

We concluded our conversation shortly after that, and I polished off my beer, feeling as giddy as a schoolboy.

For real. I hadn't felt excitement or butterflies like this since I was young, dumb, and full of cum before I enlisted.

I got up, tossed my empty in the kitchen trash on the way by, and returned to my bedroom.

I stripped and flopped down in bed and read and re-read our chat.

I had no fucking idea what I was doing. I couldn't even say I was being wholly altruistic and not a selfish fuck by wanting to see her again.

Hell... I tried to live as uncomplicated a life as I could for being a Royal Bastard – which always had its complications... but *fuck...* I couldn't tell, to be honest, but this felt a whole lot like I balanced on some sort of brink that could either be really good or really bad. I'd be lying if I said I wasn't attracted, but I was a *man* before she'd even shot out of her mother's womb.

I pulled on my neck to try and relieve some of the tension in it and sighed.

It took her a bit to get back to me, but get back to me with that ideal date and time she did.

Now, all that was left was to figure out what to do...

THE WEEK HAD DRAGGED on for what felt like forever. I dealt with some shit on some purchase orders we'd made not being fulfilled on time at the shop, but other than that one hiccup, everything else had run as smoothly as I could have asked for.

We hadn't been bothered by the cops or any prosecutors over the Bloody Scorpion thing all week. Neither had Jacksonville nor Ocala. Renegade and The Bishop had a pretty high confidence that it'd be dropped and we wouldn't hear anything more about it, which told me without telling me, they had *somebody* in their pocket.

Either that or Ormond Beach was just being smart and taking the gift that they'd been given on a silver fuckin' platter in putting some Scorpions away.

Like I said, *North Florida* was *ours...* and we weren't done yet. We were moving south as steadily as vetting new members and new chapters coming online would allow, but building an empire like ours was painfully slow going. Move too fast, and don't vet newcomers right, that's how you get rats on board your ship. Rats who would chew through the decking and the rigging. Rats who'd put holes in your hull and sink said ship.

Ain't none of us keen on a trip to Davey Jones's locker, so it was a slow and steady to win the race type of a deal.

Don't ask me why my thoughts were meandering in that direction. Probably to keep me cool and steady. My nerves were firing on all cylinders the more I watched the clock and the slower that damn minute hand made its move around the face.

I was more nervous about seeing Rarity again than I was about getting into a firefight – and I didn't know what that meant.

You're fucked. That's what it means, I told myself.

"Yo, Striker!" I heard called up the stairs.

"Yeah!" I called back down them.

"Got Jailbait down here lookin' for you!" Sounded like Adrian Hernandez – good worker, talented mechanic, and a stellar artist when it came to custom skins for a bike, but damned if he couldn't mind his own fuckin' business when it came to some things.

He wanted to move up in the world of the Royal Bastards. Had been in a hang-around tee for the better part of a year, but Renegade just wasn't ready to make him a prospect. Neither was Shadow, and neither was I. He just didn't have the street smarts to curb aspects of his outgoing personality and again, loose lips sank ships.

He had a long way to fuckin' go, but I was pretty sure if he could mature some, he'd make it.

"Send her on up!" I called down and spun in my chair to watch her crest the top of the steps. She was blushing a bright pink.

"I'm twenty-four," she said, and I grinned and laughed.

"Don't mind him. He can be a dumb fuck," I told her.

She looked good. She had on makeup today, and you couldn't even tell where she'd been clocked. A lot of us had healing bruises and cuts, purple fading on down to sickly yellows, greens, and that tan that was just off-putting to look at.

She looked good in her denim short shorts, her tanned legs almost looking long, and a pair of cute light pink Vans on her feet. She wore a fitted white tee, which was a daring choice for a woman with three brothers who were still toddler-age. I imagined that's why she wore it – no danger of sticky fingers.

It had a V-neck, short cap sleeves, and some light pink flowers along her ribs on one side.

"You look good," I complimented.

"Thanks," she said, taking off her little backpack handbag and dropping into the seat by my desk.

My phone rang just then, and she smiled and gestured for me to answer. I picked up the handset.

"Striker? This is Nightmare. Got a minute?" an unfamiliar voice asked on the other end. I racked my brain for half a second, and it clicked almost right away. Nightmare was a Royal Bastard, but out of Atlanta.

"Nightmare, huh? I've heard good things about you from Mav. He said you'd be calling. How can I help?" It'd been a minute since his president, Maverick, had called me up and told me about the dude. Said he was having some issues carrying the mental and emotional load from over in the sandbox.

As fucked up as it was, I didn't *have* any trouble with any of the shit that went on over there. I didn't know why and actually felt like *I* was somehow the one to come back fucked up for *not* having any real troubles. Still, I faked it well enough to help where I could when it came up like this.

"Mav said you might... you know, get where I'm coming from."

"I've been around long enough to see some shit and to know some shit. What's eating you?" I asked, ready to listen.

I heard the guy take a deep breath on the other end of the line, and I leaned back in my seat, giving Rarity a wink and holding up a finger to let her know this might be a minute.

"Back when I was with the Army Rangers... there was a mission. Intel was wrong, and I ended up taking out a civilian. A kid. Wrong place, wrong time type of deal. It's been years, but that shit still gets me, man. Some days, I can't even look in the fucking mirror." He sounded... rough, his voice heavy with emotion and cracking.

"I hear you, brother. I've got my fair share of ghosts, too. Different details, same load of guilt. You feel like it stains everything you do after, don't you?" That part was true, but I'd come to grips with it quick, leaving most of it behind in-country. Maybe I was better at compartmentalizing. Who knew?

"Exactly. Even now, being in the Bastards, it feels like I'm just pretending to be something better. Like I'll never make up for it."

I couldn't relate to that one, but I took a deep, considering, and yeah, somewhat cleansing breath and tackled it head-on.

"Listen. You can't undo it. That's the hard fucking truth. What you did back then ain't but between you an' God, homie - but you're not pretending. You're carrying that weight and still trying to do some good. *That's* what matters."

"Yeah, I get that, but some days, it feels like I'm handling things. Other days, it feels like I'm dragging a ball and chain."

"That's to be expected, but bad days don't last forever. It's simple. On your bad days, you lean on your brothers. On their bad days, you hold them up. That's how this works. You feel me? You're not alone in any of this, and you can't live like you are."

He made a scoffing noise and said, "That shit's not simple. Can't have them thinking I'm not solid."

"You think being vulnerable makes you less solid?" It was my turn to scoff. "No way, Nightmare. It makes you *real*. A brother respects that a hell of a lot more than any front you try to put up. If they don't, it just means they ain't been there like we have. When that happens, it's on us to make sure they don't go through the same hell. And if they do? It's our job to show them how to wade through this shit, just like you are now."

"I guess so." He sounded solemn but also like some of the weight had lifted, or at the very least, shifted into a more manageable way for him to heft it.

"Look, what you're dealing with is part of the package. When it happens, you have to remind yourself why you're still here. Why you fight. For me, it's the brothers I've got now. The people I can still protect. If you look around, you'll see you got that too." I met Rarity's eyes and wasn't at all startled or surprised to realize I somehow meant her in that, too. Her blue eyes sparkled. Her face was solemn as she listened, but she remained respectfully quiet as though she wasn't hearing a thing. I appreciated her for that, more than I could express.

"The thing is, it's hard to focus when the past keeps dragging me down." He sighed, and he sounded under load again. "It never lets go, and I'm constantly haunted by the images from that day."

"You'll never change the past," I told him, and it was true. You couldn't. "But you can honor it by how you live now. You're already doing that every time you show up for your chapter," I told him. "For some guys, the concept of having a battle buddy was so ingrained that when they got out, they sought out the structure and commitment they'd felt when they'd served. When they joined up with the Bastards or got involved in any other group thing, it was familiar enough to bring comfort but different enough that it was easy to forget that the club was their unit now. Their brothers, whichever one or ones they chose to lean on? They were your battle buddy now."

"I try, but some nights... it just feels like it's not enough."

"On those nights, don't try to carry it all. Write it down. Punch a bag. Hell, scream into the wind if you have to. But don't bury it. That'll only eat you alive."

"Writing, huh? That's your thing?"

"Yeah, sometimes," I admitted. I mean, I kept a journal, but it wasn't something I talked about with anyone. I also did this other thing that Pope suggested when I had the odd time of being troubled by something. "Sometimes I write letters to the people I've lost or to my younger self. Sometimes, I burn them, and sometimes, I keep them. It's not about fixing it. *It's about making peace with it.*"

"Not really good on putting my thoughts down on paper, but I'll think about it," he said.

"Good. And remember this. It's not about the mistakes you make, Nightmare. It's what you choose to do after you make them. You wouldn't be the man you are today if you hadn't lived it. Remember that. All the good that comes after for the people around you? It's there. I know you can't see the forest for the trees when you get down bad like this, but there are a lot of people who wouldn't be alive and unscathed if it weren't for you, either. The scales may never balance out. I have trouble with that, too." *I didn't.* Not anymore, but at one time, I had a bit of an existential crisis about it. I kept talking. "But use what time you got left to do what you can, and who knows, after we kick off this mortal coil for good? Maybe it'll make a difference, maybe it won't. Like I said, that's between you an' your God, but at least we fuckin' tried, yeah?"

"Thanks, Striker. That actually helps," he said after almost a full minute of silence while he parsed through what I'd said.

"Anytime, brother. Call me whenever you need to, and when the bad days come, lean into the Bastards. We're your family now, and we've got your back."

"Guess I need to take my own advice, huh? I'm always telling them the same thing."

"Exactly. Now go take care of yourself. You've got a lot of road ahead, and you're not riding it alone."

"Thanks, man. I owe you."

117

"No debts here, Nightmare. Just Royal Bastards watching out for each other. Stay safe out there, and keep the shiny side up."

"You too," he said and ended the call. I sighed, hung up my end, and looked back to Rarity.

"Sorry about that," I said.

"No worries," she said softly. "Sounded important."

I nodded. "Yeah... kinda was," I said.

"You field a lot of calls like that?" she asked. She looked a little uncomfortable as if she wasn't sure if it was okay to ask such a thing.

I smiled. "Not a lot, but I like to be there when someone needs it. Truth be told, I've wrestled with some things, but for the most part, I've gotten cozy with my demons. It's... I don't know. Sometimes I feel like I'm faking it to make it, and I can't relate with how hard someone takes some of the shit they've been through over there."

She cocked her head and looked at me, searching my face, and finally said, "It's like you told Nightmare. You balance your scales however you can. Maybe you've compartmentalized things enough to get by, but I think you can relate more than you let on. If you didn't, you wouldn't know what to say."

I searched her face right back and found myself nodding slowly.

"How'd you get so smart, darlin'?" I asked her, and she smiled.

"I don't know," she murmured. "Guess I had good parents."

I smiled and nodded. "Mine weren't all bad," I said. "My dad was a good man."

She lit up.

"Mine, too."

"My mom and I never did get along, though," I said, grinning, and she laughed.

"My mom and I do alright," she said. "I just wish she didn't worry half so much."

"I think every parent worries about their baby no matter how big or old they get," I said. I felt a momentary flash of guilt, like I should maybe *call* my parents or something, but then my mother's nagging voice hit the back of my mind, and I decided, *yeah, no. I'm good.*

"So, what adventures are we off to do today?" she asked. I smiled and felt my head bob on my shoulders.

"First, we go for a ride," I told her.

She tried to suppress her smile but gave up, laughed, and said, "Not great for my mother's nervous system."

"It's cool. I think we can keep it between you and me," I shot back, and she laughed.

"You're a bad influence," she accused.

"Guilty," I told her.

CHAPTER EIGHTEEN

R arity...
We went back down the stairs and out through the garage, several of the men down there looking up and or stopping what they were doing to blatantly stare.

I was both excited and terrified to go for a ride. The only person I'd ever ridden with had been my dad. We'd sold his motorcycle after he'd died. Mom couldn't bear to look at it, even though it hadn't been involved in the accident in any way.

She used to go on long rides, just her and my dad, while I'd stayed at Grandma and Grandpa's. I think it honestly broke her heart that she couldn't anymore – not that I think she would if the opportunity came up. That had been her and my dad's thing. Totally. Completely.

I had no idea what Striker had planned for the day, but just being out in the sunshine, sunglasses on, snugged up to his back as he carefully took us through traffic and over bridges... it was nice. We weren't going terribly fast. Traffic wasn't permitting it, but *oh*, the view from the bridge of all the sailboats out on the water was lovely.

It was nice to just relax and not have to be in charge for once and to just go with the flow. Did I think Striker was doing it just to get in my pants?

I didn't know. I mean, it was likely, but my intuition was telling me that he was being cool. That he was attracted, sure, but he wasn't being handsy or anything at all like that.

I was curious when we pulled into a little strip mall off one of the main streets heading toward the beaches.

When he parked and tapped my knee lightly twice, I hopped off. He heeled down the kickstand to lean the bike onto it. He shut off the beastly engine and got up himself, wincing at a little stiffness.

"You alright?" I asked.

He grinned at me and said, "I'm getting too old to be taking these ass whoopin's."

I laughed and looked up and down the row of businesses curiously.

"Why're we here?" I asked.

"For your appointment," he said, striding up to the door we'd parked in front of and holding it open, gesturing me through.

I furrowed my brow, went through and blinked, surprised at the strong smell of chemicals and acrylic.

"You're taking me to get my *nails* done?" I asked.

"Yep. Booked you a mani and a pedi. Off you go, enjoy yourself, I'll be right here." He dropped into one of the waiting room's seats, and a girl came to get me. He told her my name and the appointment time.

She nodded and said, "Ah, yeah, we fix your nails nice." She enthusiastically took my hand and led me into the salon toward the big deluxe massaging pedicure chairs.

My flabbers were *ghasted*. I had no idea how to deal with this input of information. No one had ever done anything like this for me except for my mom, back when we'd had the money for such luxuries. We didn't anymore, except on the rare, rare occasion, and I *missed it*. So much.

I didn't want to seem like an ungrateful brat, and Striker was smiling and watching me go, waving his hands at me in a shooing motion as I reluctantly trailed along after the salon lady.

He waited patiently in the waiting room, scrolling on his phone and laughing occasionally at something he read or watched in a video, and I just observed him.

He was incredibly handsome, and I felt a nervous flight of butterflies take off every time he smiled and that dimple on the one side appeared.

I liked his rings. He wore several large, chunky, silver rings. One looked like a class ring, but I couldn't tell from here if it was actually a class ring or some kind of military ring. He'd said he'd enlisted right out of high school but never mentioned how long he was in for or if he maybe went to school *after*... you know? He'd lived almost twice the life I had, but it was hard to remember that, just looking at his face.

He did *not* look like he was in his forties. Thirties, *maybe*, but not forties.

Honestly, I had no idea what I was even doing here, except it'd been a while since I'd remembered having a friend. I'd had plenty in high school, but after graduation, almost all of them went off to college or to travel abroad. I'd opted to stay home and take a year off. I wanted to work and save some money, take a trip somewhere... then Mom got pregnant, and we were *so* excited... and then... well... we were broken.

I didn't think there was any real life left after Dad.

I hadn't felt anything *close* to being as vibrant as I was before he... *died*. I used to say *left* because I couldn't bear to even say the word.

I let the women in the nail salon work on my hands and feet and felt a bit of a stirring in my chest. Like there was a glimmer of the old me, just there on the horizon, that I just might be able to *catch* with a lift from Striker on the back of his bike.

Silly, I know... but this?

I looked down at where my nails were being carefully filed. I opted for a French tip on both fingers and toes. Something simple that hopefully wouldn't chip at the bar. I missed my acrylics, which could withstand just about anything, but affording them was a pipe dream anymore. I just couldn't fathom dropping fifty bucks or so every other week at a good salon. That was a hundred bucks a month that could go to much better things, like keeping the three growing little monsters in clothes that *fit*.

Lord, that was a chore in and of itself! It felt like we had only just bought them shoes, and they were in another size a couple of mere months later.

"You good, baby girl?" I heard from across the empty salon, and I blinked and shook myself as if coming awake. I said, "Oh! Yeah! Just thinking really hard."

He got up, wandered over in my direction, sat sort of funny in the chair next to mine, and asked, "What about?"

His voice was gentle, soothing, and I flashed back to how he'd used it on the phone with the ex-soldier who was having a hard time.

"You're a good listener," I said, and he had a slow smile grace his lips.

It was a knowing one, as he licked his bottom lip and said to me, "Don't try to change the subject."

I laughed a little and asked, "Why is this so much easier over text rather than in person?"

"That's easy. There's something anonymous about typing into a screen and sending a message out into the ether. You were talking to me, sure, but there's an almost disconnect about it. Now..." his voice dropped into a lower register that sent a shiver down my spine in *all* the right ways. "Don't change the subject."

"I was thinking about how much I miss getting my nails done," I said. "I just can't justify the cost with the boys, you know?"

"No, yeah, I get that," he said.

"How did you even know?" I asked, and I couldn't help the smile curving my own lips.

"The pictures in your bedroom," he answered.

I cocked my head to the side, curiously and in silent question.

His smile grew, and he raked a hand through his hair, those heavy silver rings sparkling under the harsh overhead lights of the salon.

A skull with a crown, so like their club's logo. That class-looking ring with the red stone. The Harley Davidson logo, and finally, one that was a round-looking seal with a skull in the middle of it with *memento* above it and *mori* below it.

His other hand was likewise decorated in rings, and it wasn't lost on me that they more than likely served as something very akin to brass knuckles in a fight.

"I'm the chapter's road captain. Do you know what that means?" he asked.

"Vaguely," I answered truthfully. "You pick some things up working in a biker bar for the last three years."

He laughed, nodded, and said, "Yeah, I suppose you do."

"You're in charge of mapping out and leading the runs, right? You're the man with the plan."

He nodded and eyed me like I'd said something both interesting and that'd pleased him. As stupid as it may be, I glowed from the pleased look.

"That's about the right of it," he answered. "The devil's in the details when you're the man with the plan. You gotta be the one up front, the head of the pack. It's a position of a *lot* of responsibility. Not only do I need to know where the fuck I'm going – I need to have alternate routes planned and am responsible for the safety of the *whole* ride. Situational awareness is a must. If shit's going sideways up ahead, I'm responsible for alerting every rider down the line."

I nodded. "Okay," I murmured. I hadn't realized there was *that* much to it.

"I guess the whole hypervigilance and situational awareness thing was drilled into me in the Army. It was practically our religion on the Stryker brigade, and once that switch got flipped?" He shrugged. "It never went off again. I notice things that most people wouldn't. I noticed at the bar that you didn't have your nails done, but in all the pictures in your bedroom, they were *always* done, and in quite a few of them, yours matched your mom's."

He'd noticed that?

"You've been through a mess of shit. I figured it would be a nice treat."

"It is," I breathed. "Thank you."

He winked at me and got up.

"Relax, enjoy yourself, think about what you might like to eat. We'll grab a bite after a while when you get hungry. On me – no arguments."

"You're going to spoil me," I tried to protest.

All he said as he walked back to the sitting area was, "Yeah, and? You deserve it."

CHAPTER NINETEEN

S triker...

She looked softly contemplative for the rest of her service at the nail salon. She was oddly quiet as I paid and left a hefty tip for a job well done. That thoughtful silence didn't change when we stepped back out front of the salon.

"What's wrong?" I asked her gently, skimming fingertips along the underside of her arm from elbow to her fingers, holding her hand loosely in my own.

"I guess I just don't understand *why* I deserve it. I didn't do anything..."

I snorted and asked, "You're joking, right?"

She shook her head, genuinely mystified.

"You *are* a rarity, little miss Rarity," I said with a smile. "How you gonna stand there and tell me you don't deserve a little spoiling yourself when you do so much for everyone else?"

She stared up at me and didn't say a word. We stood like that for a long moment, each of us just soaking in the silence and each other's presence until I let her out of whatever predicament she maybe thought I had her in by saying, "Have a taste for anything in particular for lunch?"

"You're a confusing man, Striker. Wonderful, but confusing," she said finally, and I had to laugh at that.

"Thanks, I think," I said.

"Oh, that absolutely was meant to be a compliment," she responded, and she grinned.

"Well, alright then," I said, putting on my sunglasses. "I like the sound of that."

I got on the bike, walked it back out of the parking space, and waved her in to climb aboard. We took the ride back through the sun-soaked streets, and I took us up over the Lion's Bridge that spanned the Intracoastal waterway that divided St. Augustine. It was the stateliest bridge around, proud and precious, and gave some of the best damn views and photo ops that wasn't the lighthouse or the *Castillo de San Marcos*. The Castillo was the old Spanish fort built from coquina.

While St. Augustine was reaching its four-hundred-and-sixtieth year of existence, and the fort had pretty much always been established on the spot, it hadn't started being built until 1672 – over one hundred years *after* St. Augustine was founded. It'd taken twenty-three years to complete the old building, and its weathered and crumbling coquina was something to behold at any distance.

Coquina was a local composite made from limestone and seashells – a sort of cement made by Mother Nature herself. It was a material that was somewhat special to the area, had been surprisingly resilient to cannon fire, and made a good structure for the old fort that'd been built, initially, as a deterrent to pirates and shit.

As soon as we were over the bridge, I passed by the main drag and took the narrow, one-way street up the back of the buildings comprising it. There was a small lot back here that had a few narrow slots specifically for bikes, but wouldn't you know it? They were all full up. I slid into a spot meant for a compact car and parked, because fuck it. I'd done my due diligence. Rarity was just about to get down when I spotted a scooter about to pull out of street parking.

She got down, and I went for the scooter's spot, which was closer to our destination anyway.

Rarity stood in the lot, her eyes as big as saucers, and I called back, "Why pay for it if you ain't gotta?" She laughed, put her sunglasses on the top of her head, and jogged to the sidewalk. She looked both ways on the one-way street, hopped off the low curb, practically floating across the old bricks that formed the street back here, and stopped by my side.

"Thought you maybe decided to ditch me," she said with a smile, but I didn't laugh. I didn't even come close to chuckling.

I just shook my head, expression grave, and said, "I would *never.*"

Her face softened, and I wondered what gave her a taste of abandonment that it would even cross her mind to worry about that.

I filed it away as something to maybe explore later. Right now? I was low-key starting to get *hungry*, and we were here.

It was a Cajun-style seafood grill and bar that was popular in town. It sat on the corner of the A1A just before it turned into the bridge of lions over the Intracoastal waterway. I liked it, not because of the view – because it didn't really have one, but because the food was good and it was a step up from something fast and easy but wasn't so over-the-top fancy that I couldn't get away with wearing my cut.

We were parked at the back of the building that housed the restaurant, just shy of the courtyard that was open dining beside it. I took Rarity's hand and led her through the back gate set in the stucco and terracotta painted wall surrounding the patio and passed into the cool shadow of the building and greenery they had throughout the outdoor seating area.

There was a winding, cordoned-off path that threaded through the tables out here from the back gate to the front gate. The restaurant's entrance was closer up in the third of the building, closest to the front gate – a hostess' stand under an umbrella in the courtyard.

It was good weather, and the place was in full swing, which likely meant some kind of a wait, but truthfully, we ain't had nothing but time.

The wait was shorter than I thought, mostly owing to us not caring where they sat us, inside or outside. We were led to a small, two-seater table in the back corner of the courtyard, tucked up underneath some greenery in the shade. Despite being outdoors, it was nice and cool, and we couldn't have asked for a better spot.

We settled in, ordered drinks, perused the menu, and made our decision. Then, it was just her and I staring at each other once again.

She laughed, and it was a bit nervously. I just smiled and said, "How'd this suddenly get so awkward?"

"I don't know," she said.

"So, when you aren't bartending or babysitting, what do you do?" I asked, expecting to learn more about what she did for leisure, but not Rarity.

"Oh, I work at the craft store in Ormond Beach at the cutting table."

"Cutting table?" I asked.

"Yeah." She grinned. "You know, for like fabrics and sewing projects."

"Oh, shit. Now I feel dumb." I laughed, and she joined me.

"You sew?" I asked.

"Mm." She nodded, lowering her glass of water back to the table. "My grandma taught me. She likes to sew all kinds of things. She makes really fun Christmas stockings and sells them at local church bazaars and sometimes at the flea market over in Daytona."

"No shit?" I asked.

"Yeah, I started working there to hook her up with my employee discount whenever she came through."

Shit, even finding a *job,* she was thinking about how to best benefit *other people.* Was there no end to this woman's generosity?

"Not gonna lie, I asked that question expecting a much different answer," I said.

"Oh yeah?" She raised an eyebrow. "What'd you expect?" she asked.

"Oh, I don't know. Maybe something like, *what you actually like to do for fun?*"

She laughed wildly at that one as our ordered drinks were set on the table. We took the time to order our food, and she gave a gusty sigh as the waitstaff left us again.

"Fun," she said, and there was nothing fun about the tone in which she said the word. If anything, she sounded a cross between wistful and melancholy. "Can you use the word in a sentence?" she asked.

"We're going down to the beach to have some fun," I said, and she grinned.

"Well, that's one thing we *do* on the regular," she said. "Mom is a sun worshipper, and we take the boys to the beach all the time. It's free, lets them burn through their loads of energy, and let me tell you – we build some awesome sandcastles. Shells for windows and everything."

"Okay." I nodded slowly and asked, "What else?"

She scoffed and said, "Honestly, this is the most fun I've had in a minute."

"Yeah?" I asked.

"Yeah." She took a sip of her soda through her straw.

"Not going to lie, that's kind of pathetic," I said, and she scoffed and threw her napkin at me. I jumped and laughed, handing it back, but I didn't let go right away. She tugged on the cloth, and I leaned an elbow on the table and said, "Now you can have this back, but only if you promise to be a good girl."

Her blue eyes widened, and her lips parted in surprise as she blushed a pretty pink and murmured, "Yes, Daddy," in a way that *did things* to me.

Holy fuck, that was hot, I thought to myself as I relinquished the cloth.

She spread it in her lap demurely, and I had to fight down my stirring hard-on.

I leaned back in my seat mostly to give it more room as my jeans were getting uncomfortably tight, and said, "We're going to work on that."

"What?" she asked with a wry twist of lips. "Me having more fun?"

"Yeah," I said, and her smirk bloomed into a smile.

"Not going to lie," she said. "I like the sound of that. When do we start?"

I felt my smile grow larger and said, "I thought we already had."

"Okay." she nodded slowly. "I concede that one."

I grinned and said, "Good."

I took a drink of my soda and set it down with a satisfied *'ah!'* and said, "And so you know, I like the way you called me Daddy just then. It may just so happen to be one of my things..."

She choked on her drink, and I reached for her, patting her on the back as she coughed into her napkin until her eyes watered.

Shit, I thought to myself. *Wrong thing to say!*

She caught her breath, looked at me, and said, "Sorry, I'm so sorry! You caught me off guard with that one – but duly noted."

I grinned. "So, no problem with that one?" I asked.

"I mean, I've never done it, and it's never been *my* thing – but I'll try anything twice," she said, swiping at her under eye with her middle finger to try and keep her makeup from blurring and smearing too much.

"Didn't mean to make you choke, baby. You sure you're alright?"

She laughed. "Only thing hurt is my pride," she promised, grinning, and she winked at me.

Well, alright then...

CHAPTER TWENTY

Rarity...

I got over my embarrassment and made sure my makeup hadn't suffered too much in my compact mirror and things settled down pretty quickly.

Lunch was great, exceptionally filling, and the food was *so good*! After, we took a walk up the street behind the restaurant, strolling up the sidewalk and talking. We found ourselves in an open, almost a pedestrian square type thing that held an old schoolhouse with a big boat anchor and chain around it and a multitude of shops, boutiques, and sweet shops.

"Did they really think that was going to stop a hurricane from blowing down the schoolhouse?" I asked, eyeing the boat anchor and chain wrapped around the building and the hand-painted plaque explaining the thought process behind it.

"I have no idea," Striker said, laughing. "People are strange, I have to imagine some of 'em did, but I can't imagine all of 'em did, you know?"

"I feel like this is like, pre-internet meme, like real life meme-ing," I said. "Like how that government opened up a website to name their newest research vessel and how it ended up Boaty McBoatface because of it."

He laughed and nodded and said, "I'm sure it made front page news in some old-timey newspaper, for sure."

We kept strolling, stopped for ice cream, and kept on pushin' as we enjoyed the cool confection, licking quickly before our cones could melt in a sticky mess. I didn't think it was just me that Striker was paying extra close attention to me, specifically my mouth, as I licked at the scoop of ice cream on my cone.

I know I paid more attention than I probably should have to his tongue and wondered idly to myself, what it would feel like to have it between my legs. A thought I tried like hell to keep off of my face. I mean, we were just friends – right?

Ha!

We found ourselves at the old city gates, and paused after we passed through them to look across at the cemetery surrounded by its old, rickety, cast-iron fence and gate, and turned to look at the old historical Spanish fort to the right of it across the busy boulevard.

"Wanna go check it out?" he asked.

"The fort or the cemetery?" I asked, just to clarify.

"Unfortunately, the cemetery is closed, you can't walk through. I was talking about the fort," he said.

"Fuck yeah!" I said enthusiastically. "You used to be able to go in, can you still?" I asked. and we walked along looking for the cross-walks to cross the busy roadways to get there.

"Yeah, you can," he answered.

"Awesome," I said then circled back to our earlier conversation with a; "What about you?" We found the signal and pushed it.

"What about me?" he asked and I felt foolish – he wasn't a mind reader, of course he wouldn't follow my inner thoughts at all.

"Sorry," I said. "I meant to ask, 'what do you do for fun?'"

"Oh, shit – well, I just recently started something new," he said.

"Yeah, what's that?"

"I started hanging out with this pretty and pretty cool chick, which has been more fun than I've had in a while."

I laughed and said accusingly, "That was really corny."

"Did you like it, though?" he asked with a grin.

"I think I did, yeah," I relented and he laughed and said, "Good! Good..."

The light turned and we hustled across the boulevard, stepping up on the much better maintained sidewalk on the other side, turning left to make our way toward the fort.

"What else do you do other than hang out with me?" I asked, genuinely curious.

"Long rides to nowhere, sometimes – just hit the road with no real destination in mind. Usually, when I do that, I find myself on the A1A all the way down to the light on Ponce Inlet. That's where I was the day I stopped by to give you that post card."

"Why *did* you stop by just to give me that card?" I asked.

"Truthfully," he said, finishing the last bite of his cone and tossing the napkin in the trash on the side of the road. "I couldn't stop thinking about you."

I stopped, too, and finished the last of my cone, too, and tossed the wrapper and napkins from it into the same trashcan.

"I had a hard time, too," I said softly, and he reached out and threaded his fingers between mine.

"Can't say I'm terribly sad about that," he said softly and I smiled.

We took up walking again, over the grass and the permanent structure of a pedestrian bridge over the trench of the old, but empty moat.

"Me either," I confessed and he flashed a grin and raised my hand to his lips, pressing a kiss to the back of it that made all sorts of butterflies take off in my stomach.

"You're not worried I'm too young for you?" I asked after a few steps.

"You worried about what people might think?" he asked.

"Of you, not me," I said. "Someone sees an older guy with a younger woman and they don't think *'stud'* anymore," I sighed. "They think *'predator.'"*

He laughed at that and plucked at his leather vest, lifting it off his chest and letting it fall back down.

"They already look at me and think 'predator,' and they aren't necessarily wrong about that fact."

I bowed my head and thought about that for a minute and said, "I'm not really sure what I'm doing," I said, "but..." I trailed off, trying to get my thoughts in order.

"But?" he prompted finally, and it was gentle in such a way that I felt comfortable finishing my thought.

"I can see your point," I said finally. "I mean, maybe I used to think that myself – which I admit now, was totally biased and unfair!" I rushed out. "You definitely schooled me different. I hope you can forgive me for ever thinking that way about you."

He pulled me into a hug then and kissed the top of my hair.

"You'll find I can forgive a lot of things, baby girl – but that one? No harm, no foul."

I looked up at him, stiff in his embrace at first, simply because it was so new, but eventually, I felt myself relaxing. I put my chin on his chest and stared up into his hazel eyes and asked out of morbid curiosity, "What are the unforgiveable sins, then?"

"Lying," he said evenly. "Cheating. Not asking for help when you need it. Not taking care of yourself," he added after a pause to think.

"What like not drinking enough water?" I asked teasingly.

"And not eating regular and healthy meals, getting enough exercise," he said without a hint of joking. "See also, not asking for help when you need it – there's more to keeping yourself healthy than keeping your body healthy."

I blinked at him and drew my head back saying, "You're being serious."

He nodded and said, "I am."

I felt a little thrill go down my spine and stammered a bit as I asked, "Are you – is this you like, legit asking me out?"

His serious look dropped and his smile took its place.

"If I was?" he asked, and I could tell he was being cautious.

Honestly? Same.

I blinked again and said, "I would have to think about it."

He nodded and said, "I ain't going anywhere. You take as long as you need to think about it and I'll be here." He let me go except for the fingertips of my right hand and stepped back to give me some breathing room.

"You promise?" I asked hesitantly, surprised at myself for feeling a little bereft at the distance he'd put between us.

He cocked his head and searched my face and nodded, "I promise, baby girl," he said.

I swallowed hard, unsure why I'd even asked that, but grateful that he didn't laugh or make fun of me for it.

"Come on," he said, shaking my hand just a bit, "I wanna show you something about this place before they close it."

I smiled then, and nodded, and let him lead me into the fort.

From above, the Castillo de San Marcos was shaped almost like a ninja throwing star. Silly, but true. The fortress was in the shape of a square, but the four points of it had these almost diamond shaped protrusions off of them. Only one of them had a rounded watchtower with a dome on it, though – the one facing the mouth of the intracoastal waterway, to watch for approaching enemy ships.

I'd been here plenty of times before, on school field trips, but that had been ages ago in like *elementary* school. Still, I was curious as to what Striker was keen on showing me. I half expected it to be the part of the fort where the leader of the Seminoles was killed, but no – he took me to a different part of the fort, away from that side.

"You ever hear of the 'lost lovers of Castillo de San Marcos?'" he asked.

I squinted and put my sunglasses atop my head and said, "Vaguely. I don't know the full story."

"Okay, well, legend has it, when the fort was still being built there was this Spanish fucker that was running the show here, right? Some big military general or high baller."

"Okay," I said laughing at the way he put it.

"Story goes, he brought his wife here, and she was a *looker*, like... He wolf-whistled, and I laughed some more. "She was *smokin'* hot and this dude's pride and joy."

"Ew, you make that sound like he's one of those dudes that married his wife and then treated her like his property." I wrinkled my nose.

"BINGO," he said. "That was exactly it. Anyway, she was here but she didn't like it – in fact, she was terribly homesick and fucking *hated* it here – which who could blame her? It was unbearably hot, humid, and the mosquitos were *wicked bad*. So were things like yellow fever and dysentery, right?"

"Right," I nodded and didn't even realize I'd just sort of naturally cuddled into his side, my fingers finding the spaces between his and my other arm curled around the same one we held hands with.

He smelled good, I noticed it then. Like sunshine, salt air, clean laundry, and something woodsy. He smelled distinctly masculine and it tickled my senses, turning me on and making me want to melt into him – which low-key made me feel kind of stupid, like *girl! Get it together!*

He kept talking, like he didn't notice my internal struggle with myself over just how hot I thought he was, and how bad I was leaning toward wanting him.

"Make matters worse, her husband wasn't spending like *any* time with her and she was terribly lonely."

"Right," I nodded, and hoped like hell I was being subtle and cool, that I wasn't throwing super bad mixed signals – good lord, how did this man simultaneously make me second guess *everything I did,* but at the same time, made me feel so comfortable that I was cuddling into his side like it was as natural as breathing?

"Now, from every story I've ever heard or read about it, she *tried* to tell her husband – 'look, yo, you *need* to spend some time with me. I'm lonely, I'm miserable, and like you can either spend some time with me to make it better or if you don't want to do that, then at least let me go *home.*' Now her husband did what most dudes nowadays do and just kind of waved her off and said 'yeah, yeah, yeah, bitch; *whatever.*' The more she persisted, the more he pushed her off, until finally he basically told her, 'Look, I'm in charge of this place, suck it the fuck up, because I'm *busy* and like it or not – you're here, because you're not going home to Spain!'"

"Oo, so he was a *real* peach," I said, all sarcasm intended.

"Basically, yeah," he said.

"What a choad," I said and he snorted caught off guard and laughed.

"Absolutely," he said.

"No offense, but when it comes to stories like this, I hope she cheated on him. Sounds like she was doing everything to communicate that she needed some attention or whatever from her husband and he just wasn't listening."

"Exactly," he said, "and that's the thing – she did. She communicated in every way what she needed short of interpretive fucking dance, and this guy was just ignoring her. So, and spoiler alert, she did. There was this young buck in the military or whatever, closer to the wife in age and with a lot in common, and they started talking and one thing led to another and they fell in love and started carrying on."

"I think I remember this story now," I said smiling and stopping.

"Yeah?" he asked.

"Yeah," I said. "They ended up cheating and then disappeared together, right?"

"Right."

"Except they didn't. Husband found out about the affair and had them chained up here in the fort and sealed them in."

"Exactly," he said. "Here."

I looked around us, "Here?"

He pointed at a low opening and said, "Technically, in there. Feeling brave enough to go in?"

"Hell yeah," I said and I went first, crawling into the room and leaning up against the wall. He climbed in after and sat across from me and looked at me, finishing the story.

"It wasn't until a hundred or two hundred years later," he said, "that they found them in here, and the only reason they did was because a cannon they were moving fell through the ceiling and when they went down to retrieve it, they realized that they couldn't find it – that there was a secret room."

"Because the husband had them manacled to the walls and walled up in here," I said.

"Yep," he sighed. "With a bunch of his wife's favorite flowers – roses."

"Probably to mask the smell," I said. "When they finally died and began to rot."

"You watch too much true crime?" he asked laughing.

"I do!" I agreed. "But that's how it happened if I remember the story right. He walled them up in here and left them to die of thirst or to starve together. Sold some story about him going AWOL and that she went back to Spain and no one was the wiser, because who was going to question Dear Leader?"

"You're right," he said. "That's exactly how it went down, and the mystery of their disappearance wasn't solved until all that time later when this chamber accidentally got opened up."

"I thought there was an old ghost story associated with this place," I said. "You know, other than the one about the floating head of the Seminole leader that died here."

"There's a few," he said, "but yeah, this is one of them."

"I can't remember the details on the ghost though," I said.

"Phantom smell of roses in here," he said. "Sometimes, you come in here and get overwhelmed by the smell of roses."

I closed my eyes and breathed in deep and said, "Nope. Just the smell of old musty fort."

He smiled and said, "I like to think that when they died, they went together, and went into whatever afterlife free of suffering and pain."

"Yeah," I agreed, leaning my head back against the coquina blocks that made up the fortress walls. "Bet you they're living their best un-life in Elysium or whatever."

He cocked his head, "Elysium?" he asked.

"Ancient Greek myth originally," I said. "Their version of heaven or the garden of Eden. The place set aside in the Underworld ruled by Hades for the heroes of Greek myth at first, but then it turned into the place where anyone that led a righteous life belonged after they died."

"Is that what you believe?" he asked. "In the ancient Greek gods and goddesses?"

I shrugged and then shook my head.

"I honestly don't know what I believe," I said. "Religion was never really a part of my upbringing. My dad was staunchly anti-religion and my mom has always been more spiritual than religious."

"That's legit," he said.

"What about you?" I asked.

He studied my face, "Not particularly religious," he said. "Had it shoved down my throat a ton by an overbearing mother in the heart of the Bible Belt in Arkansas growing up. Pretty sure my dad just went to church every Sunday to appease her, too."

"Yeah?" I asked.

"Oh, I did it all," he said and his expression was pained. "Youth group, Bible camp, revivals, you name it."

I laughed and said, "Oh, come on, it couldn't have been *that* bad."

"Worse," he said and my high and bright laughter echoed back at us within the tight confines of the chamber we were in.

"After you," he said and gestured and I rolled my eyes.

"You just want to look at my ass," I accused.

"Guilty," he said, grinning, and I couldn't help but grin too.

I almost fooled myself into thinking I smelled roses as I shifted to go back out of the small chamber.

Almost.

CHAPTER TWENTY-ONE

S triker...

You awake?

I pulled my phone off my chest and read the message. It was late. Like *really fucking late.*

Yeah, baby girl. What's wrong? I asked.

Bad dream, she texted back.

Talk to me.

It wasn't like her to be so openly vulnerable. I sat up on the couch and leaned my elbows on top of my knees, my phone held between my hands.

I guess I just miss my dad... finally is what she'd texted back and I had to think. It'd taken an awfully long fuckin' time to arrive at just those seven little words.

I'm sorry, baby. As much as I'd like to be your daddy it certainly isn't like that! I tried levity. I didn't honestly know what to say.

I got nothing back for a lot of minutes. I worried that I'd said the wrong thing there... and then...

I'll be honest. I've never actually met anyone into the whole sugar daddy thing – is that what you're talking about?

I chuckled.

No, baby girl. The sugar daddy thing is similar but vastly different at the same time. One, most of those guys are lonely and rich; and there isn't always a sexual dynamic to it. Most of the time it's just a bored old rich guy looking to have some conversation and spoil a girl. What I want is... different.

Again, a long, long silence for just so few words in return.

What do you want? she asked.

A relationship. I sent simply. I thought about it, *hard,* for a full minute. Literally sitting there watching the digital clock in the top corner of my phone. Staring at the last number, until it changed, and staring at it some more... knowing that if we went down this rabbit hole, I could scare her off pretty quick, and I wasn't at all surprised to feel an almost real physical pang of pain in the center of my chest at the thought.

Granted, I didn't know Rarity super well, we'd only hung out the once or twice, but *shit fire motherfucker,* had she grown on me in such a short amount of time. She was so beautiful and selfless... fierce and plucky.

But like, one where she calls you daddy?

I chuckled at that.

That's oversimplifying it.

She sent a laughing so hard it was crying emoji and said, *You're the one that opened up this line of conversation! Now I want to understand.*

I cocked my head and texted back, hating how all nuance was lost when texting...

Why? I asked.

She gave me the right answer.

Because it seems important to you, and I like you, and I would like to understand and extend the same patience and understanding that you've extended to me.

I thought about that, and swallowed hard.

You sure? I feel like we can't un-ring this bell once it's been rung.

She took a while to answer and that was because it was a novel of a text.

I'm sure. I mean, it's already kind of been rung, hasn't it? Besides, just talking about something else is helping so much. It was a really bad dream and after knowing you, even for such a short time, I have a feeling you're about to school me on some things that people just easily wave off or make fun of when it's honestly kind of wholesome and I guess now I also want to understand because FOMO.

FOMO: Fear of Missing Out. Interesting.

There are some wholesome aspects to it, I said. *There are a lot of unwholesome aspects to it too. It's definitely not as black and white as people make it out to be.*

I waited; I was stalling like a pussy here. I really didn't want to lose out on talking to her. She had quickly become the highlight of my fuckin' day when my phone went off and it was her on the other end.

Why do I feel like you're afraid to tell me? She asked the question with a smiley face at the end. The one with the open mouth.

I was honest with her: *I am. I don't want you to stop talking to me.*

You're serious?

As a heart attack baby girl. Talking to you is the highlight of my day.

She sent back the emoji where the thing was tearing up and about to cry and I laughed to myself.

Don't waste any tears on me, baby. Not worth it.

She came back with: *They're happy ones, though!*

For real? I asked.

Yeah! Nobody's ever said anything like that about me before.

I resisted the urge to tell her that was because she'd only fucked with insecure little boys and hadn't had a real man, yet – but that shit would have come off as arrogant and douchey, even if it was the truth.

Well, I'm glad I could be the first, I said, and hoped it sounded humble enough.

I had almost convinced myself that I'd gotten her off the subject of the Daddy Dominant/Little Girl dynamic, when she circled right back around to it.

So... are you going to school me, Daddy? She put the little purple smiling demon emoji behind it and I felt a low growl crawl up my throat.

First of all, I said. *It's Daddy, with a capital 'D' always. It's a title or honorific, if you will. Secondly, be careful what you wish for, little girl... some lessons come with spankings.*

I smiled, I was teasing, but also a little worried that with the loss of nuance, that it might come off wrong via text.

LMAO! OMG! So why isn't 'little girl' capitalized, then? she asked.

It was fixing to be a long fuckin' night at this rate, but if she was game, then I was game...

Because in this dynamic, you're the little girl, or the submissive.

A GIF started loading and I lost my shit, it was the 'shocked Pikachu' one where it was the little cartoon that was just all *'huuu-uh?'* mouth hanging open and the camera zooming in.

So, this is totally like, a Fifty Shades of Gray BDSM thing? The question was so cute, and innocently asked. I couldn't help but smile until my fuckin' face hurt.

BDSM, yes – Fifty Shades of Gray? Fuck no. The only thing that kept that shit from being a Criminal Minds mini-series was the fact the dickwad was a billionaire.

I think she put in so many crying from laughter emojis because she held down the button on them as she laughed uncontrollably on the other end of things for a solid, few minutes. I could get behind that – because for real, that whole saga was nothing but manipulation and sort of abuse. Not to mention pretty fuckin' vanilla.

Okay, that was funny, she came back with. **For real, though, I want to understand... so teach me.**

Okay, we weren't going to un-ring this bell. I guess in for a penny, in for a fuckin' pound. I would rather she know from someone that knew what the hell they were talking about and had a mind to keep her safe, rather than some fuckin' bitch ass wannabe out there that could and would manipulate and hurt her under the guise of kinky fun times.

Let me get ready for and into bed, then let the lesson begin, I guess.

CHAPTER TWENTY-TWO

R**arity...**

"Rarity, you okay?" I blinked and snapped out of my thoughts about Striker and pushed myself into a standing position behind the cutting counter at the craft store.

"Sorry, what?" I asked, Meredith. She was seventeen and worked part time after school. She was a goth girl, in Florida, which I couldn't fathom all that black and all those layers in this heat but to each their own.

Surprisingly, she wasn't a moody teen, but rather bubbly and bright in this weird Wednesday Addams meets a Disney Princess kind of a way. She and I got along famously – but didn't get to work together very often. It was a rare treat when we did. I was usually gone and at the bar in the afternoons and evenings when she came in after school.

"Where have you been all day?" she asked, wrinkling her nose and grinning at me. I turned and stuffed my hands in my green apron pockets and leaned my butt against the edge of the counter behind me.

She gave me a dubious look and put her own apron over her head working on tying it in the back as she was back from her break.

"Just got a lot on my mind," I said. "I promise, everything is all good. I actually... met somebody," I said and I knew I was blushing by the heat creeping up my neck, my chest flushing and my cheeks growing warm. I couldn't help it. It was pretty much what happened any time I thought about Striker anymore.

"Ooo, so what's he like?" she asked and I couldn't help but stuff my hand against my mouth as I giggled.

It was ridiculous being this... I don't know! *Girly* about it, but we'd been talking... about all sorts of things.

It'd started when I'd texted him late several nights ago, after waking up from this *awful* dream where I was standing there, as my dad drove by and I was just helpless to watch him get slammed into in that awful accident all over again – which was nuts. I'd already been walking into class when he'd been hit, getting some of my early stuff done and out of the way before deciding on a degree and a course of action for the rest of my education...

Of course, that had all come crashing down when he'd been crashed *into*.

"He's a biker," I said reluctantly.

"Are you serious?" she asked, her face going blank as she thought about it, and I was about to cringe, fully expecting her ask me if I was *insane* because that would *totally* be what my mom or my grandmom would demand, but she focused back on me and said, "That is *so* hot!"

I let out a breath I hadn't known I'd been holding and laughed a little nervously.

"Yeah, well, they aren't exactly known to be *good* guys... but he's... different from I expected."

She shrugged and said, "If he's good to *you*, that's all that really matters, right?"

"Ha, wow! I mean, yeah, I guess but I don't think my mom or anyone would be half so understanding."

"They don't know yet?" she asked.

I sort of half-winced and said, "You're the first person I've told."

"Really?" she asked and she looked so excited under her pale makeup.

"He's a lot older than me, and I'm really worried about what people would think," I said and she cocked her head and asked, "How much older?"

"Like eighteen..."

She frowned, "Months?"

"Years..." I said and her mouth dropped open.

"Wait, that makes him like what? Fifty?" she asked.

I laughed.

"Wow, you're bad at math!" I cried, laughing until tears gathered at the corners of my eyes. "He's forty-two," I wheezed.

"And you're what?" she asked.

"Twenty-four."

"I mean, it's not *that* bad," she said. "It's not like he's forty-two and hitting on *me* at seventeen. That would be so *gross!*"

"Yeah, but a lot of people would look at it the same, wouldn't they?" I asked and no, I had no idea why I was asking Meredith. She was *seventeen!* If I wanted a more accurate picture, I should have asked any of the older ladies working here with us, but I just wasn't freaking brave enough. I certainly didn't want *Wanda's* perspective on things. She was almost as bad as my grandmother on the being older and set in the ways of the past.

Judgmental and awkward is just the tip of the iceberg, and my gran came in here and shopped because everyone here knew she was my gran and to give her my employee discount. I knew Meredith would keep my secrets. Anyone else? They would let slip in a heartbeat.

They were older, they were bored, and gossip was totally their main form of entertainment.

I didn't feel like being judged or raked over the coals for exploring things with Striker, simply because he was a biker and an older man. I could leave. I could cut contact at any time. It was something my dad had *always* drilled into my head. It didn't matter where I was or who I was with, it didn't matter if society deemed it rude to not take the drink or to say 'no.' The word no was not only *always* a viable option, it was also a complete sentence in most cases and I was not responsible for how the other person felt about my saying 'no' or extricating myself from any situation that made me uncomfortable.

Period, point blank, end of discussion.

I could leave. Call an Uber or a Lyft. Hell, even though it would be uncomfortable as hell, I could call my mom, or my grandma, but let's be honest – I would probably call my grandpa before either of them... but that was the thing.

Striker wasn't the one I was uncomfortable with.

Quite the opposite, actually. I felt freer to be myself with him than I did in front of Mom or Grandma and yeah, even Grandpa.

Probably my dad, too, if he were alive and I were being completely honest.

I think when my dad instilled the lesson of 'no' and that I could leave, he didn't anticipate it potentially ever applying to him, Mom, but definitely figured it could and would apply to my grandma someday.

My grandpa was chill, and my grandma had her good moments, don't get me wrong – but man could she be an overbearing pain in the ass when she wanted to be... and where Striker was concerned? She would be polite to his face and a pure savage behind his back and I didn't want to deal with it.

Meredith screwed up her face in a grimace at my last question, about a lot of people looking at things the same way when it came to mine and Striker's age difference and said what I knew to be true but really didn't want to hear; "Yeah, you're probably right... I'm sorry."

I sighed.

"Me too, it's why I haven't told anyone yet – at least not really."

"Really, I'm your first?" Meredith looked entirely too excited about *that*. I mean, Gemma had a clue, but she wasn't going to tell anybody, and we weren't exactly seeing each other on the regular right now, not with the bar's liquor license suspended.

"Yeah," I said with a sheepish grin and she squee'd and hugged me.

"That's so cool!" she whispered excitedly. "I swear, I won't tell a soul. Especially around here." She looked around us making sure no one could overhear and I laughed.

"Thanks," I said.

"Still, you gotta tell me *everything*! I wanna know what he's like. For real, he has to be cool to get you to notice him."

"What's that supposed to mean?" I asked, laughing.

She rolled her pretty brown eyes and said, "You are *laser focused* on your mom and brothers, to the point I wasn't entirely sure you knew there was a whole wide world out here with you. Girl, when was the last time you had fun that didn't involve your family?"

I thought about that and made a dour face and said, "Touché, you got me on that one."

"Exactly, so if you got to go out, what did you guys do?" she asked.

I smiled, I couldn't help myself, I hadn't gotten to talk about it like *at all*, with anyone, and it was nice to be able to be *excited* about it rather than just nervously keeping everything all bottled up.

I spilled the beans, carefully, both of us clamming up when anyone else working or any customers came by, and before you knew it, our shift was ending and we were both packing it in for the night.

"Thanks for listening, Mere," I said, and she smiled impishly at me.

"Hey, I live vicariously through you," she said. "At least on this and for right now. Hopefully I'll meet my dark and handsome prince someday but not around here and I sure as hell don't think any time soon."

"I feel you, there," I said rolling my own eyes and sighing. "Still, stranger things have happened."

"True, seems like you have yourself a prince charming."

I smiled and wondered what Striker would think about that.

"Later, girl," I said and she waved at me and made for the bus stop, opening up her black lace parasol to shade her fair and pale skin from the harsh sun.

I went and got into my Jeep and drove back to the house. Mom wasn't home yet, and grandma and grandpa were up to their eyeballs with the boys. Both of them looked relieved when I walked through the door to the thrice shrill chorus of "Rarity!" from the little terrors.

"You take them, I'll take dinner," Grandma declared and I put on a brittle smile and nodded.

All I wanted was five minutes to decompress, but no rest for the wicked, or so they say...

It wasn't until after dinner, after baths, and after a hell of a fight putting the three little monsters down for bed, that Mom and I had a minute.

"Drinks?" she asked, hopefully.

I said, "I'll make you one, but I really just want some time to myself tonight."

"All good, baby – I'll make my own," she said with a sigh.

"Okay," I said and we hugged. "Goodnight, Mom."

"G'night," she said.

She went for the kitchen, I went for my bedroom, and finally, blessedly, shut my door on the world and dropped onto the edge of my bed with a sigh.

I took up my phone and saw a few missed texts from Striker. A couple general just 'heys' set hours apart, and finally an; *I'm around if you want to talk. I don't want to bother you. Clearly, you're having a busy one today. Miss talkin' to you, baby girl.*

I laid out on my bed and held the phone over my face.

Hi, yeah, it's been wild... I missed talking to you, too – I just haven't had even a minute to myself all day.

It took around twenty minutes to get a response, and by the time my phone buzzed, it was through my breastbone as I'd rested it on my chest and had already begun to doze.

Hey, baby girl. You want to talk about it?

I filled him in on my day, and about the boys being your typical rambunctious four-year-old boys and he made jokes with me, and did what he always did... empathized and made me feel *heard*.

All jokes aside, he said, *sounds like it was rough. I can totally get being overwhelmed and over stimmed and just needing a fucking break. I don't know how you do it, baby girl – but you're a fuckin' rockstar for doing it.*

I felt my hard resolve soften, and I closed my eyes and just breathed for a moment, basking in the warm glow of his words.

How do you do that? I thumbed out.

Do what? he asked.

Make me feel so calm with just a few words, like a flip of the switch... For real, I've been wound up and stressed out all day and just a few minutes of texting with you I feel so much better.

I waited and what he sent back was a bit surprising, but not at the same time...

That's what a Daddy is supposed to do for his little girl...

I thought about that for a bit and asked...

Can we talk more about that?

He didn't hesitate.

Of course.

What would you like to know?

That was the million-dollar question, wasn't it? I mean, where to begin?

CHAPTER TWENTY-THREE

S triker...

It'd been a little over a week and a half since our little date in St. Augustine. The one where I'd left her gentlemanly like at her Jeep with a chaste kiss; I hadn't stopped thinking about that short, soft press of lips against mine since.

I dreamed of her petal soft kiss every fucking night, woke up to a raging boner weeping precum every morning, and yeah, had to relieve the pressure in the shower every morning, too.

All the texting and talk of the dynamic I craved more than anything else certainly hadn't been helping, but today? Today I would finally get to *see* her. Possibly even get to hold her in my arms. That was if everything was cool and went according to plan.

The Iron Horse was back open, but they were still sans their liquor license and according to Rarity, business was more than a little lackluster.

I didn't particularly care about that. They'd decided to host the Scorpions and not enforce their rules. That'd gotten Rarity hurt. I wasn't inclined to forgive that... but for one thing. I liked Rarity, I didn't want to let her lose her job, and if the Iron Horse hadn't fucked up, we maybe more than likely would have never met.

Our friendship was still a budding one, but after our day together it was now one that I was glad to find was fraught with sexual tension.

She was such a good girl, and the contents of our texts had gotten a little hotter and certainly a lot heavier since our time together. To the point that I had a wild idea on how to help out, at least for one night, with their dwindling patronage.

I'd run it by the guys and they'd been game as long as I put it together, and so a poker run it was.

The guys from Ocala and Jacksonville were game, and we'd advertised on social media for a good while, and I'd contacted a bunch of places to put the run together – it was my position within the club, after all.

The Iron Horse's owner had welcomed the idea with open arms as a peace offering. An olive branch between the club and his establishment, but he'd insisted on one thing: *no colors inside his bar.*

I'd figured that was coming and had already anticipated it. So, I'd said no problem. We'd stop out front at the gas station and divest, stowing our colors in our locked cases and saddlebags.

He'd said deal, and so it was a deal.

Riders from all over the state were set to attend. It was a fundraising poker run, after all. The start point was at our clubhouse, where we had our big tent erected, and the plan was to head down the A1A and do a total of five stops between and hold five hands of poker at each stop.

We were no strangers to doing charitable runs, and this one was no exception. We just used them as tax write-offs at the end of the year, and maybe did a little to balance our scales by running them.

This run was us being good neighbors. Florida was used to getting our shit pushed in by hurricanes. It was a yearly occurrence. Usually, we fared okay, but every once in a while? Shit got real and when it did, we all banded together and helped each other out.

Never in a million fuckin' years did anyone think *Appalachia* would bear the brunt of a full-fledged hurricane. It was about as ridiculous and as frequent as a blizzard in *Miami*. That's what happened, though. A bitch named Helene made landfall in the panhandle and cut an unprecedented swath of fuckin' destruction across something like seven states total. She fucked up Florida, Georgia, South Carolina, North Carolina, East Tennessee, parts of Virginia and West Virginia. It was wild, but nobody took damage harder than Appalachia.

She *fucked up* Western North Carolina and Eastern Tennessee like nobody's fuckin' business and those areas that she hit hardest up there were lookin' at devastation that wiped entire towns and cities clean off the fuckin' map.

It would be decades to repair the damage in the areas it could be repaired, but there were a lot of places that were just *done*. Gone. There was no fixing it. There was no starting over. There was nothing left there to start over with, there was nothing left enough to rebuild.

So, this poker run was dedicated to the hurricane relief in the Appalachian Mountains.

It was only a drop in the bucket, sure, but we knew a thing or two about catastrophic storm damage and being hung out to dry by our own government down here. Sounded like similar was happening up there. We wanted to help, and have a little fun doing it and what better way to kill two birds with one stone?

Help Appalachia, and the Iron Horse by bringing people in fuckin' droves.

By the time we reached the Iron Horse, everyone was full of beer and little else from our previous poker hand stops. We were bringing in a hungry fuckin' crowd, and the Iron Horse had their kitchens, pits, and smokers going full bore expecting the lot of us.

I was happy to say we delivered.

Tables had been set up in long lines up top, live talent was on the stage, and the *smells*. Lord, they had our mouths watering before we had our cuts off and were riding in to park.

We had the place so packed, bikes were lining the street and the Ormond Beach PD were out front directing traffic and turning folk over across the street and down some to the Broken Spoke to park.

The Broken Spoke didn't have their feelings hurt. They'd got on board and had closed down their kitchens, leaving the food to the Iron Horse. Instead, they made up for it by having their taps wide open and the beer and liquor flowing.

It was an exercise in harmony and cooperation and so far, everything was going great.

The Iron Horse's security was out front, checking ID's, turning away anyone in colors to put those colors up, and stopping anyone coming in from the Broken Spoke from bringing in any alcohol with them.

The trash cans out front were filling up, and laminated printed signs were plastered everywhere out front with 'no alcohol beyond this point – we look forward to serving you all the food you can eat.'

I was fucking starving, and posted up in line to grab a bite before heading up to look for Rarity.

She said she would be at her bar, slinging sodas, and floats.

Bar number two had been officially designated as an old-fashioned soda jerk fountain for the event. Rarity's friend's idea. The other waitress, Gemma, who'd worked at an ice cream parlor as a teen.

It'd been a good idea, and helped out parents that were excited to have their kids get a look at where they got to hang out as usually the Iron Horse was 21+.

I know Rarity was excited, because her mother and three brothers had reluctantly agreed to attend. She'd said it had taken her, *and* her mother's parents a few days to convince them – and I was surprisingly nervous to meet them.

Didn't take me long to figure out who her family was as three little boys were up on bar stools across from Rarity, each tow-headed and wearing glasses, all three in matching little outfits of olive drab long shorts, navy blue polos, and smart little high-top sneakers.

Nearby, there was an umbrella high-top table with an older couple and a woman with graying blonde hair that had to be Rarity's mother.

I didn't go there right away. I made for the bar and the last open bar stool left between one of Rarity's brothers and a woman and her man.

I slid up onto the stool and set down my food on the bar.

"Hey, you!" Rarity called and asked, "What can I get you?"

"Root beer if you got it," I said.

"Absolutely, a float or just the root beer?"

"Make it a float," I said with a grin and her smile was a million watts.

"Boys," she called out, scooping ice into a plastic cup. "I want you to meet my friend Striker." Three little faces turned up to me.

"Striker, this is Caden next to you, Braden in the middle, and that's Aden at the far end."

"Nice to meet you, boys!" I said jovially, taking a bite of my garlic butter-soaked steak tips over mashed potatoes.

God that was good!

I was met with a chorus of timid "hi's and a "hey" from her brothers.

"Nice to meet you, boys. You having fun?" I asked.

"Yeah," they all said, and the middle one slurped a spoonful of his float.

Rarity set down a float in front of me and I winked at her and she winked at me.

She and I chatted while I ate, and we all listened to the band down below.

When her mom and grandparents came over to collect the boys to head to the beach, Rarity didn't introduce me – not yet. I got that. Things were still new enough that I was just a guy she was talking to. Not enough of a thing yet to go that far. When the kids and her elders had disappeared down the steps, she turned to me and was a bright pink. I smiled from behind my float as I sipped it from the rim.

"Sorry," she said. "I feel like an asshole now for not saying anything..."

"Don't," I told her. "We definitely aren't serious enough for that yet. I get it," I said.

She shifted uncomfortably on her feet and leaned on the bar from her side and pitching her voice low, for my ears only, said to me, "It sure feels like things are... you know... getting there."

I smiled and nodded knowingly. "Glad we're on the same page, but for real – I'm not offended and my feelings aren't hurt."

She nodded and sighed. "Thanks," she said.

"Don't mention it."

The Iron Horse was going to be closing much earlier than it usually did. The party wasn't ending, it just moved on over to the Broken Spoke where the liquor flowed.

I didn't move with it, though. Even when some of the guys came around looking for me, I stayed put in my seat at Rarity's bar.

The sun was getting low when two hands clapped down on my shoulders and tightened, thumbs digging, shaking me back and forth on my bar stool in their exuberance.

"We gonna catch you two later back at the clubhouse?" I lost my tense posture at Renegade's voice.

Rarity looked up from her cleaning and sorting back behind the bar and smiled, happy-go-lucky, "Oh, I don't know," she said. "I've got to run out to Daytona in the morning and I have work here tomorrow evening for a few hours. This was great, though! Thank you guys so much for putting this all together to help us out."

"Aw, it was to help everybody, really," Renegade said, sliding up on the stool next to mine.

"Float for the road?" Rarity asked him.

"Yeah, I believe I will," Renegade declared. "You got any of that birch beer back there?"

"I surely do," Rarity said cheerfully.

"Rarity, this is Renegade," I introduced them. "Renegade is the President of our chapter."

"Hi," Rarity said. "I kind of figured, you look like a man who's in charge."

Renegade laughed and nodded, "I get that a lot," he said.

She and he bantered a bit while she made his float and handed it over.

"Thank you kindly, Ms. Rarity," Renegade said.

"I'll see you guys later, back at the club," I told him, and he gave me a nod.

"Y'all have fun, whatever you get up to," he said and took his float and went off to join a knot of Bastards at the top of the stairs.

Suddenly, it was just me and her up here, the next nearest person her friend Gemma over at bar three and a couple of the guys in charge of trash duty and security getting floats from *her* and likely shooting their shot.

"So, how much longer you got to hang around here?" I asked her.

She checked her slim silver watch, the band old and stretched to where it slid around her even slimmer wrist and she gave a gusty sigh.

"Not long," she declared. "Just have some clean up and need to check in with Rob and I think I'm pretty free to go."

"Heard my name," a balding older man with a paunch said coming up the back 'employees only' staircase around the back of the bar.

"Hey," Rarity called, tossing things in an oversized trash bag.

"What was the question?" he asked.

"No question," Rarity said.

"I just asked when she was off and getting out of here," I said.

"Ah, now if she wants to," Rob said. "Go on, I've got this," he said.

"You sure?" Rarity asked.

"Girl, with how well this went, I'm thinking about making it an all-ages yearly event so families can come enjoy some good food, good music, and some ice cream – already in talks with the Broken Spoke for them to handle the liquor like this round and close down their kitchen. The whole thing was lucrative for *both* of us."

"We can see about making it a yearly deal," I said. "Rotate charities for the poker run."

"Well, alright then," Rob said. We sat and shot the shit, shook on things, and I shot a text or two to Renegade who shot back 'no problem' and that we'd sort it out in church the following week.

All in all, it was a good fuckin' day for everybody, and it was looking like it was about to get even better for me.

CHAPTER TWENTY-FOUR

R arity...

I caught a glimpse of the way Striker looked at me and I felt a flight of butterflies take off in my stomach the likes should lift me off the ground.

Since our little date in St. Augustine, we'd practically been texting nonstop, and those texts had quickly turned... well... uh... *sexually feral* is a good way to put it.

He excited me like no other man had ever gotten me going, and part of that was his patience and precision in *asking* me. Like literally, he checked in with me *constantly* about if this was okay, or that was okay, or if this or that was too much and he wouldn't take one- or two-word answers from me. He sometimes pried until I had to practically author a whole dissertation about how I felt about some of his suggestions, or until I was pretty much spilling my guts about what I wanted or found hot...

Some of it left me flaming with embarrassment at how I *wanted* to be riled and defiled – but he never, not once *ever* made me feel ashamed for wanting the things I did. Most of the time he confessed he wanted them too, or even went a few steps further.

Some of the things were uncomfortable to think about... at first... but again with him wanting and needing to *talk* about things until some of my initial squick either calmed down or in some cases became insurmountable. I didn't know how to feel about some of the things he liked or wanted – but at the same time, he swore that some of them weren't deal breakers, like at all.

Some, he asked if we went slow, if I'd make up my final mind after we tried things out.

That sounded reasonable – and so I'd agreed; but then wondered if I was crazy and if things were moving too fast and how bad my mother might freak out and the anxiety would get up there – and still, he would sit with me, across the miles, and comfort me and calm me, and tell me that nothing had to happen, that if it just needed to stay deeply flirtatious and in text, that it could. That it was all up to me...

There was a certain safety and anonymity when texting back and for through that tiny screen, one that I didn't have now with the way Striker's hazel eyes bored into mine as he walked me out of the Iron Horse and out to my Jeep.

"You want I should come to your place and we go for a ride?" he asked.

I laughed then and asked, "On your bike, or..?"

He grinned and said, "Yes, on my bike."

"Yeah, sure," I said. "Let me just get changed and we can go."

"Sounds good, baby," he said and we were both so very awkward standing beside my Jeep.

"I want to kiss you, would, that be okay?" he asked, low and careful.

I tipped my face up to him and nodded shortly and he dipped his lips to meet mine.

God, he had soft lips, and the thrill that slid along my nervous system at the light contact he made sent a shiver down my spine – holy crap.

I felt myself lean into him, and his hands slide along my hips, and pull me closer by my lower back as my lips parted for him.

He tentatively flicked his tongue against my bottom lip, as he closed his gently on my top lip and I felt scalded by the rush of heat that went through me.

I pulled back, breath stolen, and heart racing and felt myself blush *furiously*.

"I'll be right behind you," he murmured. I just have to go back and untangle my bike from the rest of 'em."

"Okay," I whispered.

"See you soon," he said, and his hands reluctantly slid from around my body and dropped to his sides.

I opened my Jeep's door and he stepped in, caging me as I pulled myself up into the driver's seat, hands up to make sure I got in okay and there to catch me if I slipped. It was silly, I'd never had anything close to it happen getting into my dad's old rig, but at the same time, it was sweet.

"See you soon," I called as he closed the door for me, and he flashed a grin at me.

"Drive careful," he ordered, and I barked a laugh.

"It's like a mile, if that!" I protested and he gave me a gently chiding look without saying anything and I felt myself color.

Hell, Dad hadn't been more than a quarter mile from the house, at the mouth of the development when he'd gone to make his right turn and the guy on the crotch rocket had slammed into him going in excess of a hundred miles per hour.

Dad's little commuter sedan hadn't stood a chance. I'd sold my car to help with some expenses – I hadn't been able to bear the thought of parting with his Jeep. Mom hadn't even argued. She'd just signed the Jeep over to me when we got the chance; after the estate was settled.

I started up the Jeep and he stood back and watched me go, walking back to the Iron Horse only after I'd turned on my signal to go right, to head up the boulevard to the entrance to my housing development.

I pulled into my driveway to find Mom's car and my grandparents' car gone, so they were likely at the beach, playing with the boys and letting my mom indulge in her favorite pastime: sun worshipping.

I sometimes worried about her and skin cancer, but knock on wood – nothing had happened yet.

I went into my room and contemplated what to freaking wear.

I was a girly girl at heart, and loved my skin, so I tended toward whites and bright colors, sometimes pastels. With my blonde hair and blue eyes, I was a real Barbie about it sometimes, but it was fun.

I found a ladies' cut white tee that was your regular round neck and cap sleeves, but hugged my curves and really showed off the girls. I'd adjusted it at work at the craft store, cropping it using one of the sewing machines on display to create a new bottom hem.

Actually, one of the women had helped me with that bottom hem, and bless her for it, because I *sucked* at sewing at the time and was a rudimentary beginner at best. With what I wanted and was asking for, my grandmother wouldn't have helped, even though she was at sewing level *expert* – I mean, I'd asked, and she'd said the look was way too trashy for me; so I'd found another way.

The tee fit like a dream and showed my stomach above the waistband of my short/skirt combo.

I had several pairs of the short/skirt thing in just about every color they offered them in. They were super stretchy, soft material, that looked like a skirt from the back but in the front, on one side, there was a slit cut into the skirt material to show the front of the shorts on one leg. That side the shorts had a decorative slit across the thigh, and a buckle that showed and flashed as you walked. The look was edgy behind a veil of demure and I freaking *loved it*.

I went with the dusty pastel pink pair and heard the grumble of Striker's bike out front just as I let down my hair to brush it out and put it back up.

I opened up my bathroom door and opened up the front door leaving it shut to keep the cats in for now and went back to working on my hair in my bathroom mirror.

"Rarity, you okay?" I heard him call out at the front door as he pushed it open.

"Yeah!" I called around the hair tie I held between my lips and teeth in a subtle pink a bit paler than my skirt as I used both hands to brush and smoothed my hair up into a high ponytail.

He shut the front door behind him and leaned a shoulder against the doorjamb of my bathroom, his eyes wandering up and down me as a slow smile started on his lips amid his deep five o'clock shadow.

"What?" I muttered around the hair tie in my mouth.

"Nothing," he said. "I like the fit."

I felt myself blush faintly as I held my hair up with one hand and retrieved the tie with the other, pulling the long shining tail of my hair through the loop and winding it, pulling it through again. I did that three times and pulled things secure and added the pink bow barrette one of my brothers had found somewhere for me and had gifted me.

I clipped it to cover the hair tie and picked up a clear lip gloss and swiped it over my bottom lip, pursing them and rubbing them together, before swiping one more time and stood back to look.

One of the things I loved about these short/skirt things is *they had pockets.* I put my lip gloss in my right one and fluffed the skirt back down over the top of it, and voilà. All I needed was shoes and I was good to go.

"You look good," he said as I turned to go into my room.

I turned and shot him a smile over my shoulder and said, "Be right out, just grabbing shoes and switching purses."

He nodded and said, "I'll be out front."

"K," I said and I went into my room from the opposite door to my bathroom and dropped onto the edge of my bed. I pulled the shoe organizer out from underneath it and picked my pale pink Chuck's out. I wore the same white low socks that I'd been wearing at work with my bar Sketchers for comfort, and they were just fine. I slid into the flat, cooler, and more lightweight shoe, and tied the laces.

After my shoes were on and secure, I kicked the shoe organizer back under my bed and stood up, grabbing my wallet and keys off my vanity and taking down my Hello Kitty mini-backpack purse from the hook inside the closet. It was white, and had pink accents and a pink bow by one of her ears, but it also had my name embroidered in pink on the front pocket. It'd been my Christmas gift from the boys and my mom last Christmas and I didn't have it out much. It matched my outfit, though and was super cute, and I needed something secure for the ride up to St. Augustine.

I dumped my wallet and keys into the main compartment, put my lip gloss in the front pocket where my name was stitched, and swung it onto my back.

It was comfortable and lightweight and would totally do for today.

I went out and met Striker at his bike and did a little twirl for him.

He gave a low whistle and declared, "Very nice!"

"Yeah?" I asked.

"Perfectly fuckin' adorable," he agreed, and I laughed.

"Thanks for not calling me ridiculous," I said and he shook his head.

"Never, baby girl."

The words weren't what sent a thrill through me, nor what raised gooseflesh in a tingling wash down my arms and the rest of my body even though the Florida sun shone bright and the heat hung thick in the humid air – it was the look in his eyes.

I'd never seen anyone look so damn serious about something before in my life.

I smiled and nodded and he got onto his bike, settling a little closer to the handlebars than I thought he normally would to make room for me.

I settled behind him, wrapping my arms around him and cozying up to his back, and even though this wasn't the first time I'd ridden with him, after all the raw and honest and deeply flirtatious texting... it felt different. Like it was something brand new.

"Taking the scenic route!" he called over the roar of the bike starting up, and I called back to him, "What?" right as what he'd said fully registered in my brain.

"I said, I'm taking the scenic route!" he called again, and I grinned and hollered back, "Fine by me!"

I wasn't sure what the 'scenic' route was supposed to be, but wasn't surprised that it took us deeper into Ormond Beach rather than back past the Iron Horse and to the I-95.

We took the coastal byway on up, and it was nice, the breeze coming in off the water cooling the sweat that tried to collect under my mini-backpack.

I had no idea where we were going, but I didn't care.

I felt safe with Striker. Calm in a way that I couldn't describe. He'd been open with me about his likes and dislikes, and while I wasn't sure about the whole daddy/little girl thing – I continued to mull it over.

I mean, I'd always thought it was weird and meant in an incestuous way, which I think everyone thought of it that way... but Striker and I had talked *a lot* about it recently, and it wasn't that the more we discussed it.

I went from laughing at the notion, to curious about it, to *wanting* to understand it, to wondering if I *did* play with the notion with him... how far or how *normal* could it become.

That was the part that honestly worried me the most.

It was going to be hard enough coming out to my mom that I was dating someone so significantly older than me, let alone if I got too comfortable and let *Daddy* slip out of my mouth in front of her. That would be an epic fucking horror show.

Still... with as much as we had been talking about it, I was getting comfortable with the idea... turning it over and over in my mind but still so very hesitant to break the ice with Striker *in person* about it.

It was a big step, but it was one that I wanted so badly to make. I worried that made me some kind of selfish, but I didn't know how to go about things, either. I was sure it would come up at some point – for now, I just wanted to be close to him and let the wind carry the rest away.

I felt better the further we got from Ormond Beach and the closer we got to St. Augustine. It was like the layers were peeled off and blown back to flutter to the asphalt we left behind and the closer we got to his stomping grounds? The closer we got to me simply being *allowed* to be my authentic self. No judgments, just a sort of shiftless freedom.

Like wearing your daddy's tee shirt like a dress that fell to the floor the night you were small and sick, all of your own pajamas soiled with things coming out of both ends. All that was missing was the being cuddled and hugging your favorite stuffy as the blue glow of the television and the sounds of your favorite cartoons comforted you.

I wanted badly to connect with that feeling again, and the more time I spent talking with Striker, the closer I felt I edged toward it.

He'd explained that was the heart of the dynamic. That he was there to support, nurture, and comfort me. That it left me free to regress into a more childlike state without actually *being* a child and that it had nothing at all to do with being a pedo. He had no interest in minors whatsoever. He liked *women*. I was a *woman*, and at no point did he ever forget that fact.

That was comforting in its own way, and made perfect sense to me.

I didn't think the rest of the world understood it or wanted to.

I think if they put the thought into it that it honestly required, that it would make people face a part of themselves that they wouldn't want to face.

As Striker had explained it to me, for some people the dynamic was therapeutic. Allowing them to regress into a childlike state that allowed them to feel *safe* and repair some broken aspect of their own childhood. For others, who didn't have a broken childhood, like me – it was something different. Allowing them to guiltlessly tap into and enjoy things that were nostalgic to them.

For instance, the outfit I'd chosen today... it was on the cusp of being socially unacceptable for a girl my age to dress the way I was dressed. I maybe only had a year or two left for it to be considered acceptable before it became considered low rent or trashy. Hell, if my grandmother had seen me leave the house like this, I would have had a hell of a fight and argument on my hands.

I knew I'd better enjoy it while I could... but also, this dynamic, no matter what age I was, I could dress this way for Striker in privacy and we could both enjoy it as much as we wanted and fuck what anyone else thought or had to say.

There was a certain appeal to that, I must say...

We worked our way up the A1A and I just enjoyed the ride. The thrum of the bike and the air washing over me as we ate over the miles of asphalt and pavement rushing beneath the tires; it was like being reborn in a way.

We pulled up outside the customization shop, inside a gated side lot, and he parked the bike. I got off first after he tapped my knee twice, and he walked the bike back into place in an angle parking job against the wall. It looked like there were already some people here, judging by the other bikes parked along the wall on this side of the lot, and a few parked against the fence across from us.

He gently took my fingertips into his hand and led me by them toward the gate we'd ridden through.

We walked around the front of the building, past the locked door to the front office, and to the other side of the building that faced the water, climbing a set of steps to the second floor, where we stopped at the locked door there, as Striker fished through his keys. A loud burst of laughter from above us had him looking at me and shrugging.

"Sounds like the clubhouse door is open, I was just stopping at this one by default. C'mon, up we get," he took my hand again and led the way up the next flight of steps to the next landing. He dragged open the glass door that was blacked out with paint on the other side of the glass, making the logo for the Royal Bastard's MC pop, which had been painted on first, in loving detail.

We went inside, and the inside was a world away from what I thought it would be! I expected something like the Iron Horse. The wood worn and carved into roughly. License plates and bullet riddled street signs tacked to the ceiling and walls... but no, this place was... *fancy*.

The whole floor up here was open, and the spaces divided by flooring. While the majority of it was a glossy worn hardwood reminiscent of an old warehouse, there were other sections finished with pride and a loving care.

There were two red velvet topped pool tables over in one corner, with black-and-white chess board patterned tile underneath them.

Between the pool tables and the bar was a stretch of what looked almost like a bowling alley floor, with three lanes that led to three dart boards.

The bar on the left had a wide expanse of standing space between it, and the cluster of couches and recliners on a black, red, and white large geometric patterned throw rug, that sat in front of a wall with a painted rectangle of white. A projector mounted to the ceiling pointed that way.

There were wires running from it, to a cabinet by the door we'd come in through, and on the other side of the cabinet that rested against a short expanse of wall was another doorway leading to an open-air, but covered deck where we could hear laughter and voices.

There was a man in a black leather vest with no patches at all on it, front nor back, stocking the bar and doing the general bartending duties.

I asked Striker curiously, "How come his vest has no patches?"

"Aw, that's Adrien, he's just a hang-around. If he ever does move up to Prospect, he'll get a bottom rocker that says 'St. Augustine' and a top rocker that says 'Prospect' until he earns his colors."

"Oh, so a hang around is like a pre-prospecting period?" I asked.

"Exactly right," he said.

"I'd always wondered about that," I said. "I've seen guys riding around that had vests like his – but didn't know the difference between it and a prospect."

"Well, today you learned," Striker said with a grin and he tweaked the end of my nose making me wrinkle it and grin back.

"Let me give you the ten-cent tour," he said, and led me further into the room.

Ceiling fans spun above our heads, moving the air, and it was surprisingly cool inside despite the open big windows out to the deck. The open areas didn't have any glass in them. In fact, the only thing that separated them from the open deck was a stone slab counter and these built-in metal stools on either side.

There were rolls of what looked like clear vinyl that zipped or snapped down securely in case of colder temperatures, but it looked like they didn't come down too often.

Striker led me opposite that direction, to our left and stopped short of the big area of sectional, couches, and recliners.

"This here is where we watch sports, fights, and occasionally do movie nights," he said. "That door leads down the stairs to the offices where you found me the first time you came around."

"Oh! Okay," I said, nodding.

"Over here is the bar." He threw some chin to the Hispanic guy behind the bar. I couldn't guess if he was Spanish, Cuban, Puerto Rican, Mexican – or any other Latin American or other country, and here in Florida, some could be touchy when it came to their origins. Like, don't you *dare* accuse a Cubano of being Puerto Rican or vice versa. Them could be fighting words. It was much safer to just ask or keep your mouth shut until they outright said where they were from. Guessing was just rude.

"Adrian, I'd like you to meet my lady, Rarity," Striker said and the man behind the bar gave a charming smile and nodded his head in my direction.

"Nice to meet you, Rarity," he said.

"Nice to meet you, too," I said.

"Get you guys a drink?" he asked and I smiled and said, "I'll take a hard seltzer if you've got one."

"Got plenty, what's your poison? We've got Black Cherry, Mango, Watermelon, Peach, Blackberry, or it looks like Green Apple."

"Oo, I'll try the green apple if you don't mind," I replied and he brought a can up out of a cooler and set it on the bar, popping the top for me.

"What about you, Boss?" he asked Striker.

"Gimme an IPA," he said and Adrien nodded his glossy head of slicked back hair, and pulled up a pint glass and drew a beer for Striker from the tap.

"Thanks, man," Striker said and took it, dropping a few bucks into a tip jar for Adrien who grinned and said, "Thank *you*!"

Striker put a hand to the small of my back and I shivered with the delicious sensation of his rough fingertips against my skin.

"You're not cold, are you?" he asked, dipping low to murmur in my ear and I shivered again.

"No," I said on a laugh, blushing deeply.

"Good to know I have that effect," he said straightening back up and saying, "Darts, pool, *obviously* – ladies' room in the back corner here behind the pool table, and men's room here," he indicated each. "Don't go in this room without me – ever, okay?" he indicated the door halfway between the bathrooms and the open windows leading to the deck.

"What's in there?" I asked.

"Kinky fun times," he said – "I just don't want anybody getting any ideas that you're up for fun with anyone but me."

"Gotcha," I said sipping out of the cold can of seltzer in my hand. "Thanks for the warning."

"The door on the other side of the bar that we skipped? That's the Chapel – don't go in there, either."

"Okay," I agreed.

He led me to the stools up by the windows leading outside and I slid up onto the one he pulled out for me.

"Striker, who've we got here?" a man called and I put on a polite sort of half smile, and looked to Striker.

"Shadow, this is Rarity. Rarity, this is our Vice President of the St. Augustine chapter, Shadow."

"Hello, nice to meet you," I said and extended my hand. Shadow took it across the cement countertop and rather than shaking it, leaned over it and kissed the back of my hand, his light brown eyes sparkling with a bit of mischief as I blushed to the roots of my hair. His was swept back, barely long enough to pull half up, but he managed it enough to keep it out of his eyes. He was windswept and while decent looking enough, was easily lost in a crowd. He crooked a grin at me and straightened and said, "Welcome in, Rarity. Is that your name or a nickname?" he asked.

"Oh, it's my actual name," I said laughing. "I was my parent's miracle baby until the boys came – now I'm still the only girl."

"Very cool," he said. "Everybody c'mere and meet Rarity if you haven't. She's here with Striker," Shadow called over his shoulder.

That's how I met Skull, and Bones, who were a pair of Cajun brothers and who I recognized as the ones who helped Striker lead me and Gemma down the stairs and out of the fray at the big bar fight.

Skull and Bones were an interesting pair, and funny. Not as in funny 'ha ha' but funny as in *weird*. Definitely a pair of guys that if they were out on their own, I may have crossed the street to avoid them. They were mostly silent or spoke in their native Cajun-French, but they liked to *stare* and it was a fixed look that felt predatory and not in the thrilling sort of way that may have come from Striker, but in a way that creeped me out. *Thoroughly* creeped me out.

There was one girl back here, seated on the other side of the cement counter and all the way down toward what looked like a barbecue grill and smoker combo on the other end of the deck.

She was on her phone, raven haired and not paying anyone any mind and she looked to be my age, if a little younger.

"Dusty, come meet Rarity," Striker called.

"Hi," she called flatly, raising a hand in greeting but she never even looked up from her phone.

I raised my eyebrows and Striker laughed.

"Don't mind Dusty, she's Renegade's daughter. Renegade is our President and still isn't here, yet."

"Gotcha," I said.

"Sorry not sorry, I'm trying to book an appointment and this damn website is giving me the run-around," Dusty said frowning down at her phone.

"It's no worries, sorry we interrupted," I said and she looked up at me then, and gave me a sort of half grin before going back to whatever she was trying to accomplish on her phone.

Aside from Shadow, Skull, and Bones, there was Scrubs, a member of the Jacksonville chapter who was just hanging out with Skull and Bones by all appearances.

"So, what're your big plans for the rest of the day?" Shadow asked, sliding up onto one of the stools opposite ours.

"No real plans, figured we'd take the ride up this way and chill out for a bit. See where the night took us," Striker said and he was grinning from ear to ear and threw me a wink when Shadow wasn't looking.

"You give her the ten-cent tour?" Shadow asked.

"Yeah, for the most part," Striker responded. "Haven't shown her the chapel or the dungeon."

I blinked and said, "Those are two *very* different things, and I don't think I have *ever* heard them used in the same sentence."

Both Striker and Shadow laughed at that.

"Come on, I'll show you the Chapel, and let Striker explain," Shadow got up and came around the counter through the archway leading out onto the deck.

We followed him across the big room and past the bar, to the door Striker had neglected on his initial tour.

Inside was a sort of board room, with a long table, but it was *anything* but corporate.

The one wall was painted black, making it seem like the room was smaller, or tighter somehow, but with windows on three sides, it wasn't that bad. It wasn't claustrophobic feeling at all. How could it be with all that glass?

Set under some track lighting in the center of the ceiling was the table and it was impressive. It was long, burnished steel, with the club logo cut out in the center, the steel heat treated and rainbowed out around the cuts with enough room at each place around the table for paperwork or whatever else a man needed in front of him.

"Wow, that's really *nice*," I said running fingertips over the cool steel.

"Custom job, took forever for 'em to make and get it here. Renegade paid a mint from the club coffers to get it, but it's the pride of the clubhouse," Shadow said.

"Why hide it back here?" I asked, curiously and genuinely at a loss for why. It was a piece that deserved to be seen.

"This is the chapel," Striker explained, parking himself on the corner of the table and drawing me into the circle of his arm.

"This is the room that all club business goes down in. Every major or minor decision is made here according to our bylaws," Shadow said, arms crossed over his chest.

"It's as sacred of a place as you can get for us, and we don't invite people outside the club in to just look at it very often."

"To what do I owe the distinct honor then?" I asked them softly.

"You saved his life," Shadow said succinctly.

I scoffed.

"You did," Striker said jostling me a little bit. "Kept me from catching a bullet."

"Consider this a small token of our appreciation," Shadow said, grinning.

I smiled at that, and said, "Hey, we kept *each other* alive. You and yours got me and Gemma out unscathed. I can't tell you how much we and our families appreciate that," I countered.

Striker leaned in, and kissed me, then, and I felt my insides go loose. The stress and the just *whatever* that rode me melting away under the soft touch of his lips against my own.

Shadow's light chuckle broke us apart, and he asked, "Shall we continue?"

I swallowed hard and nodded, high spots of color in my cheeks that Striker had a good laugh at, even as he smoothed some of it away with a gently swipe of his thumb against my skin that turned up the heat in a whole different sort of way.

CHAPTER TWENTY-FIVE

S triker...

Rarity stuck close to me as we slipped out of the Chapel and moved back out around the bar.

She paused at the odd nook between the bar and the line of three dart lanes when she spied the sock 'em arcade game.

"I didn't even notice that back there," she said with a laugh.

"Want me to fire it up?" Shadow asked. "Let the boys show off a little?"

Rarity laughed and took a drink from her can of seltzer and said, "I dunno, what's the prize?"

"A kiss from the fair lady?" a voice called from behind us and I turned to see Skull coming our way, Bones in tow, heading for the bar.

"If we're gonna throw down for *that*," Shadow said. "We best have everybody here."

"What do you think, baby? You game. If not, then we'll definitely think of something else. We don't wanna make you feel uncomfortable."

"I think I can part with a kiss, but that's it. That's as far as I'm willing to go," she said. "All in good fun – but I'm happy right where I am." She cuddled closer into my side and Skull let out one of his shrill yips and high-fived his brother, Bones.

"May the best man win. Got more rollin' in any minute now, Cher."

"Better finish that tour," Shadow said with a wink going over to the machine to switch it on and let it warm up.

We went past the dart boards, and she trailed fingertips along the red felt and glossy black wood of the edge of one of the billiard tables. She smiled faintly at the club's logo in the center of each, and let her eyes roam the mugshots over the bathroom doors in their line down the wall toward the deck, all along the ceiling.

"That's you!" she said in surprise at my first mugshot from a couple years back.

"Arrest record, yes," I said. "Criminal record, no. It's a point of pride that they've never made anything stick," I told her.

"What was this one for?" she asked.

"Got pulled over, gave the cop a ration of shit. Nothing illegal but he hauled my ass in anyway and *tried* to charge me with resisting arrest. Got a tidy sum from the St. Augustine police for that fuck up. Can't arrest someone on no charge and then charge them for resisting arrest – lawyers had a field day."

"What was his excuse to try and put cuffs on you in the first place?" Rarity asked and I grinned.

"Turns out it's perfectly legal to give a cop the finger, it's protected under free speech. First amendment rights, baby."

We kept going down the line and she caught my second mug shot.

"And this one?" she asked.

"Bad search," I said. "Turned up some weed and arrested me for it, but my lawyer got it all dismissed because he didn't have probable cause to search me in the first place, and I didn't give him consent. Fourth amendment rights came in clutch on that one."

"You sue?" she asked.

"Ongoing, but they're gonna settle again," I told her.

"Hell of a way to make that bag," Shadow said grinning.

"Hey, get it however you can get it," I shot back and we bumped fists laughing.

Rarity smiled and shook her head, "My mom and grandparents might have a solid argument on you being a bad influence on the boys," she said, and there was something there in her eyes that was worried, and humorless, despite the soft smile on her lips.

"I can and will be a perfect boy scout," I murmured near her ear and she laughed high and loud, the sound like crystal, shimmering with magic.

I grinned and didn't say anything. I knew I was full of shit. I was glad she did too. Didn't want any accidental misunderstandings of promising something I couldn't.

I didn't know how long she would stick around, I couldn't expect forever. She was young, I was not... even though out of every woman I'd met, it was Rarity that I hoped would stick around for a long time and not just a good time.

Still. Things were new, and I didn't want to press it.

Again, she was young... I was not. I had a lot of life left, sure, but almost twenty years was a big difference. I would be lying if I said I didn't worry about it in the back of my mind, but there wasn't anything I could do. She was wild and free, and that was one of the things I loved about her. I didn't want to capture her, or put her in some kind of a gilded cage – that wasn't what I was about.

I wanted to watch her soar, and I wanted her to come back to me of her own free will. *That* was hotter than anything.

We stopped at the dungeon door, and I felt my curiosity at what her reaction would be pique, as Shadow opened it with a flourish and a devilish grin.

Rarity's eyes got wide when she rounded the door frame and stepped inside.

The room was longer than it was wide. Front to back it was probably only about eight feet, maybe – but it was easily almost twice that long.

At the one end were two St. Andrew's crosses in the corners against the back wall, left and right. A peg board with an assortment of floggers, canes, crops, and whips to choose from between them.

A spanking bench was inside and to the left through the door, and in the center of the back wall was a slightly raised dais with a life-sized motorcycle made out of rich beautiful wood. It was a fun piece, and sturdy, with two eye bolts in the floor about two feet apart in front of it, and one on the other side of it.

The bolts were the perfect width to shackle ankles to, bend the girl over, and lash her wrists together and to the eye bolt in the floor on the other side of the bike. It was solid and wasn't going anywhere. You could fuck, suck, and do whatever the hell else you wanted to her over that thing, and it was a fun time.

To the right, was a canopy bed, up against a cinder block wall, the smokers, and the barbecue pit on the other side of that wall out on the deck. The canopy bed was wrought iron and steel, with plenty of anchor points in the headboard and foot board, a king sized, and good for a couple of couples to fuck on – which yes, the parties did tend to get that wild.

The whole room was painted black, and the sheets and padding were either black or red, in line with the club's colors. It was very goth and vampy in here, and there were a few extras dangling from the ceilings. Anchor points for some Shabari and rope play for those that were into it, or to set up one of the swings stored in the bank of four lockers between the wooden bike and the St. Andrew's crosses.

"Oookaaaay," Rarity said. "This is more than a little above my paygrade. I may not be vanilla, but I'm like, maybe vanilla with a few rainbow sprinkles, not... *wow*."

Shadow and I shared a laugh at her reaction and she tucked into me a little closer. I ran my hand up and down her arm and said, "It's not for everybody," in a bid to reassure her.

"Renegade is the resident sadist," Shadow declared. "Everyone else ranges up and down the spicy spectrum from super-hot Carolina Reaper pepper to barely spicy jalapeño."

I could see the question in her eyes as she looked up at me, but that was a discussion between just me and her and dependent on how far or how comfortable she was going.

We went back out, shutting the door behind us, to more of the guys including Renegade filing in the door to the outside steps up here.

"Oh, hey! It's a party now!" Renegade called as Dusty slid in for a hug.

"Hey, Daddy," she said.

"How's my girl?" Renegade asked, kissing the top of her head.

"Good," she answered.

"You meet Rarity, yet?" he asked.

"Briefly." Rarity shot Dusty a polite smile and Dusty smiled.

"Yeah, sort of. I was trying to make an appointment with my gyno and the website was being a bitch."

"Shit, Dusty – TMI. There are some things as your father I really don't want to know," Renegade said jostling her and letting her go.

"I'm twenty-two, not *twelve*," she said rolling her eyes as she walked past us to the bar to get another drink.

"You always look five to me!" he called after her.

"My *actual* daughter," he said to Rarity, and he gave me a look.

"I gathered," she said laughing.

"We doin' this?" Skull called out and he threw some punches at the air with some damn fine form.

"What're we doing?" Renegade asked.

"Sock 'em, competing for a kiss from Striker's fair lady," Shadow filled him in.

"Alright! I can handle that; line 'em up boys! We got a wager – hardest hitter gets a kiss from the fair Rarity!"

I led Rarity over to the corner of the bar nearest the arcade game, and lifted her up to sit her on the edge where she could see and more importantly, where any of the guys that wanted to test their mettle could see *her*.

"You sure you're good?" I asked her, and she smiled and nodded once happily.

"All in good fun," she said. "Are you okay with it?"

I grinned and winked back and said, "All in good fun, and I'm gonna win it – so what do I have to worry about?"

She threw back her head and laughed, and it was a good sound. It was also pretty fucking boastful of me when there were guys like Skull and Renegade lining up, who were easily more built than me. Not to mention guys from the other chapters who'd come up this way to party.

There was a mix of Jacksonville, St. Augustine, and Ocala and the mood was good, the vibe riding on the wind light and full of good fun. If it had been anything else, I wouldn't have let my baby girl be the prize for this dipshittery – but things were good, and we'd play fair, and I meant it about doing my best to win this.

I fell in line; we'd done this before. Each man got three shots, and their average went on the scoreboard. Shadow went first, then manned the chalkboard between the billiard tables and the Sock 'em setup, his phone out, calculator going strong to average out everyone else.

After Shadow was a guy from Jacksonville, one I wasn't too familiar with, but seemed cool enough. He didn't do much of a good showing. Not with Renegade up next. Only hope I had against Ren is that he was tipsy or toasty enough to not be swinging too hard.

No luck there. He hit it and hit it *hard* on the first punch he threw. The second one was a little less, and the third was even less than that, but it was still averaged out to a number that made me sweat more than a little.

Next up was Ultra Violent, or UV from Ocala, and shit*fire*, motherfucker! I didn't know if I was going to beat his ass. Jesus *fucking* Christ!

I was next, and I loosened up, rotating my neck on my shoulders and giving a few stretches while Renegade ribbed me hard over if I fucked this up, he was gonna enjoy kissing my girl, if not watching UV or somebody else do it.

We went back and forth, trading jibes, and I appreciated his effort – he knew what he was doing, getting me worked up.

It wasn't a question of hitting the target on the bag square – I could do that shit in my sleep. It was about the follow through and hitting it fucking *hard enough*.

I socked it with everything that I had, muscles screaming in a bit of protest with residual stiffness from the throwdown at the Iron Horse and just because fuck, I was forty-two not twenty-four anymore! Fuck!

I wound up, and fared actually *better* on the second punch, which gave me some hope.

Now don't fuck this up, I thought to myself, and I fucking let rip and socked it a third time to a round of rowdy cheering.

I took the top spot, but fuckin' *barely*, yo.

I shook out my hand and looked to Rarity who was cheering and dancing in her seat, but the fun wasn't over yet – there was still a bit of a lineup after me.

I wandered over to her and put my arm around her waist, leaning back against the bar and massaging her hip while we took in the rest of the guys and their efforts.

A couple edged out Renegade in second place, and one came only a single fuckin' point behind me, and just when I thought I had it in the bag? Skull stepped up.

I was feeling pretty good; Skull wasn't a super big guy. Five foot eight, so certainly not the tallest of us, but he *did* fight *a lot,* and he wrestled alligators for a living – so there was that.

His first punch knocked everyone else's out of the running, but he had two more to go. I would be lying if I said I wasn't sweating, hoping that his second or even third would drop him enough that it wouldn't matter, but he brought the *fire,* and his next two punches edged out his first by a touch, and the third *still* out ranked my best, but wasn't quite up to the first two.

Guys were going, *'whoa'* and laughing their asses off in disbelief, and I admit – I was duly impressed, even as I was straight up nervous as to why Skull was so hard pressed to win this. It wasn't like him.

Unless it was really Bones that wanted the kiss. I could totally see Skull doing it for his brother.

Of course, Skull was declared the winner and reigning champion in short order, and I was both surprised and not when he stepped up to claim his prize.

It was all in good fun, after all... wasn't it?

Skull gave me an inscrutable look and a quick nod before he stepped in front of Rarity, and I waited impassively, to see what the fuckin' weirdo I called a brother would do.

He went to Rarity and took her hand, said a bunch of shit in his native tongue that only he and Bones would understand, and bent gallantly over her hand and kissed the back with a brush of lips and an intense look in her direction.

Rarity blushed prettily, and he backed off and walked away, to a bunch of incredulous scoffs and a smattering of laughter at his expense, but he didn't pay it no mind. He walked up to Bones and said something to him and Bones replied, but again – wasn't like a one of us could fuckin' understand them.

Rarity turned to me, wide-eyed and bewildered and I shrugged.

"Who the fuck knows with those two," I said.

"That was... confusing," she said with a light laugh.

"Who you tellin'?" I asked.

Skull and Bones had retreated to the back deck and were standing against the railing. Bones looked back at me and when he caught me looking, gave a respectful nod and then turned and spit over the railing like the classy fucker he was.

I helped Rarity down and asked, "Shall I show you the rest of the place?" and she smiled up at me.

"I'd like that," she said and I grinned.

Honestly, I just wanted her alone, and all to myself for a bit, and it was as good an excuse as any to get her away from the crowd.

CHAPTER TWENTY-SIX

R arity...

We went down the stairs and into the office area that housed Striker's desk and the offices used by Renegade and Shadow. There was weight equipment out on the deck down here, something that Striker had said was moved down from upstairs with all the visitors they'd had to the club lately.

There were shelves of smaller parts down here on the second floor, too – but the bulk of that stuff had to be down on the first floor, in the garage.

He showed me around the second floor – and there wasn't a whole lot to it. Just a few more single occupancy bathrooms for when the two upstairs were occupied, and those were down here right by the stairs up to the third floor.

He took my hand in his and led me to the set of stairs I'd come up the first time I'd ever been here, which honestly felt like eons ago, rather than just weeks.

We went down into the closed-up garages downstairs, so that he could show me the projects they were working on, and I stopped at the bottom of the stairs to run fingertips over the thinly covered project leaning near the wall. It had this wispy plastic sheeting draped over it, so thin, that the current of air from our passing made it rustle and ripple.

"Oh, this one is going out Monday – we just finished," he said noting my fingertips trailing over the thin plastic and over the seat.

"Yeah?" I asked.

"She's a beauty," he remarked. "Headed to New Orleans and Dracula themed."

"Dracula themed?" I asked. "Book or movie?"

He grinned and said, "Basically the same thing," and drew the plastic back, revealing a motorcycle done in rich blacks and reds. The tank a glossy black with deep burgundy roses that dripped blood.

There were coffin and bat accents and details all over the place, and it was beautiful – dark and rich, the whole thing screaming money and decadence.

"This is my favorite part," he said kneeling down and running a thumb around some engraving at the edge of some round engine piece I had no name for. I knelt down beside him to look and felt my lips curve into an appreciative smile at the famous quote from the movie, *"I have crossed oceans of time to find you..."*

"I've never actually read Dracula to know if this quote is part of the book, but they delivered it in the movie with," I sucked in a breath and whistled a bit and said, *"wow."*

"I know, right?" he said and he stood and held down a hand to help me to my feet.

I overbalanced, and rather than fall toward the bike that cost more than I probably made in a decade, I trusted Striker to catch me, and fetched up against him. I looked up about to apologize, but the look on his face stole my breath and stopped me from speaking.

We stared into each other's eyes for several throbbing, aching, heartbeats that were filled with a longing I had no real understanding of, and then his lips descended toward mine, and it felt as though whatever longing I'd felt took wing and his kiss unlocked the door to its cage and it flew free with a frantic beat of its wings that tickled my insides.

Our lips met, and this time, things were... *different.* More intense, *insanely intense,* my heart swelling in my chest until it pressed painfully against the cage of my ribs. Like, it swelled so hard from being so full at finally having Striker's hands on me, that it left no room for me to draw breath, even as his hands slid around my body, pulling me closer to him.

Our tongues danced, the heat building between us, until my skin flushed and a light mist of perspiration dewed my chest and upper lip.

I groaned into Striker's mouth, and swooned into him, and yeah, my foot popped up off the ground behind me like we were the lead characters in some epic romance movie in the scene where the music swelled and the kiss became this almost fever dream.

"You trust me, baby girl?" he practically growled against my lips, and the low visceral sound of it sent a shudder through me in the most delicious of ways.

"Yes," I gasped.

He gathered me close and kissed my mouth, along my jaw, and down the side of my neck, stopping and practically attacking that sweet spot when I let out a gasp and went very nearly limp in his embrace.

And no, it was not lost on me that he was practically feeding at the spot on my neck where a vampire would while I was backed up against the bike of Dracula or whatever.

I pressed into him even closer as his hands smoothed along my skin in the gap between my cropped tee and the waistband of my shorts/skirt combo before pressing into my skin and sliding beneath the Lycra or spandex of my waistband or whatever.

He slid his hands below not only my shorts, but my panties as well, and the feel of his hands against my skin in such an intimate place practically had me writhing.

He pressed one of his powerful thighs between my legs and up against me, and I unabashedly writhed against him to try and get some kind of relief from the mounting desire and growing frustration within me.

"Does my baby girl want her daddy's cock inside her?" he asked me, whispering in my ear, and *oh, God, yes – that was so hot.*

"Yes," I whispered breathlessly, on a note of pleading, my arms around his neck, my fingernails scratching the back of his scalp, pulling his mouth to mine once more.

The kissing was impassioned, little moans and groans escaping the both of us as things heated way past boiling point between the both of us.

He skimmed my panties and shorts with their ruffle of skirt like material down, pushing them down, down, down, my smoothly shaven legs and I let him go to take them from me, stepping out of the garments carefully at his urging.

He stuffed them in his back pocket, all the while his mouth moved against my skin, kissing my inner thighs, looking up at me with this insanely intent and beautifully predatory look in his hazel-green eyes as he stroked fingers between my legs, gauging my excitement, making sure I was ready.

God yes, I was ready. I wanted this like I'd never wanted anything in my life, I swear to God.

He stood up, capturing my mouth with his again, and I kissed him with a fervor I didn't know I even possessed. He put his hands to my outer thighs and dipped, and I trusted him, pressing close, wrapping my arms around his neck and shoulders, as he lifted me, sitting me on the Dracula bike's seat, spreading me open so the cool air of the garage could kiss my heated and dripping wet pussy.

I shuddered at the sensations, even as he kept himself bowed to kiss me as he scrabbled with his hands at his belt and the front of his jeans.

I leaned head and shoulders back against the wall and spread my legs further, reaching between us to play with myself, slicking my wetness all over, teasing my own clit as he pulled a condom from somewhere on his person, and ripped it open with his teeth.

I let my gaze follow his movements as he took his hard, long, and thick cock in one hand and rolled the rubber down his length, the latex straining around the thickness of the root of his dick, and I was vaguely worried about taking all of him — if I was capable of stretching that much to take him.

Granted, I hadn't fucked *a lot*, and thus felt fairly inexperienced — but also, I'd never had anything as big as he was inside me. Not even a vibrator or a dildo.

"You ready?" he asked me.

"God, yes," I said on a gasp. "Please, please fucking fill me, Daddy. I want you; I *need* you."

He chuckled darkly, and pressed at my opening, my body giving a satisfying little stretch and give throbbing shudder as he kept pressing in, hissing out between clenched teeth, the look on his face as he watched himself disappear into my freshly shaven and bald pussy from that morning one like he was absolutely hyper focused on committing this to memory for all time.

I arched closer to him, head back against the cinderblock wall, hands pressed to the leather seat that was soft as butter, and tilted my pelvis *just so* and *oh, that was fucking magic.*

He gripped my hips and started thrusting, working himself in and out of me, slicking through my wetness and setting a pace that was seriously doing things for me.

I gasped in even little puffs of breath and rocked to meet him on every thrust, careful that the big machine supporting my weight didn't wiggle too much beneath me, but while it rocked, it barely did, and it felt stable enough.

I trusted that Striker knew what he was doing, and that the motorcycle would support me and our lovemaking, but I would be lying if I said there wasn't a little thrill of fear that shot through me and somehow, some way, subtly enhanced things for me as well.

I held onto him and writhed, getting the friction just right, but still I was close but maddeningly I just couldn't quite get *there*, you know?

"Touch yourself, baby. Touch your clit for Daddy." I dropped one arm from around his neck, held onto his vest with the other while I let my fingertips find that bundle of nerves, pressing into it, rolling my fingertips through my own wetness, over my clitoris, the pressure, the friction, delicious. A tingle started in my pussy and I clenched down around Striker's pressing and stroking cock and he uttered in a strained tone, "That's it, that's my good girl. Do it for me, baby. Come for Daddy. I wanna feel you come for me."

I listened to his quiet encouragement, the intensity of his voice, the panting, the gasping, the sounds our bodies made with him sliding in and out of me, the slicking of my fingers against myself, my blood rushing in my ears, my heart thundering in my chest, the tingle in my nipples and that full feeling low in my belly – building, building, *yes!*

I threw back my head, let my hand slip from my body and held onto the seat beneath me, and pulled myself against Striker, body stiffening, his arms going around me and holding me tight, as my pussy throbbed and rhythmically pulled at his cock which throbbed deep inside me in counterpoint.

The perfect crescendo to the symphony our love made.

CHAPTER TWENTY-SEVEN

S triker...

I'd never had the moment strike me, or be so... *pure*. Did I regret our first time being down here, in the filthy garage? Somewhat – but at the same time? No. She'd been so into it, and I was so proud of her my chest very nearly swelled with it.

Withdrawing myself from her warm, silken, body was a trial, but it had to be done. I didn't want to risk the chance of someone coming down here and catching her off guard. I couldn't care less about anybody watching me fuck – but that wasn't something we had discussed or negotiated and not everyone was an exhibitionist like me.

I held the condom on myself as I pulled out, and *ee Gods,* that was sensitive! Joy going off from my cock to my brain in a string of fucking fireworks, pulsing and exploding in my chest and behind my closed eyelids in this sensation like if singing transcended sound into physical sensation.

I got a grip, stripped it off my softening cock, and tossed it in the nearest trash can.

"Let's get you dressed, princess," I murmured and helped her off the bike and onto her feet. She stood in her flat shoes on the dusty cement slab of the garage floor and I kneeled in front of her, pulling her shorts and underwear out of my back pocket where I'd stuffed them, and untangling the garments from one another and holding out her panties for her to step into. She did, and I pulled them up her legs, and out around the curve of her ass, making sure they were comfortably pulled up and in place. She giggled at me, when I went to do the same for her shorts/skirt combo, making sure I had them right.

She rested a hand on my shoulder, and let me help her, and I glowed with pride for my little girl, my princess, and got those up and in place for her too.

"Come on, baby; let's get you to a restroom."

"Okay, Daddy..." she said it almost shyly, as if she were tasting the honorific on for size, and she blushed deeply as she said it, adding color to her pale cheeks and deepening the color across her already flushed chest from our passions.

"Take all the time you need to get used to it, baby girl, I'm not going anywhere," I murmured, and then pulled her to me, holding her tight, pressing my lips against her forehead.

I felt her body soften in response to that touch from my lips, her muscles going lax, her arms going around me, her fingers tangling in the laces at the sides of my cut, beautifully childlike in her uncertainty.

She had nothing at all to fear from me, or from anyone for that matter. That was the role I longed to take. As a protector, as a leader, as someone she could trust in and trust implicitly that I could and would take care of her.

I held her for long moments, and let her soak up my love for her, and spend some quiet moments in the moment – but moments like this couldn't last forever, and I needed to make sure my little girl took care of herself and part of that was taking a pee after sex to make sure she didn't get a urinary tract infection.

I led her upstairs and to the restroom, using the one next to hers for myself. I washed up and went back out and it was only a few seconds more before she returned to me.

"What should we do now?" she asked uncertainly and I smiled.

"I'd like to take you home," I said and her eyes widened, which made me chuckle. "*With me*, not back to yours."

Her face colored with embarrassment.

"Oh," she said putting her hand over her mouth and with her other arm over her stomach she looked the picture of adorable awkwardness.

I held out my hand and she reluctantly took the one off from over her mouth and tangled her fingers with mine. I raised them to my lips, giving her a very real look of devotion, and kissed her fingers between her first and second knuckles.

Her blue eyes softened, and I could see a longing in them, as though she had been desperate for some softness and gentleness, and like she never wanted this to end.

Same, baby girl. Same, I thought to myself and tried to convey the feelings I felt with my eyes alone, unsure how I was supposed to convert any of it into words that could convey the magnitude of them.

I led her back downstairs and out the side door to the lot where my bike was parked. I didn't really feel the need to tell the boys we were off. A pretty young thing like Rarity tucked into my side, they would know. Some of them might even be a little jealous. I certainly hoped so.

The ride to my place wasn't overly long, but was humid with a breath of rain coming in off the Atlantic. We pulled into my spot by my rental a rumble of thunder right on the heels of the rumble of my bike, the machine chugging and purring to a stop just as the clouds thickened and started to roll in overhead.

We got off the bike and I keyed our way into the house, just as another flash of lightning dazzled our senses and the boom of thunder heralded the skies opening up.

We ducked into the house, laughing, and I shut the door on the rough patter of rain outside.

Rarity's blue eyes sparkled as she slipped out of her shoes and took off her Hello Kitty backpack.

"Oh, shit," she murmured and swatted at the stuffed animal and the gray dust from the shop wall on it.

"Glad it didn't get wet to set the stain," I said as most if not all the dust came off with a few smacks.

"Me too," she said gratefully.

"Don't worry, baby girl, we'll get it clean." She smiled up at me and I smiled back, stroking her cheek with my thumb, feeling her pulse jump in the side of her neck under my fingers.

I kicked off my boots and left them on the tile entryway and hung her little backpack on the hooks set on the wall behind the door. My jacket and cut went up next to it, and I had to smile. I loved the look of the two beside each other.

I turned back to Rarity, who almost looked shy, when she asked, "So, what now?"

"Now, I'd like to play with my little girl," I said with a grin I knew held all sorts of fun wicked intentions.

"Oh? And what does that look like?" she asked. It was a fair and good question.

"First of all," I said drawing her into my arms. "If I ever do something you're unsure of, we talk about it until either you are sure or you decide it's a hard no, okay?"

"Okay..." She drew the word out and the inevitable follow-up question came. "Like what?"

"Like when we're in this house, alone, just you and me? I want you nude and ready for me. I'm going to tease you, *a lot*, but I won't always give you what you want. I want to use toys on you, play with that pretty little pussy of yours, put jewelry on those perfect tits to accentuate those pert little nipples, and I may even bend you over and play with your ass a little, maybe put a plug in there, one with a gem or a cute tail to it. I promise to go slow with that, though. Start real small, with something you'd hardly know is there."

She scoffed a bit of an incredulous laugh at the last and said, "I don't know about that last one."

"All I ask is that you try for Daddy. Can you do that for me, princess?"

Her face softened, her blue eyes deepening with an unnamed emotion as she pondered what I was asking.

"How about now?" she asked softly.

"You get naked," I told her, "I'll get the toys."

"Okay," she whispered.

"Hang your clothes up right here, kitten."

"Yes, Daddy," she declared.

I let her go, reluctantly, my hands itching to be on her body at all times when she was near me. I went through the living room, past the guest bath, and into the main bedroom suite and to the old foot-locker by the bedside table I kept all manner of toys and things in.

I picked out a set of three graduated plugs wrapped in black velvet with ice blue round gems that were the match for her eyes. I also found myself a bottle of liquid lube and took both out to the main rooms.

She was just hanging up her bra, and I stopped to admire her nude profile, at her perfect round peach of an ass and her heavy breasts.

She had a *figure,* and I liked that, the rest of her flat and toned with youth and what could only be a combination of hard work and regular exercise.

"C'mere baby," I crooked a finger at her and she padded over to me, bare feet sinking into the plush cream carpet,

I pulled a chair out from the glass dining room table and said, "I know it's cold, but I want you to bend over and press flat to the glass, keep that ass up for me, okay?"

"Okay, Daddy," she swallowed hard, the honorific still difficult for her, and fuck yeah, I understood why. I was proud of her for using it, for trying it, but if she ultimately found she wasn't comfortable with 'daddy,' I had no problem choosing something else. Something sacred to the both of us, something that would work for the both of us and suit us just fine. Nothing was set in stone here. We had all the time in the world to figure it out.

I set the things I'd brought out with me down, on the table behind her and she was leaning back from me, clutching the edge of the glass, unsure. I took a seat in the chair and pulled it up and asked, "How you feeling, baby? Talk to me."

"Nervous," she said, and her voice shook, and was indeed nervous in tone.

I smiled at her, "Nervous bad, or nervous good?"

She laughed a little and asked me, "There's a difference?"

"Nervous bad, you're scared – and scared in such a way like you think I'm going to hurt you, or let something bad happen to you."

"And nervous good?" she asked, looking at me with a soft wonder.

"Anxious, excited, like you're about to go on a roller coaster ride."

"Definitely the second one," she whispered softly, "maybe just a little bit of the first."

I let my eyes rove her beautiful, soft skin, and drew my gaze back up to her face, letting her see in my eyes and my expression that I meant absolutely no harm. I had no interest in hurting her. All I wanted was to open doors she never knew were closed, take her to new heights of pleasure that she'd never even dreamed was possible all the while indulging myself at the same time. Availing myself of her sweet, tender flesh, and feeling wrap around my cock like it had just an hour or so ago.

I also wanted to take her ass at some point, but that wasn't for today. No, today was just light training. The first step in working her body up to taking my cock someday.

"You trust me to be a good Daddy to you, my sweet girl?" I asked, smoothing my hands up her lithe body, over her delectable skin, to cup and massage her breasts.

She groaned, her eyes slipping shut and I corrected her gently, "Ah-ah, look at me."

She opened her eyes and answered, "Yes. I trust you."

"Turn around then, sweetheart," I turned her in my hands, and she faced away from me.

Hands on the table. She put her hands on the table and I pulled up my chair better, and lightly tapped her feet apart. "I know the glass is cold but bend over for me, please. Let me see that beautiful pussy and that tight little asshole."

She giggled and bent, gasping and shrieking a bit at the contact of the cold glass against her skin. The table did what I wanted, though. It put her on her toes, and tilted her pelvis *just so*, to put that beautiful pink pussy and her tight little starfish on display for me.

I rubbed her right ass cheek with my hand and she writhed and I gave it a light smack, not enough to hurt but definitely enough to sting a little and grace her fair skin with a red handprint for a minute. She yipped and jumped and made this slightly annoyed squeal that was just fuckin' *adorable.*

"Mm, that's my girl," I praised her. "So pretty, so wet for Daddy, hmm?"

She writhed a little and let out this little moan and I liked that. Loved that my words had an effect. I unraveled the holder and slipped the smallest plug out of its pocket.

"I'm going to decorate this little asshole of mine and make it sparkle. How's that sound?" I played with it, pressing the tip of my index finger against the ridged tissue and rubbing it in a small circle, just enough to tantalize and titillate her.

"Mm, that feels weird. Weird, but good," she said and finished her sentence on a little gasp as I dripped a drop of the silicone-based lubricant directly on her asshole.

She jerked at the sensation and complained, "Cold!"

"Sorry baby," I said on a chuckle, but I wasn't sorry at all. I liked to make her squirm and she did it so beautifully for me.

I teased her asshole with my fingertip again, getting it nice and slick, but most importantly, used to my touch before I pressed just enough to get my fingertip in, up to the first knuckle.

She jerked and squealed, but not in a bad way – rather on a delighted giggle that was part discomfort, part... I want to say *joy* at discovering a deliciously dirty, new sensation.

"You like that?" I asked, working it in and out just a little bit, just enough to let her feel it.

"Yes," she purred, and she relaxed, letting the table take a little more of her weight.

I kept playing with her, for a while, adding another drop of lube when this one became scarce and with the distribution of this second drop, I forced my finger in just a little bit deeper, up to the second knuckle, but I didn't make her take the joint, not yet.

The slender, stainless-steel plug shone on the black cloth beside her hip, and I gauged it. I would say the widest part that she would have to take on the plug was just a teensy bit bigger in girth than my second knuckle would be, so I would get her nice and comfortable with that, before switching out.

She was moaning softly, her hips writhing as I finger fucked her tight little ass and she barely even jerked when I forced it in past the second knuckle.

"Good girl," I praised on a proud laugh, and she let out a little gasp. I held the plug in my left hand to warm it, while I gave her longer strokes with my finger before pulling it from her ass altogether.

She made a noise of protest and I chuckled and said, "Hang on, baby. I'm not done yet."

"Mm, okay," she whimpered and I dripped some lube on the plug and spread it around.

"Here we go," I slipped it right into place. *Boop!* With nary even a gasp from her and sat back in satisfaction as the jewel sparkled under the overhead light.

"Now that's pretty," I said and rubbed her ass with my left hand.

"Stand up for me, baby," and she did as I told her, sucking in a

sharp breath at the new sensation of having something in her ass –
even if it was small.

"How does that feel?" I asked.

"Good," she said turning around slowly.

"Good, now this is what I want you to do..." I instructed her to go
to the couch and to pick a movie for us to watch. I didn't care what,
at all, while I washed my hands really well and made us popcorn.

I wanted to snuggle my nude little girl and play with her pretty
pussy until she came all over my hand and begged me to fuck her.

I also wanted to see if, at any point, I could up the size of the plug
in her ass to at least the second one – I didn't anticipate getting to
the third today, but the second would be nice. I wanted to bend her
over and take her eventually from behind and watch her little
asshole glitter while I filled her and dragged more of those succulent
little moans out of her lovely throat.

I wanted to do a lot of things to defile her, and then I wanted to
give her a bath, wrap her up, and hold her against me all night safe
and snug as a bug in a rug – even though I was pretty certain that
wasn't going to happen *tonight*... I knew she had to get back at some
point.

She scrolled through my streaming services while I scrubbed up
and popped a bowl of popcorn, and when I came around the kitchen
island and went to the couch she looked up and asked, "Is this
okay?"

I didn't know what I expected her to choose, but was surprised
when it was the live action *Little Mermaid*.

"I haven't watched it yet," she said and I sat down beside her on
the couch, set the bowl of popcorn down and said enthusiastically,
"Let's do it!"

We settled in, polished off the bowl of popcorn before the first
ten minutes of the movie had rolled by, and listened to the rain pelt
outside.

We both got more comfortable, me laying the length of the
couch, her draped over my chest, on her stomach, as I touched her all

over – smoothing my hands everywhere I could reach on her until I noticed she shivered and it wasn't just from all the touching?

"You cold, little one?" I asked gently and she nodded. I smiled and pulled the blanket off of the couch and asked, "Why didn't you say so?"

She shrugged, her attention rapt on the television and the singing mermaid and I had to chuckle. I snuggled her and put a finger against the plug in her ass and wiggled it, asking, "How does this feel?"

"Okay," she murmured.

"Just okay, or does it still feel good?" I asked.

"Good," she responded and looked up at me. I smiled and kissed her forehead and when she shifted again, made sure I shifted enough that her wet little pussy was within my reach.

She gasped and whimpered, writhing against my clothed body as I slicked my fingers through her wetness and played with her clit.

She groaned and wiggled her bottom back against the curve of my lap, and yeah, my cock was hard and ready – but I wasn't. I wanted to wring enough orgasms out of her that when I did finally take her, she was limp and barely able to move beneath me.

This was the shit I delighted in. This was the shit I lived for – and I would take Rarity on the ride of her fuckin' life for as long as she was willing to stick with me and entertain my pervy fucking bullshit.

CHAPTER TWENTY-EIGHT

R**arity...**

He teased my pussy until I came, writhing against him, my ass pressed back against the erection pressing against the front of his jeans. I reached behind me and fondled him through the stiff fabric, the heat coming off of him incredible – but he wasn't ready to give me what I wanted.

He gave me a rest, and kissed the side of my neck, his fingers playing through the wetness between my thighs, slicking against my folds, sweetly torturing my clit. I shivered, but not with cold, and after a bit and my breathing had come back down and returned to normal? He started the sweet and welcome torture all over again.

As the movie credits rolled, he got me up and asked how my ass felt, when I said fine, he went to the kitchen, washed his hands, and fixed me a glass of something to drink. He brought it to me and said, "Hydrate, baby. I'm not done with you yet."

I smiled and drank the red liquid in the glass of ice and felt my eyebrows go up when I realized it was red Gatorade or some other electrolyte drink.

"Got a favorite?" he asked after I'd downed half the glass.

"The white one, Cherry Frost I think they call it. I just call it the white Gatorade," I said.

"Noted, I'll keep some on hand. Right now, I'd like to try the next size up in your ass if you're game."

I nodded carefully, apprehensive, but I would try it. The first one wasn't so bad at all. I mean, I barely felt it now. Just a sort of hardness in my asshole now. I stood and the plug shifted with the movement, and it was a little more noticeable when I walked. I turned my head and assumed the position bent over the table as I had before and he gently tugged on the plug, thrusting it a little. I giggled at the strange sensation, and he plunged a middle finger up inside my pussy and I gasped, thrusting my hips back to meet him.

"Good girl," he praised. "That's my good girl."

I swallowed hard, and felt my knees tremble and breathed in and out slowly as he teased around inside my pussy, jerking when he found that spot inside me that sent waves of shimmering sensation rippling through me.

I moaned and closed my eyes, resting my cheek against the glass, my tits pressed against the glass. I bet it'd look comical from underneath, but oh what he did to me made that an entirely fleeting thought.

"Feel good?" he asked me.

"Yes," I whispered.

"Gonna cum for your Daddy?" he asked.

"You keep doing that, yes," I said pertly and he pull his hand from the toy in my ass and gave my ass cheek a smack. I yipped and jumped, my pussy clenching around his invading finger and he chuckled.

He went back to manipulating the small plug in my ass, and fervently worked that spot inside me until I came again, sagging, letting the table take my weight, and watching the glass fog in front of me with my panting breaths.

"Push out," he ordered and gave a little tug on the anal plug and I did, and it popped free with no trouble. He instantly replaced it with a finger and worked my ass and my pussy both.

I writhed against his hands and sucked in a sharp breath and held it as he slipped a second finger in my ass to join the first. I made a small noise of protest as he stretched me beyond the scope of comfort, but *oh God*, did it feel good having him in both holes. Like, I never knew it could be this good – and even after what? Three? Four orgasms, since being here in his little house with him? I still craved the feeling of his cock inside me. I wanted to feel him so deep that when he pushed into me I felt him in my womb. Hell, I wanted to feel him fuck me and fill me so bad I felt against the back side of my tonsils!

"Please," I begged. "Please fill me with your cock."

"Mmm," he made a satisfied hum, "I like it when you beg me like that, baby girl."

He pulled his fingers out of my ass, and cold lube dripped on my asshole. Soon after, cold metal pressed and I pushed out, relaxing, letting it slide into me. Making a small noise of protest as it once again, stretched my tight little asshole beyond what was comfortable, but it was such a fleeting discomfort as my ass swallowed the plug and the flared base settled snug against the puckered flesh at my opening.

"How does that feel?" he asked.

"Good," I moaned, thinking about it a second and sighing out, "full. Definitely more intense than the last one, but not uncomfortable – yet. Feels hard, and I want your cock inside me so badly now, Daddy – *please?*"

He chuckled and said, "You stay right there, just like that – be good, don't move a muscle, and I'll give you what you want, okay?"

"Okay," I moaned breathlessly.

I was so turned on. Turned on to the point I would do whatever he asked of me, suck his dick, let him put it in my ass, just *anything* to have him inside me. It was like all orgasms paled in comparison to the one in the garage earlier, where I'd held him in my body. Where he'd filled me so perfectly, made me feel like I was so tight, I could barely contain him.

He went into the kitchen and washed his hands again, thoroughly, and I appreciated that – I wasn't keen on ass to pussy and getting an infection; so, I would take him being careful of that. I liked it. I wondered, vaguely, how we would handle it when he fucked my ass for real – and I found that I was more turned on and curious about having him there than I was nervous or scared.

Did I think I could take him right now? Oh, hell no – even the biggest plug that sat beside my hip on the table wasn't as thick at its thickest point as he was. It would take work to get me up to that – but I also found myself desperate to know what it would feel like to have his cock inside me with this already much bigger plug than the first one I'd had in.

The first one had been small enough that just its presence had been... noticeable. It'd been *different*. Foreign, but not in a bad way. Just in an interesting and unique way. I'd liked it. Just the feeling of it in my ass had made me feel sexy, and brazen in a way that I'd never felt before.

This one felt more intense. As though it was stretching me. Less simply present in my ass and more that... like my training had really begun.

We'd talked about this in particular, a lot, to the point that I had so been looking forward to trying it for him and he did *not* disappoint by making it the first dirty and outside the box thing we'd tried together.

We'd talked about so many other things, too. Remote control vibrators out in public. A plug in my ass, and a vibe in my pussy while taking a slow walk somewhere. Nipple torture was something he wanted to try as well. Starting simply with some nipple jewelry that hung from them while he watched my tits bounce as we fucked – and that had sounded hot. He wanted to try different clamps, too –

not to hurt, but more to stimulate... but he wasn't beyond punishing me if I was a bad little girl.

We'd talked about that, too and both agreed, no matter what, no marks should be left. That marks were going too far.

I jumped when he touched my hips and massaged my lower back with his thumbs.

"Stand up and come with me, baby. I want you in my bed. I want to make you cum for me some more."

I stood up, and turned in the circle of his arms, wrapping mine around his neck and leaning into him. He smiled down at me, his hands smoothing up and down my back, cupping my ass, squeezing its globes and asking me, "How does that one feel now? Still good?"

"Yes," I whispered and I pulled his mouth to mine, tangling my fingers in his hair.

He obliged me, kissing me, lifting me, urging me to hop up. I wrapped my legs around his hips, and moaned into his mouth at the interesting things that it did to the plug in my ass as I ground my soaking wet pussy against the front of him, seeking out friction with his erection pressing at the front of his jeans.

He turned us both, and powerfully, carried me up the hall, turning at the last doorway on the right and taking me into a fairly sparsely furnished bedroom, laying me on the rumpled covers of his bed.

I let him go with my arms and stretched them over my head, letting my legs fall open as he pulled the tee shirt he wore off over his head.

"Touch yourself, play with that pussy baby," he instructed me, and I reached down, dipping my fingertips into my wetness and teasing my clit lightly with my fingertips as he shucked himself out of his jeans and socks.

He gripped his cock, and stroked it with his fist, and it was the first real, unabashed, un-obfuscated look that I got of Striker and the long, lean, muscular nude front of him.

Fuck, he was hot. My blood heating as I watched the temperature rise in his eyes. I loved the way he looked at me, letting his eyes devour me from my head to my toes, staring at my tits with reverence, following the hourglass curve of my body to my hip before settling hungrily on where I played in my own wetness at his command.

He reached into the bedside table's drawer and pulled out a condom, ripping open the packet with his teeth and rolling it on.

I watched, squeezing and rolling a nipple between my other set of fingers while I plunged the other set up inside me.

"Oh, fuck... Rarity," he groaned and he collapsed over me, and lined himself up with my opening.

I pulled at his ass, trying to get him to put himself in but he resisted, going slow, and once he pushed in just beyond the entrance to my pussy, I realized why.

I sucked in a sharp breath as his cock pushed on the plug in my ass, making me feel even more impossibly tight.

He worked himself back and forth a little and grunted, pulling out.

"On your hands and knees, baby," he ordered, and I obediently rolled onto all fours.

He put his thumb against the jewel in my ass and I gasped at the sensation of the larger plug moving inside of me, and then his cock was pressing in again.

I moaned, groaned piteously, and arched my back low, pressing my stomach and tits to the bed, offering myself up to him and begging silently for more. God, I needed *more*.

I needed that thick cock inside of me, pressing against that plug, filling me, stretching me impossibly large, it felt so *good*. I needed it, I wanted it, that building *pressure*, that full feeling like nothing I'd ever felt before. It was so, so, good – it hurt, vaguely, but I adored it. Loved it. Was more than willing to take it for Striker who seemed to hit the mark with me in every fucking way – he pushed into me and bottomed gently out against the end of me, and hissed out from between clenched teeth.

"Fuck you're so fucking *tight*, baby girl. My cock fits so *nice*. Are you good?"

I panted from the extremely full feeling and not trusting my words, just nodded rapidly, and held back my hands making grabby hands motions to indicate I wanted more.

He laughed, grasping my hips and pulling out, quickly putting his thumb back on the jewel in the plug to keep it in my ass as he struck a thrusting rhythm and *oh God yeah*.

It was a lot, not going to lie. It was like, *a lot, a lot,* but I wasn't willing to cry *uncle* just yet. It was intense, bordering on painful, but —

I cried out when one thrust went particularly deep and more than a little astray to the point it didn't feel good, it just plain *hurt*, and without pausing, without missing a beat, he took his hand away from the anal plug, kept thrusting, and the plug popped free. He threw it down on the floor, replaced both hands on my hips, and slowed way down into slow, sensual and much more even, much less frantic strokes.

I panted, relaxed some into the mattress, and took what he gave me and that sharp, momentary pain faded into oblivion, swept away on a blissful wave.

"Oh, God, oh, Daddy, oh, *yes!*" I cried and he slowly worked his pace back up.

I reached a hand between my thighs and played with my cunt, feeling his slide in and out of me, listened to the music our bodies made, and teased my clit; ramping up the pleasure once again, knowing that when I came this time, with Striker so deep inside of me, that I was going to be absolutely *spent*.

I was okay with that. I *needed* the oblivion that only his touch could bring, and I was positively *desperate* for it. Ready for it. Needing of it in a way I'd never needed anything before.

I was vaguely aware of my mouth making feral noises, of sound pouring from my throat, and I knew they were words — but I was wholly ensnared by what Striker was doing to me to the point that when I did come? It was screaming his name as lightning crackled outside and the stars themselves fell from the sky, streaking behind my eyelids as a pleasure so pure burned through me, scorching me from the inside out.

CHAPTER TWENTY-NINE

S triker...

"Oh, God, oh, Daddy, oh, yes!" she cried, and her pussy was doing that thing. That thing where she was growing hot around my dick, her muscles tightening up around me, making it harder to press in and pull out, but I put some more power into my thrusting, my thighs burning, my hips flexing, and I knew I was hitting everything just right, because her cries amped up, echoing back off of the ceiling and slamming into my chest, urging me on faster, harder, stronger.

"Yes! Yes! Yes, yes, yes, yes, *yes!*" she cried, and her voice was pure operatic fantasy, reaching a crescendo and descending into animalistic and feral cries that *God, fuck, yes* - sent me right over the edge with her.

I pulled her back onto my cock as I let loose inside the condom inside her, her body rhythmically gripping and draining me, her body collapsing forward onto her stomach, and I wasn't ready to pull out – so I collapsed right along with her, over her back, pressing her into the covers, and lacing my fingers with hers, holding her down, kissing her shoulder as her ass rose and fell and she moved me inside of her, just like she couldn't hold still and it was *so good.*

I hummed in appreciation, and nuzzled behind her ear, breathing her in deeply, the scent that was sweet like cotton candy.

"I think I'm done," she gasped. "No more, I can't take any more."

I laughed and felt a frisson of pride split my chest wide open.

"Glad I still got it," I mumbled, and she sighed out in pure satisfaction and wiggled under me, pulling my arms around her like she would use me as a blanket and could go to sleep right then and there.

"Ah, nope – you gotta get up and pee," I reminded her, reaching between us to hold the condom on myself and shuddering as I pulled out of her snug, warm, wet, and all-around delectable twat.

She moaned, whining, and smacked the bed by her face and I crawled backward off of her and off of the bed.

She rolled over and looked up at me and I held my hands down to her, the condom secure enough and momentarily forgotten as I reached down and took her hands and hauled her, protesting in this adorable little whining, to her feet.

"Go pee, then get your ass back here so I can tuck you in," I ordered. She gave me a baleful look, a half-assed little salute, and thrust her butt back at me before walking out the bedroom door to the bathroom in the hall.

I disposed of the condom in the trash, sighed in satisfaction, and turned back my half-assed made bed for her return.

She dutifully took her leak, washed her hands, and came back to me. I took her hand and guided her alongside the bed and she laid down obediently enough. I tucked the blankets over her and sat down at her hip.

Her makeup was a bit streaky and her hair was mussed in their twin pigtails and I chuckled and reached up to take them out and let her hair down. I massaged her scalp and she closed her eyes and groaned.

"Stay right here for Daddy, princess. I'll be right back."

"Okay," she whispered, the small word sounding... vulnerable.

Yeah, she was done. Poor thing had probably never experienced such an intense intimacy before. She was young, beautiful, and I was glad to be her first in that arena even if I wasn't the first to ever be inside of her.

I went to the kitchen and got me a bottle of water and made her a juice, refilling her glass and adding a bit more ice. I stuck a bendy straw in it so she wouldn't spill, and brought both back with me to the bedroom, my own urge to pee becoming imminent.

I set my bottle down on the bedside table and handed down her glass and said, "Both hands, princess. Don't spill, okay?"

"Okay," her voice shook a little and I kissed her forehead. I could almost feel the uncertainty drain from her, and when I pulled back, yep, her eyes were closed and she looked more centered.

"Sip on that like a good girl, and Daddy'll be right back, okay? I want to hold you."

She smiled shyly up at me from behind the rim of her glass and took the straw between her lips, and *damn, down boy, she's done for tonight,* I had to tell my cock before he got too excited.

I picked up the plug off the floor on my way out and went into the bathroom. I took my piss, cleaned up, and went back to the bedroom and got into bed with my sweet girl, who didn't hesitate to cuddle into my side.

"So sweet," I murmured and kissed her bright blonde hair and she snuggled closer as I stroked the soft skin of her back. The wind was howling, the rain still pelting out there, and I closed my eyes and listened to the rain.

I don't think it was long before either of us were out.

I know I roused a little bit later, just long enough to switch out the bedside lamp that I always left lit in case I got back late.

God, she felt good in my arms...

The next morning, I woke to the birds chirping and the sun streaming in through the slits around the edges and through the middle of the bedroom curtains.

Rarity, and I both hadn't moved an inch, and she was still tucked tightly into my side, her head on my shoulder and her leg draped across my own. I cleared my throat and she jumped slightly, sucking in a deep breath, and when those blue eyes of hers opened, they pinned me to the spot with their beauty.

I don't think I would ever get tired of waking up to those eyes, and the thought of looking down into them while her lips wrapped around my cock had my morning wood twitching beneath the sheet.

"What time is it?" she queried breathily, and I looked behind her at the flashing lights on my alarm clock.

"Dunno," I said, voice deep and rough with disuse from our long sleep. "Power must have gone out in the night at some point."

"Oh, *shit*," she muttered and turned to look for herself. "I told my mom I would be home last night!"

"Oh, shit, is right baby. Were you supposed to look after the boys or something?"

"No, I just hadn't planned on staying out so late, let alone overnight. I bet she's worried sick."

"Go get your phone," I ordered and she leaped up and padded out of the bedroom and down the hallway. She returned with her phone in her hands, chewing her bottom lip nervously.

"Like sixteen texts and seven missed calls," she said unhappily. "I'm lucky she didn't show up here – she has me on a family tracker app – we're all on it just in case."

"Good plan," I praised even as she texted something out.

"I told her I fell asleep watching a movie with you and you didn't wake me up," she winced as she looked at me and I chuckled, motioning for her to come back to me, to come back to bed. I lifted the sheet and she eagerly crawled in with me as her phone started to ring in her hand – or buzz, rather. Her actual ringer was off. Silenced in favor of the vibration function.

"Hi, Mom," she said, closing her eyes and looking pained.

"You had me worried sick!" I heard her mom admonish through the phone.

"I know, I'm sorry! But really, I'm fine – we watched *The Little Mermaid* live action and I fell asleep."

She and her mom went back and forth and her mom finally admitted, "I figured you were just having a good time. I saw you were at the same place for a while and when it didn't change. You're lucky I had more sense than to come up there!"

Rarity laughed and said, "I'm glad you didn't. That would be *really* embarrassing, Mom."

"I know, which is why I didn't do it – but Rarity, you're my only daughter and I couldn't handle it if anything happened to you, too. So text me every once in a while, okay?" I could hear her mom's voice cracking from here, and I hugged Rarity around the shoulders as she leaned into me and she sniffed, guilty tears starting in her eyes.

"I promise, I was having a good time and I was being selfish, I'm so sorry. I'll be home soon, okay?"

"Don't rush – I know you don't get out much. Grandma and Grandpa have it for now."

"No, no; I'll head home soon. It's okay!"

They argued a bit and finally Rarity said she wouldn't hurry *too much*, and they ended the call.

She looked at me, and burst into tears, and I held her tight, resting my chin on the top of her head and let her have her cry.

Mom was right, it was okay for us to both feel shitty for a minute; but it wouldn't be okay if we made the same mistake twice, and I loved my little girl enough to make sure that it didn't happen again.

"New rule," I said. "You text your mother every now and again when you're up this way, okay?"

She sniffed and nodded and said, "Okay, Daddy," and I chuckled and held her tight.

"That's my good girl," I told her and she sighed, a shuddering thing, and got it together.

I was so proud of her.

CHAPTER THIRTY

Rarity...

"So, I gotta ask," my mom said, handing the joint back to me as we sat on the back porch several nights after my impromptu overnight and amazing fucking sexcapades with Striker. She held her breath a second longer and let out a plume of green smoke. "How serious are you about this biker?" She raised her eyebrows, and I coughed like a bitch caught off guard. I'd been walking on eggshells, wondering when she was going to give me the third degree and she had gotten me! I'd been lulled into a false sense of security, thinking she wouldn't make a big thing about it – but *nope*. Not my mother. *God dammit.*

I sure as *hell* wasn't going to tell her about the Daddy/little girl roleplaying shit we were up to – she wouldn't get it, and would lose her shit; but I couldn't explain it if I even wanted to try, like for real – it didn't feel creepy or incestuous *at all*. Like we totally got it, we were both *consenting adults,* and it wasn't about him *actually* being my daddy. My daddy had died, and there was a hole in my soul that no one or nothing would ever fill... but the way Striker cared for me, the way he cuddled me and was gentle with me, and the way he made me feel safe to go back to that almost childlike state?

It was intoxicating. It felt so fucking *good* and I wanted *more of it, please and thank you.*

Still... no way was I telling my *mom* any of *that.* It was about to be hard enough explaining the fucking age difference... I didn't know how bad she was going to freak about the eighteen-year gap in our ages but I damn sure knew Grandma was going to freak the fuck out.

"I really like him," I said and tried not to let on how serious we were already.

"Yeah?" she asked, "How much?"

Her smile was genuine and I just didn't have the heart to come clean about even our ages – not yet anyway. She hadn't gotten a really super up-close look at Striker yet to notice. He'd been wearing his sunglasses when she'd met him at the Iron Horse briefly on the poker run/family day thing we'd thrown together and she hadn't been home when he'd returned me to the house.

"Like... a lot," I said with an awkward shrug. "We like a lot of the same things, and he's super smart. I learn things from him all the time and talking to him is fun."

"Learn things like what?" she asked, grinning.

"Mom!" I cried and threw one of the patio couch pillows at her. She caught it, laughing, and stuffed it behind her.

I took another hit, and handed her back the joint and she took it to finish it off.

"What's his name, again?" she asked.

"Striker," I said after a long pause in which I held in the green smoke long enough. I could feel the tension in my back and neck start to loosen as the high started to take effect.

"What kind of a name is that?" she asked, wrinkling her nose.

I rolled my eyes, "Quit acting brand new – you've lived around this shit longer than I've been alive. It's his road name."

"What's his real name?" she asked.

"Zachary," I said.

"Zachary..." she drew out his name, fishing for a last name and I snorted.

"I know his last name," I said. "What're you gonna do? Run a background check on him?" for some reason, likely because we were high, we both started laughing at that and the giggles became infectious until both of us were nearly pissing ourselves laughing.

"You know your daddy would," she said and for a fraction of a second my heart seized in my breast and the thought flashed through my brain; *she knows! How the hell does she know?* That was, of course, *before* it clicked, that she meant 'Daddy' as in my *actual father.*

"Oh, pfft! For sure!" I agreed, hoping my face or body language hadn't given anything away.

"It took everything in him not to threaten your prom date, he *hated* that kid."

I snorted and laughed at that – *I* had hated my prom date by the time prom actually happened. I would have been *much* better off going stag or whatever, because *fuck Riley Acosta.* Jerk.

He'd gone around telling *everyone* how he was going to knock me up with a prom night dumpster baby and how he didn't give a fuck. He'd be at the University of Tennessee before I could even come up with a positive pregnancy test.

Creepy fucker.

I told my mom about it and she stared at me aghast.

"This Striker guy better not be anything like that," she said.

I smiled in spite of myself and said, "Not even remotely. Striker is more mature than that, for one, and part of the reason I like him so much is... I don't know... I feel safe with him. He's not like that at all, otherwise I would have already dropped him like a bad habit."

"Yeah, well, if he ever turns that way you'd better."

I smiled at my mom and told her the truth as I stretched and felt a few satisfying pops in my back, "Don't worry, Mom, all I have is you and Dad to look to as examples. You guys were pure couple's goals. I won't settle for anything less. I promise you that."

Shit, it was the wrong thing to say, because she stared at me for several moments and then broke down right into tears.

"Oh, Mom, I didn't mean it like that," I said, scooching down the couch at her and wrapping her up in a tight hug.

"No, no!" she said, waving me off some. "I know, it's just – I'm so damn proud of you!"

I sniffed tearing up because *she* was teared up and said, "What?"

"I'm so proud of you! You know what's right and what not to put up with, and I'm proud of you!"

Ah, shucks...

"I love you, Mom..."

I mean, what the hell else was there to say?

CHAPTER THIRTY-ONE

S triker…

My girl was cagey, and didn't like to ask for help. It was one of her more endearing, yet frustrating qualities about her – her fierce independence. I kept trying to tell her that, *yes*, I understood that she *could* do it all by herself – but that didn't mean I *wanted* her to. That I was here, and I *wanted* to help.

She just wasn't great at cooperating with me on that front – which also suited me just fine because it led to some awesome and sexy funishments. No, you didn't read that wrong. I mean, sure, I could punish her but why punish someone for a quality that you actually appreciated? No, I introduced my kitten to the word *funishment* – which was a consequence of her not asking for help, sure – but it also wasn't too unpleasant for her to be considered a true *punishment*.

Example: she didn't call me when her kitchen sink backed up and she needed to take it apart underneath. She should have. She wasted the better part of two whole days on the problem – battling with do-it-yourself online tutorial videos and going back and forth to the hardware store for parts, getting the wrong things and not being able to return 'em, and a whole host of other headaches. All of which she could have avoided if I'd known the fucking problem... but *nope*.

I asked why her granddad hadn't helped her out, and she'd laughed and said he was some kind of retired NASA guy and wasn't very handy.

Could he math out a bunch of physics shit to the nth degree and bring an astronaut home out of space? Yeah, in his head, almost as fast as a calculator, but put a wrench in his hand? He would ask which end to use – so no dice, there.

So, to teach her the benefit of having me around, I taught her a lesson in just what I could do with my hands and I didn't get tired.

I made her orgasm until she complained the next day about feeling like she'd had the worst fuckin' ab workout in the known world rather than a series of never-ending orgasms that had rocked her shit.

So, when my phone rang in the middle of the day and her smiling face flashed across my screen, I was glad I'd just dropped the handset to my desk phone back in its cradle and that I could take her call.

On picking up, I didn't even get so much as a 'hello' before one of her brother's screaming and crying came through the line. My smile dropped right off my face and I demanded, *"What's wrong?"* before she could even draw breath to speak.

"Aden got his little butt busted and is being *way* more dramatic than things call for," she said and I heard her blow wisps of her blonde hair out of her face on the other end of the line.

"Oh yeah? What'd he do?" I asked, leaning back in my chair.

"Flushing things down the toilet that don't belong in the toilet – and now it's stuck, Mom's freaking the fuck out because we can't afford a plumber, the boys' bathroom isn't working, Pops and Mimi are out of town, and it's not like they'd be much help anyway and I'm officially over here waving the white flag. I need help. Please tell me your offer on emergency plumbing work is still good after the last fiasco?"

I was trying not to laugh, because of course it would be the boys doing and yeah – no, my girl definitely didn't need to be dealing with icky toilets.

"I've got you," I said. "I can head over in about a half an hour as soon as the shop closes down. Just let me run home and get my truck and throw some tools in the back."

"Might not need them," she said. "My dad's got a garage full of everything you could possibly need for a house. He was the handy guy and could fix just about anything around here and did. I just wished I'd paid more attention."

"Oh, hey now – don't beat yourself up, Princess. You've got me for all of that now. You know I'm just a phone call away."

"I know," she said, but sounded both slightly nervous and I figured that was what was up.

Her mom.

She wasn't ready for me to really come out into the light as her boyfriend. She was worried about what her mom would think, but honestly – from the little I'd seen of her mom, she seemed like a smart woman if'n a little overprotective. Which I got that.

"No time like the present to rip that Band-Aid off," I said softly.

"Say what now?" she asked.

"Me meeting your mom as more than just your biker friend..." I said gently.

"Oh, God – you don't think I'm *ashamed* of you or something stupid like that, do you?" she sounded aghast.

I chuckled, and said, "No, I know you aren't baby. Cautious; worried about how your mom is going to feel about it, I get it – believe me... I know how awkward shit can get. I'm down for whatever you need me to be."

She sighed and it was a defeated sound.

"Right now, I need you to be my knight in shining armor on his iron horse and come slay this toilet dragon," she said and she sounded tired.

I had to laugh.

"Toilet dragon?" I asked.

"That's what we think he flushed, a plastic toy dragon figurine, among other things."

"Wonderful," I said dryly.

"Oh, don't even get me started right now. We thought these three skipped the terrible twos and went right over being three-nagers. Nope, apparently, they wanted to pop off at four and they've been just awful lately."

"I think that might be partially my fault," I said. "I'm taking up a lot of their favorite sister's time lately."

"Oh, shit..." she whispered softly.

"Pretty sure I have an idea on that, too – I'll see you in..." I checked the time again, "About an hour and forty-five tops. I'll slay the toilet dragon and meet the family and try to be everyone's sparkling hero."

"That's Forks," Stormy said walking by and overhearing me, and I covered the mouthpiece on my phone and snorted giving him the finger and hoping I didn't accidentally upset Rarity by having her think I was laughing at her.

"Okay," Rarity said and she sounded relieved. "We'll see you then."

"Okay," I told her. "See you then, baby girl."

"I love you," she said softly, as though trying to hide it but needing to say it none the less.

"Daddy loves you too," I said with all the fondness and heart melting sentiment that went with it.

"See you then, bye..."

"See you then. Bye-bye."

We ended the call and I sighed.

"Trouble in paradise?" Stormy asked, and he came back over and dropped into the chair by my desk.

"Ah, nah," I told him. "Boys decided to flush things down the toilet and got it blocked but good. She was just calling in the cavalry."

"Ah," he nodded, "I gotcha."

223

"What's on your mind?" I asked him, knowing the thoughtful look in his deep brown eyes.

He pursed his lips and shook his head and said, "Nothing, brother. Seems like you have it in hand. You happen to need one with the," he cleared his throat, "toilet dragon, you call on the rest of your knights. You got it?"

I laughed and nodded, "I hear you, King Arthur."

"...and the knights of the round toilet bowl," he said and got up, clapping me on the shoulder. We both had a decent laugh and I appreciated him checking on me.

King Stormy and the Knights of the Round Toilet Bowl... Royal Bastards were we.

Jesus Fucking Christ. I couldn't wait to tell Rarity about this one. She'd definitely get a kick out of it.

CHAPTER THIRTY-TWO

arity...

R I opened the door to the house and let out the breath I hadn't known I'd been holding at the sight of Striker on the other side, tool belt slung over his shoulder and a smirk on his full and sexy lips.

God, the way my heart seized in my chest at the sight of him... and *God*, how I just wanted to fling myself into his arms and hide from all the adulting that'd had to go on over the last several hours with the boys being serious butt heads and Mom being in a foul mood and just *all the things*.

It'd been so bad and I thought Mom was going to have a heart attack or stroke to the point I called off of work.

Striker's smile never faltered, if anything it grew as he took me in from behind his mirrored aviators as he said, "You look frazzled, babe."

"You have *no idea*," I told him rolling my eyes and stepping aside as he stepped over the threshold and into the house.

I shut the door behind him, my nerves riding high and a fine buzz settling just under my skin. I felt like any second the shit was going to hit the fan – but I literally had no reason to be so jumpy other than I didn't know what Mom would do. She was going to know Striker was older than me just by looking at him. I just hoped she sort of guessed lower than what he was and I would be happy to, you know, low-key entertain her on her bullshit right up until I couldn't anymore.

Of course, I was hoping by the time things came to light and the air was cleared, it wouldn't matter anymore – you know? I just really hoped that she could and would give him a chance.

"Take me to your toilet dragon's lair," he said and I laughed a little and shook my head.

"This way," I told him.

We passed the kitchen on the left on the way to the boys' bathroom, and Mom glanced over her shoulder at the sink. The boys were in their room on a major time out.

"Hey!" my mom called out. "Hope you like steak and shrimp – dinner is the least I can do for these little monsters fucking up your evening plans."

"It's no problem," Striker said, grinning at her. "I'm happy to help."

She nodded but was pretty wholly absorbed in her grill prep at the sink.

"This way," I said and ushered him quickly down the hall. I touched the boys' bedroom door and said, "Boy's room," and went up the hall a few more steps and touched the opposite door just down from theirs giving it a little shove open, "The dragon's lair."

Striker laughed and slid past me into the bathroom, "Go do whatever your mom needs help with for dinner, fair Princess," he said using his pet name for me and giving me a wink after raising his sunglasses on the top of his head. "I'll slay this dragon."

I grinned and shook my head and couldn't help myself, laughing with him.

"Be brave my valiant knight," I leaned down and smacked a kiss on his lips and he set his tool belt down and started his explorations of the problem.

I went back out to the kitchen and quietly started picking out three good sized potatoes and three little ones for the boys. When Mom grilled, everyone liked her baked potatoes to go with things.

The boys liked steak, but they wouldn't be getting any. Mom was making them teriyaki chicken breast instead. You didn't get steak for acting like little buttholes – plus, steak was expensive and these had been on sale which is the only reason she'd snatched them and there were only three in the pack.

Striker was in there earning his steak for sure right now, the boys could deal with chicken. It wouldn't kill them, and yet I still felt bad for them.

Mom's steak was just that good.

"Don't forget to butter and salt crust those before you wrap them," my mom said as she coated the chicken breasts with marinade.

"Did you want me to even make the boys up potatoes, or did you want me to get the rice cooker going for them?" I asked.

She stopped and thought about it, and said, "You know what? Rice cooker – no potatoes for them tonight."

Eek, Mom was *really* miffed.

"Okay." I didn't even try to argue on their behalf. They'd pretty much done it all today. Hitting, kicking, cussing, throwing things at each other, flushing things down the toilet – and just generally being destructive little dicks.

Terroristic tots had replaced my sweet angel babies today, and it seriously felt like only a goddamn exorcism would bring them back.

"Have they been quiet?" our mom asked and I froze.

"Shit," I said.

"Fuck," she echoed and she went.

A moment later I heard her, "Oh, my God!" and when the crying *instantly* started, I knew it was bad.

"Need help?" I called.

"No!" she hollered back and *swat!* There went one of them screaming at the top of his lungs.

Well, shit.

"Whoa, whoa, whoa!" I heard Striker holler – "Just what did you get into little man?" and the chaos just burbled over from there.

I abandoned my prep work with a heavy sigh and went to see what was going on now and Jesus Christ!

"Where the hell did they get a permanent marker!" I cried as my mom finished giving the next boy a swat. I caught the third before he could make his escape. Striker had the first on the bathroom counter and was doing his best to scrub marker off his skin but yeah – that wasn't happening.

Mom got the one I had a hold of and gave him a swat and I took Caden with me to the kitchen. He was squalling like we'd put both his brothers through a woodchipper in front of him and I could see Mom was *this close* to losing her shit – and truth – as the one who had been dealing with this bullshit *all day* while she'd been at work?

I could feel the frustrated tears gathering in my own eyes as I sat Caden on the kitchen island and took his glasses off his little ink smeared face.

Striker came in a moment later with Aden under one arm and Braden under the other, my mom stalking past the both of us and going out to the back porch.

"I told her to go have a puff – you need to go to?" he asked.

"Yes, but no," I said through gritted teeth.

"Right, let's get them scrubbed off, and put them into pajamas. It's getting to be about that time."

"Yes, it is," I agreed. Way past time if you asked me.

We got them in baths, scrubbed the worst of it off through protests, screaming, and squalling, and got the boys into clean pajamas while Mom tried to sort out their bedroom.

It was a tomorrow problem. Just too overwhelming for tonight.

Once in PJs, they got a plain, hurried dinner of chicken and rice, and then it was *straight* to bed.

It was a damn whirlwind of activity – but Striker was our hero.

"You got kids of your own?" my mother had asked him, and I knew her suspicions were valid – Striker had been *really* good with the boys.

"Nah," he said. "I'm just everybody's favorite crazy uncle," he told her and I had to smile at that. I could definitely buy that.

"Had a lot of practice wrangling the smaller kids at church growing up – and my mom ran an in-home daycare, so I've had a lot of practice. For sure, though – your three tiny terrors have been enough to keep anyone from wanting any just like 'em tonight," he shook his head. "I don't know how y'all do it."

"Me either sometimes," my mom said. She heaved a big sigh.

"If you ladies don't mind, I'm going to get back to what I came here to do and wrangling those little demons has worked up quite the appetite."

"Shit, God, yeah!" My mom shook her head as though coming out of a daze and said, "Rarity – potatoes and salad. I'm sure the grill is hot and ready and good to go."

"Potatoes are already on and have been for..." I checked the time. "Shit, they're probably ready."

"Good girl!" my mom crowed.

"I'll get on that salad and you get on the steak and shrimp and it shouldn't be long at all before dinner is up," I said.

"Sounds good. Teamwork makes the dream work – go team," Striker said and he disappeared back in the direction of the boys' bathroom.

Mom took the platter of seasoned steaks and shrimp skewers out with her and I set to work throwing together a quick and dirty garden salad in one of our big bowls.

Mom came back to wash the platter and reuse it, calling out to Striker, asking how he liked his steak. Medium-rare, just like us, so that was great.

Before long, I was calling for him to wash up and while he did, I set the table for three.

We were all three so worn out we didn't have it in us for small talk around the table for which I was grateful. Striker said he was going to have to pull the whole toilet, and may have to replace the whole thing if he couldn't get the stupid toy out of it. He was frustrated, too – and the food definitely helped out *a lot.*

He told me and Mom to go to bed. Mom said, "I'm going to have to. I have work tomorrow."

"I'm good for a while longer," I said. "Go to bed, Mom. I've got clean up."

"You are my golden child right now," she said and I snorted.

"Don't ask me how I know," Striker said, "But Axe body spray takes permanent marker right off of any wall."

"Okay, why?" My mom asked. "Why would *anyone* know that?"

Striker laughed, and I laughed too and he shook his head.

"I'm a boy who hangs out with *a lot* of boys – and all of us have been dumb at one time or another. Pretty sure I got a can of it out in my truck – again – *don't ask.*"

"You know what?" my mom said. "I'm not going to. I'm just going to say, 'thank you' to the both of you, take the win, and say goodnight."

"Night, Mom," I murmured and hugged her back as she awkwardly hugged me.

She went to bed, and I was glad that she wasn't so stressed that she hadn't eaten, that most of her plate was clear except a little baked potato and the fat from her steak which we saved for the cats as a treat to find in their bowl.

Striker leaned back and looked at me after he'd said his own thanks for the fine meal and that he hoped my mom would get some rest.

We stared at each other for a long minute and he reached out and cupped y cheek, smoothing a thumb over the soft skin and murmuring, "It's okay if you need to fall apart a minute, baby girl. I've got you, now."

I sniffed and breathed deep and shook my head.

"Maybe after clean up," I said and he nodded.

"Need a little help?" he asked.

I shook my head.

"No, you go on."

"Trust me, I'll get it fixed, even if I have to call King Stormy himself, and all the rest of the Knights of the Round Toilet Bowl."

I snorted and started laughing. I couldn't help it.

"The Royal Bastards are we." He thumped his fist over his heart twice and held it up like some kind of ancient Knight bro code and I lost it into an absolute *fit* of giggles to the point I had to stuff both hands against my mouth to keep from completely losing my shit and disturbing my mom.

He grinned at me and winked. I couldn't help but feel *much* better about things.

CHAPTER THIRTY-THREE

S triker...

I left Rarity to clean up the kitchen from dinner, after holding her for a time and leaving her with a kiss to her forehead at the sink.

This fucking toilet was fixin' to slay *me*. I wasn't going to be able to fix it tonight. I was seriously about to take it out back and smash it with a fuckin' hammer just for the fuckin' satisfaction – when it happened. There was a noise, and a pop. When I picked the fucking thing up off its base, there was this goddamned rubber dragon like a rubber ducky for bath time or whatever – but not a duck.

"Motherfucker," I swore.

"Everything okay?"

"Jesus, princess!" I pressed a hand to my chest after jumping sky high. She was lucky I was in an awkward position with nothing at hand. I could have hurt her.

"Shit, I'm sorry – I didn't mean to startle you," she said.

"Just make some fuckin' noise or something next time, I'm a vet and we all got some sort of sand demons just looking for an opportunity to ruin us and everything we love if we're not careful. I would never hurt you on purpose – you know that, but *damn*."

"No, I know!" she said quickly. "I get it, I'm sorry."

"All good," I reassured her.

"Whatcha got?" she asked.

I picked up the dragon.

"The head, body, and the rest of your mighty foe, my princess. Your dragon has been slayed!" I tossed it in the sink. "I'm taking that fucker with me, too – I earned its ass."

She laughed and said, "My hero," before rolling her eyes.

"I'm not going to be able to put this back in tonight. I wanna get a new wax ring and make sure it gets a good seal. If I was a less stable man, I'd smash the fuckin' thing on principle it was that big of a pain in my ass – but a penny saved is a penny earned and not worth the price of a new john."

"I wouldn't blame you if you did smash it," she said, crossing her arms and leaning her hip against the sink top – "or if you ran screaming from the chaos that is my life with these three little bridge trolls."

"Nah," I said, shaking my head, and turning to wash my hands thoroughly with soap and water at the boys' sink. "Why would you even say that?" I asked.

She didn't say anything for such a long time I had to look over my shoulder to make sure she was still there at the other end of the counter. She wouldn't look at me, and gave a sort of shrug, which was a total non-answer.

I shut off the water, shook off my hands in the bowl of the sink, and grabbed the hand towel out of the ring, turning to square up with her and try and get it out of her what was eating her.

"Just feeling insecure, I guess," she said and I pulled her to me.

"How can I help?" I asked and she rested her forehead against my chest, letting her hands slip from beneath her arms and go around my waist. She melted into me, and I took the weight she carried and hefted it like it was nothing – knowing that to her, she carried the weight of her family's world on those delicate slim shoulders.

"I love you, Rarity Mitchell," I said finally, into her hair. "You're sweet. You're kind. Your brothers are a handful, sure – but today was just a real bad day and tomorrow will be better."

"What if it's not?" she asked piteously.

"Then the day after that will be better," I told her with a chuckle.

"How can you know?" she asked petulantly.

"Because the bad days like today? They don't last forever," I reassured her.

"I'm scared my mom isn't going to get the chance to know you and love you as much as I do before my grandmother ruins it all."

It was one of the rawest things I'd ever heard come out of her mouth and it made me freeze.

"What do you mean?" I asked innocently, but I already knew and my heart cracked right down the middle for the soft and fearful tone she'd used to make her initial confession.

"My mom's mom is nothing like me or my mom," she said. "She's very... particular... gossipy and judgy. Like I don't tell *anyone* at the craft store *anything* about my home life or life outside of work because I know those old biddies would narc me out to gran in a heartbeat."

"Okay," I said carefully.

"The *only* reason I waved the white flag today was because they're out of town," she said. "I'm just not ready for World War Three to break out in the house because gran *will* pitch a fit and I don't want any fighting... but mostly I'm scared my mom's opinion about you will be colored by what Grandma is going to have to say about us and I'm just not ready for the peace I feel with you to be disturbed or for you to rightfully say 'fuck this shit' and walk away because of all the drama."

I chuckled then, and held her tighter and said, "I like a little chaos. Thrive on it, actually – I wouldn't be a Royal Bastard if I didn't."

"I'm afraid we're going to be too much chaos for even the Royal Bastards," she said miserably and I had to fight not to have a fit of laughter loud enough to wake anyone in the house.

"We'll cross all of those bridges when we come to 'em baby girl," I promised, stroking a hand down her long, smooth, blonde hair.

"Promise, Daddy?" she whispered so quietly I barely heard her.

"I promise," I assured her out loud since she hadn't caught the promise in my voice alone.

"I love you too much to want to let go," she said and she sounded on the verge of tears. "You make my life so much better."

I smiled at that, and held her tight, "Who else you gonna find to come slay your toilet dragons at a moment's notice?" I asked, and she snorted and buried her face in my chest to keep from laughing too loud.

Of all the dragons I had to possibly slay for my fair princess, I hadn't expected her grandmother to be the one. She'd seemed nice enough at the Iron Horse on the family day for all the exchange was pretty brief.

I wondered about some things now.

It was definitely some food for thought.

I tucked my girl into bed not long after and it tore me apart to leave and not get beneath the covers with her – but there would be plenty of opportunity for that later.

I went home, got some sleep, ground through a half a day at work the next day and took care of the more pressing shit, and ducked my head into Stormy's office to let him know what was up.

"Yeah, man – go ahead," he said. "It's quiet enough around here."

"Thanks, man," I said and I'd left early. A quick run past the hardware store, and I was on my way back to Rarity.

I didn't need my truck, so I'd left it back at St. Augustine. The tools I'd left at her place could easily fit in the saddlebag of my bike for the return trip. I would re-install her toilet and see if her brothers would behave for a chance at an all-expenses-paid trip to the Gator Farm up my way.

She was radiant when she answered the door, even if she was still frayed around the edges some.

"How goes it? Crew pull another mutiny today?" I asked.

"The beatings will continue until morale improves," she said rolling her eyes and stepping aside to let me into the house.

The living room was a war zone of toys and little boys playing robots, one of the Transformers movies on the screen.

"Who's dat?" one of them asked, running up.

"Guys," Rarity called, and the other two stopped their WWE wrestling moves long enough to scramble over and join their brother.

"I was here last night. Don't you remember?" I asked them.

"Yeah," three little voices chorused back at me.

"Aden, Braden, and Caden – meet my friend Striker. Striker, these are my little brothers who were being stubborn little billy goats last night."

"Ah huh." I nodded sagely. "I remember that. Have you boys been good today?"

"Yes," they all chorused.

"No," Rarity recited with them and frowned.

"Well, how come they say 'yes' and you say 'no'?" I asked.

"Throwing food at each other at the breakfast table is being good?" Rarity asked her siblings with an arched eyebrow.

"No," they all chorused sadly and I fought not to laugh.

"Tell you boys what. I'll make you a deal."

They all perked up.

"You behave yourselves the rest of the week and this weekend, I'll take you, and your sister – your mom, grandparents – whoever you want, to the Alligator Farm up by where I live."

"Alligator farm?" Braden asked.

"Real life dinosaurs," I said, nodding wisely.

"What?" That definitely got Aden's attention and Caden was just as curious.

"Only if you're good for sissy," I told them. "And your mom, and your memaw and pop-pop."

The boys all looked at Rarity who said, "Don't look at me. The deal's with him!"

"Can you do that?" I asked them.

"Yeah," I got back from all three.

"Okay, go back to your movie and sit quiet now while I finish fixing your potty."

"Okay." All three went back to the couch and climbed up on it.

Rarity looked after them for a moment and then turned to me.

"That's awfully expensive," she tried to argue, and I chuckled.

"Not when two of your club brothers practically run the place. The Boucher brothers got us handled. All it'll cost me is snacks and drinks."

"Are you serious?" she asked.

"As a heart attack," I told her.

"I'm going to text Mom," she said and she looked both so grateful and so relieved.

"I got you, let me get started on getting their toilet back in."

"Thank you," she said, and she sounded grateful to the bottom of her heart, which did mine some good.

"Anytime and anything for you, princess," I said softly and made my way in the direction of the boy's bathroom.

She broke for the kitchen and her phone sitting on the kitchen island.

I meant it, too – anything for her. My love for that girl was growing with every passing moment, let alone every passing day; and the more I saw her interact with her family, the more I wanted to do for them, too.

CHAPTER THIRTY-FOUR

R arity...

Grandma and grandpa were back from the Keys, and so it was all seven of us for the Gator Farm that weekend.

Striker was meeting us there, and we all piled in to my mom's van for the ride up to St. Augustine. I brought a backpack full of things for an overnight if I could somehow manage to get left behind. I knew Striker would be good for a ride home.

I really hoped that things went well, but Grandma was already in one of her moods, nit picking about *everything* from the passenger seat up front as Mom drove while Grandpa and I say back in the third-row seating behind the row of boys in front of us in their car seats.

While they hadn't precisely gone back to being pious little angels, their fits and bouts had rapidly and diminished in the extreme enough that we were a go for the outing. Plus, how often could you get free admission to a place like the Gator Farm? We weren't able to afford many experiences for the boys like that – so there was no way we could pass it up.

Striker was waiting for us outside in the parking lot, leaned up against his bike in the sparse shade from one of the flowering tall bushes planted between rows of cars in the parking lot.

He pushed off and started walking toward us as my mom crept down the lines of parked cars looking for an open space.

"Who is this man, again?" my grandmother asked, peering over her shoulder past me and Grandpa out the dusty back window as he strolled up the lane behind us and Mom turned us into a wide-open spot at the end.

"Rarity's new boyfriend," my mom answered and I felt the weirdest conflicting emotions. Like I both blushed and had the color drain out of my face at the same time!

On the one hand, my mom saying it so casually, and with not so much as a hint of having a problem with it in her tone, elated me. Of course, the fact that Striker and I were clearly outed in front of my grandmother gave me such a damn fright! It made everything feel like it was much higher stakes than it had the moment before.

The noise and the chaos of my family piling out of the van matched what was going on in my heart and my head as the panic rose and my grandmother's voice, laced with a mixture of curiosity and disapproval just made my nerves jangle harder.

All of it was silenced when I hopped out of the back of the van, the last one out, and overbalanced, pitching forward only to be folded right into Striker's arms.

I swear, the second they closed around me? Everything just... stopped.

I was home. The one and only place that made all the noise stop and that shut out all the bullshit. My brothers. My mom. My grandparents. The bar. The stress. The overwhelmingness of it all just gone – *poof!*

"Hey baby, you doin' alright?" he asked close to my ear and I smiled and twined my arms around his neck and hugged him to me tight and said, "Never better, now."

"Good to hear," he said with a chuckle and I lowered myself from my toes down flat on my feet again.

Mom, Grandpa, and Grandma had one of each of the boys in hand, and Striker had mine in his as we traversed the sun scorched blacktop in the direction of the red building with its frescoes of swamp and alligators in bright muraled panels between the red painted supports and the like.

We went through the front door, and Striker stepped up to the ticketing window with me.

"Striker, party of eight," he said. "It's on the Boucher Brothers."

The person behind the window checked a clipboard, got on a radio, and a minute later, Skull slipped into the box office from a door in the back, and plucked an envelope off the clipboard and slid it out the slot to Striker.

"Come on back, y'all – I got something good for the kids," he said and he gave me a wink. I smiled and Striker stopped long enough to hook us all up with special guest wristbands before we went through the turnstile and into the park, or zoo, or whatever you called it honestly.

The building was sort of hollow, or a ring, around a big central depressed pool or lagoon surrounded by fencing. There was an observation platform that had a set of stairs up to it and Bones was up there, fiddling with something or other.

We went around the pool, the stink of lizard – or really rather gator, hanging thick on the humid air and boy did it *stink*. The mustiness of a giant lizard tank with underpinnings of rot and decay from the swampy brackish water the gators were in.

We followed Skull up the steps to where his brother, Bones, was tying rotten pieces of chicken to long, bamboo poles, like a fishing rod.

"Wanna feed some gators?" Skull asked the boys who all looked at each other and lit up like I'd never seen before.

"Yeah!"

It was fun watching the boys get to engage and do something so cool. Mom, Grandpa, and even *I* got in on the action and for real, even standing so high up above, *feeling* the gator snap on the end of the line on that piece of stinky chicken was something. The way the pole jerked in your hand as the animal did its death roll or whatever – *lord.*

I'd lived in Florida my whole life, had even seen some swamp puppies in the wild, sunning themselves on the banks of the waterways near the house – but I'd never been *this close* nor had I ever been on the other end of a pole or anything they actually had a hold of.

It was a whole new type of fear and respect I'd learned on that platform because *holy Christ!*

Aden, Braden, and Caden were *bursting* at the seams with questions; all of which, the Boucher brothers answered with patience and kindness that surprised even me. Striker winked at me when I looked up and marveled at him, and I couldn't help but grin.

"What say we get washed up, have a little lunch, and see the rest of the place?" Striker suggested. "Catch the Butcher Brothers' next show?"

We couldn't argue with that.

The Gator Farm had a seating area and sort of a built-in kiosk with snack and lunch food items. You know, the kind of stuff you'd find at any ballpark. Hot dogs, nachos which were just tortilla rounds with the fake liquid cheese sauce in a cardboard boat. We all sat down at one of the big round tables, made for a big family, but still had to pull chairs from other tables to be able to all sit.

It was busy, in here, families and kids milling about and some looking at us with envy for what we'd gotten to do with the showrunners and the gators.

"So... Striker," my grandmother said, and I felt myself freeze with a nacho halfway in my face. "What do you do?"

"I work in the warehousing and accounts division of my buddy's custom bike shop here in St. Augustine," he answered truthfully.

"Oh! And does that pay well?" she asked.

"Barbra!" my grandfather sounded horrified, even as my mom spat; "Jesus, Mom!"

"What!?" she exclaimed. "I'm just curious, that's all."

"It's all good," Striker said affably, putting a reassuring hand on my knee beneath the table. "I actually do better than you might expect. Our shop is one of the best in the country. One of those places that gets recognized internationally, even."

"Really?" my grandmother asked, and didn't bother to keep the genuine surprise out of her voice.

Like we were some kind of family with pedigree or whatever. *Don't make me laugh...* Grandpa had done well for himself when he'd worked for NASA; and my dad had done well with what he'd done when he was alive, but Granddad was retired now, and that only went so far. His pension had been good, but the more that time went on and the more inflation rose, and the tougher things had gotten it didn't go nearly as far as it would have, in, say, the 1990s.

They were with Mom and I because they were struggle-bussing just as much as we were and we were helping *each other* out... but to hear my grandmother tell it, it was her and grandpa and his retirement funding my mother, myself, and the boys after her son-in-law's tragic death. Like we didn't contribute at all. Like we were orphan waifs and desperate... and yeah, we kind of were screwed; but it wasn't like I didn't work two jobs, my mom didn't hold down a fairly decent job of her own or any of that.

No, it was all my grandparent's charity.

Like I could roll my eyes any harder...

It was so complicated though. Like, I loved my grandma, and I wanted her to love all of us back – but sometimes it just didn't feel like she could... I mean, if you love someone, you can worry about them without the whole nitpicking them apart, or complaining or wildly gossiping or bandying about your disapproval of this, that, or the other – right?

When Dad was alive, interacting with Grandma had been much easier for both Mom and myself, being that he kind of acted like a shield for the both of us... but with Dad gone? It was like Mom was starving for Grandma's approval all over again and she would bend the knee whatever it took, and most of the time? It took me going under the bus. Or at least, so it felt like to me.

I knew it was coming... but it was like any accident or collision – you knew it was coming, you could see it was coming, the dread and suspense and anxiety of it was building, the utter horror at what was to come – knowing it would be bad. Knowing that bones would crunch, blood would spray, and it would be all kinds of gory and you wouldn't be able to unsee *any* of it, but God dammit, you still couldn't look away.

I could do confrontation all damn night at the bar. I could even do it all damn day at the craft store... or when it came to keeping the boys in line, but when it came to my grandma or my mom – I couldn't tell you how much I avoided it and didn't want to deal with it.

My grandmother ran through a bunch of seemingly innocent questions with Striker, but I knew she was fishing and it would only be a matter of time before she found something to be unhappy about.

"How long have you been doing that? Working for your friend, I mean," she asked.

Striker was polite and succinct in his answer, and I put my hand over where his rested on my knee and gave it a warning squeeze.

I'd come clean about what she could be like, had spilled all of my fears, and he was honestly the only person I felt like I was free to do that with, you know? He was certainly the only person I was comfortable doing it with.

"And before that?" she asked and I swear it almost felt like my throat was closing up.

"US Military service, Army Stryker brigade. I've done several tours," he said and he definitely was clipped talking about his service. I knew he didn't like talking about it. Hated the hero worship that came with it, because as he'd confided in me in one of our late-night talks – he didn't feel like what he'd done over there was any type of 'hero shit.' His words, not mine.

"Well, thank you for your service!" my grandfather said, and all Striker did was give him a tight nod, once up, and once down acknowledging the thanks politely.

I could see my grandmother doing the calculations in her head, like that one internet GIF of the woman with that just *look* of confused concentration as the math equations in sheer gibberish went up around her head.

"How old are you, Striker?" my grandmother asked.

Shit. Fuck. Goddammit, here we go, I thought.

"I'm forty-two," he answered honestly and the table suddenly went very still and very quiet as Grandma, Grandpa, *and* Mom all traded glances.

"Forty-two?" my grandmother asked innocently, as though she hadn't heard him plain as day.

"Yes, ma'am," he said.

My mom surprised me then. She met my eyes and with a faint smile said, "I always knew my Rarity would see older men, she's got an old soul."

Aw, Mom...

I took a deep breath, and tried not to tear up, because I hadn't expected that. My mom hardly ever stood up for me where Grandma was concerned but she'd clearly just put out her flag on top of this hill and proclaimed she was going to die on it with that endorsement.

I stared at my mom and tried to telegraph all of my gratitude and love with that one look, and she smiled over the top of Caden's head who was seated in her lap, and gave a slight nod back.

I don't know why she did it, but it meant the world to me that she was on my side with this one.

Striker and my grandmother traded questions and answers, and I could tell Grandma was getting worked up and didn't like things one bit.

I guess Striker saw the signs, too and rather than continue engaging to where my grandmother caused a scene, he said, "Why don't y'all enjoy the park some more, I'd like to take Rarity over on yonder to see something cool about this place. We'll meet back up at the bleachers for the show at three o'clock."

"That sounds great," my mom said with a big smile, heading off my grandmother's argument which she had barely gotten to draw breath to try and make.

Striker stood up right then and there and held a hand down to me, I took it, even though I wasn't done eating and I was still hungry. *Anything* to extricate myself from my grandmother feeling like she was some kind of bloodhound on a scent.

We excused ourselves and wandered in whatever direction he wanted to take me.

"Sorry, Princess," he murmured softly as we went up over one of the boardwalks around the main alligator pit where the shows happened.

"It's okay," I said with a nervous laugh. "Anything is better than sitting through one of gran's humiliating third degrees."

"Still hungry?" he asked.

"Yeah," I said ruefully.

"Come on, there's another concession stand thing over on this way, I'll get you a cinnamon sugar pretzel."

"That sounds really good," I confessed. "What did you want to show me?" I asked. "Or was that just a ruse to get me out of there?"

He chuckled, "I actually *did* want to show you something. The accidental rookery."

"Accidental rookery?" I asked.

"Yeah, you see all the nesting birds up over the gator pits," he said pointing up into the trees over the ponds and enclosures.

"I wondered about that," I said. "I thought it was a feature – you know? Like they brought the birds here."

"Some of 'em that are in enclosures, sure – but look up, past the trees, there's no net keeping these birds in here. They build their nests over the alligators to keep 'em safe from things like predatory raccoons."

"Oh, shit!" I did a double-take, "That's wild!"

"It gets really cool the other end of the park over this way," he pointed in the direction we were going. "The birds are so used to the people, they got their nests at eye level and a little below.

"We can see eggs and baby birds?" I asked.

"Yup," he grinned at me.

"Aw, yay!"

I wrapped both my arms around his one and laced my fingers through his and he chuckled.

"I thought you might like that," he said, and the further I walked with him from my family, the more centered I felt. The more I felt like I could *breathe*.

CHAPTER THIRTY-FIVE

S triker...

Giving my girl the breather from her grandma had been the right call. The further into the park we wandered, the higher we climbed the varying levels of steps and onto platforms and boardwalks into the aviary, the more she seemed to relax.

We stole some kisses in the shade, and I held her hand in mine for as long as possible, kissing her knuckles every chance I got.

Eventually, we ran back into her family as, of course, Grandma had insisted on coming around this way with the boys to see what was over here.

She was a conniver, that one – thrived on drama. I knew the type. My mother was just like her. Like my mother, I'd bet even money that Rarity's memaw had been one of the mean girls in high school back in the '60s or whenever she'd gone.

The thing about mean girls is they pretty much top out at their peak in high school, and then spend the rest of their natural lives in the same damn mindset. They weren't smart or talented enough to do anything else.

I kept Rarity under my wing and we went and enjoyed the show,

Skull and Bones putting gators through their paces and demonstrating their formidable and awesome power. Bones coming on through the audience with a baby cayman on its back, little snout taped shut, to let people stroke its belly and watch it fall pretty much instantly asleep.

The boys were rapt, and Mom looked like she was enjoying herself as thoroughly as her kids, meanwhile, Grandma tried and failed to pry while myself and her granddad stone walled her the best we could.

Finally, it was a trip through the giftshop where I sprang for four stuffed alligators. Three green ones and a white one for my girl. It was supposed to be a match for the white gator they had here – but it wasn't an albino. It was something else entirely as it didn't have the red eyes of an albino but rather blue. Something about a pigmentation mutation in its genes or some shit.

It was what'd gotten Skull and Bones on board with this place. They'd caught the thing in the wild, practically just coming out of the nest. Had brought it here and the rest was pretty much history.

They were born trappers and hunters, and they made regular trips on down into the Glades to help thin the over population of invasive species reptiles and shit that'd gotten loose in the aftermath of Hurricane Andrew and had proceeded to breed wild and decimate the local eco-system.

A whole wing of the Gator Farm was shit that they'd caught and brought in up here to display and educate about the ecosystems and shit of the swamp. They'd really been the ones to turn this place around from a rundown roadside attraction with just a few alligators and snakes, into the wild attraction that it was now featuring species from all over the fuckin' world and then some.

It was impressive shit.

"Well, it was very nice meeting you Striker," Grandma declared in this tone that made me straight up believe that butter wouldn't melt in her mouth.

"Likewise, ma'am," I said. "You wanna grab your bag?" I asked

Rarity and she nodded, going for the back of the van and where she'd stashed her backpack.

"What?" her grandmother looked surprised, "No, you're coming home with us," she said and I tried not to snort and laugh at the look Rarity's Mom and Granddad exchanged behind the woman's back.

"I'll be home tomorrow," Rarity said and came back over to me.

"Today is a *family* day, Rarity Jane," her grandmother said, tone dripping with disapproval, and she gave me a faint, brittle smile, that just plain pissed me off as she said to me, "You understand, of course."

"I surely do," I said. "Family day was fun, and it's over now – so if you don't mind, I'm going to take Rarity here for a walk on the beach and a meetup with some of our friends for dinner tonight."

"But—"

"Oh, Mom, just *let it go!* Rarity deserves some time off and to have some fun with people her own age!" Rarity's mom glared at her mother as she turned around from buckling the last of the boys in.

"Except he's *not* her own age!" her grandmother said ruthlessly.

Ah, and there it was...

"Rarity?" I asked. "You happy?"

"Very," she said, hugging into my side and giving her grandmother a worse than a withering look. She wore a sad and disappointed one.

"Well, the boys..." her grandmother tried to argue, but it was Granddad to the rescue with a firm, "Barbara."

Her grandma looked pissed and Rarity stood up just a little straighter and said, "I'm twenty-four, and not *five*. I'll see you all *tomorrow*."

I smiled and gave her a bit of a squeeze, but I could tell, the fight with Grandma was far from over. Grandma glared at me, a wintery look, but here was the thing – I ran my own life. She didn't dictate what I did, what Rarity did, and I was damn sure looking forward to defiling her granddaughter every which way from Sunday tonight, just for the satisfaction of knowing how much it would piss *Barbra* off if she knew just what we got up to.

"Get in the car, Mom," Rarity's mom snapped, and I had a feeling she was about to give her mom and maybe even her dad some hell on the way home. Didn't matter how old they were – they deserved it as far as I was concerned. Barbara for being Barbara, and Gramps for, well, being such a fuckin' pushover and letting his wife run roughshod over everybody. I mean, for fuck's sake – *be a man.*

Rarity cast a grateful look to her mother and I steered her away toward my bike.

"Jesus Christ, that woman doesn't know when to quit, does she?" I asked.

"I am *so* sorry," Rarity said, stopping at my bike to set her backpack on the seat to open it up and put her prize snowy gator stuffy into it for the ride.

"Baby, you ain't got nothing to be sorry for. I have a feeling ol' granny's met her match. I don't give a fuck if she likes me or not. I'm in it to win it with *you*, not her."

"Yeah, but what about when she doubles down?" she asked. "It wears on you, and fast – believe me."

"Shit, she wants to fuck around, she can find out," I told her.

"What's that supposed to mean?" she asked, shrugging back into her backpack.

"It means, whatever you want and need to do, that's up to you and I'm here for it. If she wants to get so insufferable that you spend more time up here and less down there, I'd be happy to make that happen. It's whatever's good for you, baby girl."

"You really mean that, don't you?" she asked softly, staring up at me with no little wonder on her face.

"Damn straight. She can fuckin' try me," I said. "I mean, shit; she's just like my mother; in fact, my mother is arguably *worse* – so to be perfectly honest with you, better bitches than your grandmother have tried and look how that worked out. I'm here, Mom is back in Arkansas, and I don't have fuck all to do with her."

She snorted and covered her mouth with both of her hands in this adorable way to keep from laughing. I got on the bike; she settled on behind me and wrapped her arms around me and I fired it up.

"God, I love you!" she called over the chug of the motor and I wondered where that'd come from, even if I wasn't complaining.

"What's that for?" I asked.

She shook her head, and watched her family go by, waving at the boys who waved wildly at us as they went by, her grandmother stiff in the passenger seat and not looking in our direction. Her mom wore an annoyed look, but didn't look our way, either – preferring to focus on driving.

We pulled out of the lot shortly after her family did, although I took us the opposite way they headed on purpose.

I took her to the beach for a walk and to let the breeze carry a bunch of the bad vibes off down the way, over the sand to swirl out over the water and drown.

We were having a barbecue out at Stormy's place, some party time by the pool, and I was looking forward to good food, good beer, and my baby girl in my lap.

We held hands as we walked the beach and talked about things.

All sorts of things, really.

Her hopes and dreams were simple ones. She eventually *did* want to go to school, as soon as the boys were in school themselves, and I loved her even more for the way she'd put her life on hold for that. She knew childcare was expensive and worked as much as she could and had taken on roles that were far too adult for herself at an early enough age when she should have been starting life for herself.

She did so much and asked so little in return, and it ground my gears that even though her grandmother was supposed to be there to *help*, she usually did far more to complicate things.

We talked about projects around the house that her dad had wanted to do, and hadn't gotten to, and I made the decision to take a few of those on if it would make her and her mom's life easier.

All in all, Rarity was an easy girl to love, and part of loving her meant loving those boys and her mom and yeah, even her complicated and messy grandmother and her poor granddad that was more often than not affable and forgotten somewhere in the background.

It was wild, but it was also organic, and easy, and wholesome in a way I hadn't expected my life to take a turn for.

I was alright with it, though. I liked planning with my baby girl. I liked scheming and dreaming with her. I liked that her dreams were simple enough without a whole lot of flash and that she was a calm to the general storm that was life with the Bastards.

It was nice, and just walking barefoot along the beach with her like we were now, was almost a surreal and freeing experience in and of itself.

We laughed and she bumped shoulders knocking me off balance, when I told her we needed to find her a hobby *other* than her little brothers, when she couldn't come up with anything that she did outside of working and caring for them.

Although, truthfully, those boys were a hoot, and I'd loved watching their little faces light up at the Gator Farm.

"Where to, now?" she asked me as we dusted off our feet as best we could and donned our shoes again.

"We're off to Renegade's for a club dinner and just to relax and hang around the pool," I said. "Then when you've had enough food and enough of people, I'd like to take you home to my place and snuggle my little girl and just have a low-key evening."

She grinned and nodded and said, "I like the sound of that."

The ride to Renegade's was refreshing, and it was probably a little eye opening for Rarity. I mean, I was used to this shit, but I could tell as we rolled along the big, gated mansions and houses as we delved into one of the richer neighborhoods of St. Augustine, she was *not* prepared.

I rolled up to the gate and hit the intercom button.

"Who goes there?" a voice came over the speaker box. I revved the bike twice, which was the proper response, and the gate swung open for us.

Rarity giggled behind me as we swept down the long drive and pulled into the circular drive at the end. She hopped off so I could back the bike into the line already up against the curb.

She stood on the front step, staring at the fountain in the center of the drive as I shut off the bike and pulled the key, looping the ring around my index finger and catching the bundle of keys in the palm of my hand.

"This is Renegade's place?" she asked, and she looked a cross between intimidated and suitably impressed.

"Yep. When I said his custom shop was one of the best in the business I wasn't exaggerating," I said.

I went to her and took her hand.

"This place is... a lot," she said and I chuckled.

"Wait'll you see the *inside*," I said dryly.

I went to the front door, arm around my girl, and put my hand to the latch, depressing the button with my thumb and going right on in. We didn't stand on ceremony, the guys and I when it came to Renegade's place. As our President, he made it clear to each and every one of us – fancy digs aside, *mi case et su casa...* or whatever the saying was.

Rarity stepped over the threshold, and I smiled to myself faintly.

For me? This was more of a coming into the inner sanctum than being at the club or hanging in my own home.

Renegade's wasn't for club bunnies and sweet tits to come around. We only came around the manse with real ones, and by bringing her here, the boys would know – Rarity was as real as it got for me.

CHAPTER THIRTY-SIX

R arity...

Holy shit... I thought to myself, *if my grandmother saw this place, she would shit a brick sideways!*

I had a moment of pause in my inner thoughts, and then: *God, I almost wish that she could – it might shut her up for a damn minute.*

I wasn't feeling very charitable toward my grandmother today for trying to stir the pot where Striker was concerned. *Especially* considering he'd saved us all a gang of money fixing the boys' bathroom for free.

He didn't have to do that. Nor did he have to help with the boys and their out-of-pocket behavior that night, nor did he have to bargain with them and treat our whole damn family to the day at the Gator Farm like he had, only for her to turn around and throw a fit because she didn't like *our ages?*

It'd made me mad. It'd been beyond rude, and I was forever *team Striker* over team Grandma after today – for real.

Striker stood behind me, guiding me through the giant house with its stone floors and beautifully neutral-colored walls with their smooth, spotless paint, by my shoulders. Making baby steps behind me, standing close at my back, and bumping me lightly with every step, making me giggle.

I don't think he knew how much I loved when he just naturally sort of fell into guiding me around like this. Like I was his precious little girl. It was something so small but also made me feel so special at the same time.

We found Renegade in the kitchen on the phone, the brick of electronic tucked between his ear and his shoulder as he poured some type of marinade over some meat in a glass baking dish.

"Oh, hey, put a lid on that and into the fridge for me, would yah?" he said in our direction and turned to rinse the bowl and whisk he'd been using in the sink.

"Yeah, yeah! I got you," he said. "Look, I'm gonna get it handled and I'm gonna do it my way, and the minute that I fuck up and it goes pear-shaped is the minute you can tell me 'I told you so' and take a shark bite outta my ass – now I'd love to do our usual little dance here – but I got a guest that just showed up and I'm no longer free to speak on it. So, we need to table this for now if you don't mind."

I watched as Striker put the lid on the glass dish that came with it and he slid it into the refrigerator which was chock full of veggies and things.

"Great," Renegade said, his broad back turned in our direction. He was shirtless in just a pair of black swim trunks with white piping at the pockets or whatever other accents.

"Yeah, fuck you too," he said with a laugh. "Bye now." He pressed the button on the phone to end the call and tossed the device on the counter in its heavy case with a gusty sigh.

"Fucking asshole," he muttered, before he turned around, spotted me, and his whole expression brightened up.

"Hey! Rarity, come give us a hug," he said and I laughed a little uncomfortably but obliged him. "You guys have a good day with the family?" he asked.

"Oh, it was *wonderful*," I said. "Skull and Bones were really great with the boys."

"Never would figure it with those psychopaths, but they sure are good with the kids," he said. "Striker, what's up, man?" he came around the kitchen island and clasped hands with Striker and they pulled each other into a bruising hug.

"You bring your suit?" Renegade asked me.

"Oh, hah, nah – I didn't expect to wind up at a pool party today, so..." I trailed off.

"Hey, no worries!" he went to the sliding back door leading out onto the patio and out to the pool and opened it up to yell, "Yo, Dusty! 'Mere a minute!"

The girl from the clubhouse that I'd met looked up from whoever she was talking to and she jumped up and padded this way.

"What's up, Dad?" she asked, tossing her long black braid over her shoulder.

"Rarity needs a suit, you got something?"

Dusty rolled her eyes and said, "I've spent entirely too much of your money on bathing suits, so yeah – I'm sure I've got something." She smiled at me warmly and said, "Come on."

Striker nudged me in her direction and I followed her through the house to a set of stairs and up to the second floor.

"You a one-piece or a two-piece girly?" she asked.

"Two," I answered and she said, "Ah, thank God. I don't think I've owned a one-piece suit since I was like twelve."

I laughed and said, "Girl, same."

"So, you and Striker, huh?" she asked, letting herself into a room. I followed and tried not to let my jaw drop at the gothic elegance inside.

"Yeah," I said as she went over to her black dresser and pulled open a drawer that was brimming with swimsuit pieces.

"What's that like?" she asked.

"Really nice," I said with a smile.

"Isn't he into that whole 'call me Daddy' thing?" she asked, and snorted when I blushed and blushed *hard*.

"I mean, to each their own, I'm not judging – I know entirely too much about these guys. It's just a little weird for me getting to know their girlfriends typically because it's like... well, they're literally like all my uncles and sometimes, like with you, it's like... you're my age and it's less like you could be my auntie and more like my cousin. You know?"

I laughed a little and said, "I can see how it gets weird."

"Not as weird as when one of my dad's girlfriends he had for a while lied about her age and was actually younger than *me*," she said and rolled her eyes. "That one was – eugh. When he didn't dump her lying ass, I didn't talk to him for like a month or more. It was ridiculous."

"What happened?" I asked.

"I caught her stealing, kicked her ass, and he dumped her after that," she said with a shrug, then she stopped and really looked at me.

"Good thing you're with Striker. Doesn't matter what we put you in, the other guys will keep their hands off since you're his."

I blinked and she sling shot a pair of purple bikini bottoms at me off her finger. I caught them and she said, "Your tits are huge compared to mine, it's gonna be a trick finding something to fit them."

She wasn't wrong, but *wow – no filter much?*

We found something but it was a lot less than I was used to, and barely held my chest in and kept my nipples covered. I went back down with her, leaving my things in her room for when I came back to change again later.

The suit I was in was white and had an almost rainbow irides-cent shimmer to it. It was pretty, and I bet it cost a mint with its designer label.

Out at the pool, Renegade was standing at a grill in the corner of the patio, getting it heating, and Striker was standing near him in a pair of red swim trunks that hugged his thighs just a little tight — either an old pair of his, or a borrowed suit like mine, although I don't think he'd borrowed them from Renegade. Renegade's thighs were even bigger than Strikers. His chest and shoulders even broader and more defined along with a set of washboard abs.

Not bad for a man in his late forties, possibly even his early fifties.

I folded into Striker's side and he sipped on a beer, asking, "You good?"

I laughed and nodded and said, "Feeling a little exposed but yeah, I'm good," I said.

"Shit, you could run around back here topless if you wanted to. Wouldn't bother anybody none and nobody'd better bother you," Renegade declared.

"He's right," Striker said, and kissed my temple. "Best get some sunscreen on that fair skin of yours," he said.

"Dusty's got some," Renegade said.

"Cool," Striker said, steering me out toward the lounge chairs by the side of the pool. Dusty tossed him a spray can of sunscreen on request and went back to watching whatever show she was watching on her tablet as she lounged in the sun.

Striker sprayed me down and rubbed the fine mist of sunscreen into my skin, making me giggle when he sprayed his hands and rubbed it into my face like I was a child.

There were other club members back here, a couple in the shallow end of the pool, sitting on the stairs drinking beer and talking bikes.

Everyone was just sort of keeping it low key and relaxing.

I sunned, and swam with Striker, holding onto him, wrapping arms around his neck and legs around his waist as we bobbed in between the shallow and the deep end of the pool and talked and laughed.

Dinner was kebobs, and grilled to perfection, and before long, the sun was setting and I wasn't able to keep from yawning only minutes apart from one another.

"I think that's our cue to go," Striker said as I covered yet another yawn with the back of my hand as I stared into the fire in the propane firepit over under an arbor nearby the pool and patio.

It'd been one of the best days ever, but I was tired, and so very ready to lay down and cuddle with my Daddy for the night. It sounded perfect, to be honest.

I liked hanging out with him and the rest of the club by the pool today. It'd been nice. Cozy, and I'd liked getting to know some of the rest of the guys.

I changed back into my clothes in Dusty's room and left the swimsuit in the bottom of her bathroom sink like she'd asked.

Striker was waiting at the bottom of the stairs for me, and immediately folded me into his arms, holding me close and kissing my temple.

"You okay baby?" he asked me.

"I'm really tired, Daddy," I whispered back and he chuckled.

"Come on then, kitten. Let's go home, get a quick shower, and get you tucked in. Sound good?"

"Sounds like the best," I said and we said our goodbyes and left. Thank God, he'd managed to keep the goodbyes short, because I was really afraid I would fall asleep on the back of his bike – and I certainly didn't want to do something stupid like that and fall off.

I was pretty sure it was just my fear of doing just that, that kept me awake for the blessedly short ride.

We pulled in the gate of the mansion property that Striker lived on and stopped in front of his little carriage house or whatever. Just inside the door, he stopped me just inside the door and kissed me softly and carefully.

I let my backpack slip from my shoulders, and he hung it up on the hooks set just inside the door.

I could barely breathe with the way his hands hovered over my face, my neck, just to where I could feel the heat from them, but not touching. No, not yet. The only part of him that touched me was his lips, so soft, so careful against mine.

I forgot to breathe, when his hands finally made contact with my skin, to smooth up and down my arms in a light and careful caress.

"Let's get you out of these clothes, hm?" he whispered softly, his voice so gentle it was like music played in another room to my ear.

I nodded mutely, desperate to be nude and pressed against him, my body almost as hungry as my soul for his touch.

"That's my girl," he said with a glowing pride to his tone that very nearly made me swoon.

He undressed me, slowly, taking his time, his touches like gossamer whispers against my skin. Oh, how he punctuated each clothing item's removal with a soft press of his lips! I felt worshipped, cherished in a way I couldn't even begin to describe, and I wanted that for him, too.

I captured his face between my hands as he rose up and kissed him, slipping my tongue past his lips and tucking myself into the front of his bigger body as his hands smoothed over my back and went to my waist, hauling me more firmly up against him.

"I love you," he growled into my mouth, and I tingled from head to toe at those three little words.

I whimpered into his mouth, my body exciting, tired though as I was.

"Mm," he pulled me against him and I gave a leap, clinging to him like a spider monkey as he walked us through his house with assurance.

He laid me on his rumpled and hastily made bed and pulled his shirt off over his head, discarding it to the floor before pressing more fully against me, skin on skin contact – which is what I had craved to begin with.

Somehow, he managed to get rid of his pants, which – *yes, please!* And before I knew it, he was pressing into me, sliding inside of me, and I couldn't help but arch beneath him and let my eyes roll into the back of my head.

Yeah, I know, I know, we were flirting with a danger of pregnancy or whatever – but I loved this. The feel of him, with no barriers between us was intoxicating in a way I can't even begin to describe, and I wanted it. I wanted him, so badly in that moment, I was willing to throw caution to the wind.

"Please, Daddy. Please!" I begged. "Love me."

He growled, and bowed over me, thrusting deep and deeper still, my legs falling open, his cock damn near reaching the end of me, and then he pushed in just that little bit more and bottomed out and *God, that felt good!*

I sank into the bed behind me and loved when he pressed me into it. I wrapped my arms around him as he kissed me, and ground into me, giving this twist and a little back and forth to his hips that *oh, my God,* did more than a little something for me.

He loved me with passion, and tender care, and I just couldn't get enough – I didn't ever want to, either.

He was just that amazing to me.

CHAPTER THIRTY-SEVEN

S triker...

I loved her for hours this way, just getting into that sacred rhythm that pleased us both and held us on that precipice where time stopped and it all just felt so fucking good that you almost couldn't stand it. Still, no matter how long you went at it this way, it wasn't enough to send you sailing into that warm, golden abyss, either.

It was a beautiful madness, an exquisite torture, and a passionate edging that when the pinnacle was reached, would guarantee one of the most graceful falls. That when we reached the top, it would be as though touching the divine itself.

I loved bringing her like this, I loved her soft skin against mine, and caring for her, and doing things for her to make her life easier. I loved her and her family, complicated though some of the relationships she had with them might be...

I wouldn't trade my little princess for the world.

The way she wrapped her arms around me, the way she twined her legs around my hips, caressing my calf with the bottom of her foot as I loved her. She wholly participated in joining with me, and the way she did it so sweetly, and so naturally, turned me on like nothing else.

I delved my hands beneath her, holding her close, kissing her chin, the side of her neck, lavishing attention against the beating pulse in the side of her lovely throat until the combination of that and the way I moved my hips and by extension my cock, inside her, had her coming completely undone.

She unraveled so beautifully, her pink lips parting, a cross between a moan and a sigh escaping them, and I don't think I would ever get tired of that sound. I don't think it was possible to ever grow tired of making her come for me so beautifully... and the things I wanted to do to her and with her were just beginning.

She was so incredibly perfect and sweet, trusting and loving, so full of compassion and grace, I couldn't hardly stand it – and the best part?

She was mine. Now and for always. Now and forever, as long as she wanted to *be* mine – and I swear, I would *never* give her a reason to want anything else.

God, I loved her.

ALSO BY A.J. DOWNEY

Sacred Hearts MC Novella

Christmas with the Brotherhood

Indigo Knights

1. Her Thin Blue Lifeline

2. His Cold Blue Command

3. A Low Blue Flame

4. His Wild Blue Rose

5. Her Pained Blue Silence

6. A Cold Blue Call

7. Her Reluctant Blue Cavalier

8. Forged Under Fire

9. Under A Blue Moon

10. Sound of Blue Thunder

Sacred Hearts MC Pacific Northwest

1. Over the High Side

2. Wind Therapy

3. Apex of the Curve

4. Low Sided

5. Eating Asphalt

6. Hammer Down

7. Only Fool Riding

The Voodoo Bastards MC

1. Bourbon & Blood

2. Whiskey Shivers

3. Moonshine Lullabies

4. Cognac Secrets

5. Tequila Damnation

Iron Wraiths MC

1. Original Syn

2. Love & Fear

3. The Hangman's Rope

Paranormal Romance (with Ryan Kells)

1. I Am The Alpha

2. Omega's Run

3. Hunter's End

Indigo City Darker (with Jared KingPacal Lain)

1. Triple Threat

2. Double Shot

Standalones

Synchronicity

ABOUT A.J. DOWNEY

A.J. Downey is a Pacific Northwest girl living in an East Tennessee world who finds inspiration from her surroundings, through the people she meets, and likely as a byproduct of way too much caffeine. She specializes in real and relatable romance stories featuring that real-life kind of love that everyone craves.

Stalker Information:

Website
www.ajdowney.com

Sign up for her newsletter at
http://eepurl.com/dkQiIH

Facebook Group - AJ's Sacred Circle
https://www.facebook.com/groups/authorajdowney/

f facebook.com/authorajdowney

instagram.com/ajdowney

BB bookbub.com/authors/a-j-downey